A Christmas Wish

A Manhattan Dream novel

By
Engy Neville

Chapter One

T HE SUMMER HEAT rolled deliciously over her skin, and Amy soothed the first prickles threatening with a generous dollop of sunscreen.

She loved everything about summer from the long bright days to the blue skies to the spontaneous beach trips. Being a Los Angeles native, she had never missed the beach until recently. It was always there, available and waiting. After moving to New York at the tail end of the coldest winters on record, yearning for the beach and warm temperatures was suddenly a real dilemma.

She couldn't believe her lucky stars when Megan, her coworker and friend, invited Amy and Amy's best friends Miranda and Lisa to the Hamptons for a whole week. The beach house belonged to Megan's parents. They'd planned a summer in Europe, but their regular dog sitter had already scheduled a vacation herself for the week, so the duty fell to Megan. "You can't make this stuff up," Amy said, more to herself than anyone.

She could barely contain her enthusiasm; her only hesitation was the preplanned staycation with her best friends from LA for a week of sightseeing in the city. Granted, a week in the hot and humid city didn't compare to a beach house in the Hamptons, but she still didn't want them to feel slighted. They'd been inseparable since college, and this was the longest stretch of time they'd ever been apart. She missed them.

To her relief, when she called Miranda to explain the slight change of plans, Miranda's didn't hold back her excitement.

"What? Are you kidding?" Miranda screamed into the phone. Someone in the background shushed Miranda, and she muttered a quick apology. "I'm listening. I'm just stepping outside to talk to you," she whispered.

"I'm not kidding. It's all set. Do you remember me mentioning my coworker, Megan?" Amy asked, her voice rising with excitement. "Long story short, her parents need her to watch their dog while they're in Europe, and she thought it would be fun for us to join her. So I said yes on our behalf. I hope you don't mind. If you hate the idea, we can always back out. It's not a big deal."

Reaching for her wine, Amy took a generous sip and leaned back into the chair, glass in hand. An entire week at the beach house sounded heavenly. Amy couldn't be more grateful or more excited to get out of the city and experience a real summer in the coveted Hamptons. A beach vacation. What could be better?

"It sounds really cool. That's so nice of her. There's only one small problem... I know our original plan was for Lisa to come too, but she can't make it anymore. She's on some crazy deadline and she's hoping to make partner. So it's just me. Is that okay?" Loud honking muffled Miranda's voice. Impatient LA drivers.

"Of course that's okay. Bummer about Lisa. She'll miss out on a great trip," Amy said, her enthusiasm waning a bit. "I'm glad you're still coming. We're going to have a blast, and you're going to love Megan. She's so sweet and mellow."

"I can hardly wait. I can't tell you how much I need this getaway. I've been teaching back-to-back classes since you left and have worked almost every weekend. Between people taking vacations and calling in sick, I seem to be the only one available to teach vinyasa. Anyway, let me run. I need to air out the studio before my class. The instructor before me never cracks open a single window, ever. It's so disgusting in there," Miranda said before blowing kisses into the phone and ringing off.

Now, a few weeks later, Amy was fully embracing the aristocratic lifestyle of East Hampton, practically feeling like a local as she woke up early to practice yoga on the beach with Megan in tow and Miranda at the helm. She wasn't sure how long their ritual would last, but it was day two, and their dedication hadn't wavered yet.

Amy hardly recognized herself these days. The sudden shift in her life after accepting a new job in a city so far away from home proved to be a positive and a rejuvenating change. As the marketing manager at Glitz, a popular Los Angeles based lifestyle magazine, Amy was often the punching bag for her incompetent and inexperienced young boss who had landed the position because of family connections, not merit. Amy had hit a low point in her life and career when Sarah began targeting her, issuing insults and verbal assaults as a form of sport for her own amusement.

Lo and behold, a dream job at her favorite magazine opened, and despite some unforeseen hurdles along the way, Amy nailed the interview and landed the job. The leap of faith required to move her entire life within a matter of weeks was the catalyst for other positive changes. Instead of snoozing the alarm a million times before dragging herself to the office, Amy now woke up extra early to squeeze in a yoga class before work. Ironically, Miranda taught yoga daily at a local studio not far from Amy's old apartment in Brentwood, CA, and yet it took moving cross-country for her to embrace the healthier lifestyle. She gave up the gazillion cups of coffee a day and switched to Jasmine green tea—unsweetened. She found herself smiling more often than not, the light in her brown eyes shining brightly. She pinched herself at least once a day for her good fortune.

"Amy, Amy! Come into the water. It feels amazing," Miranda shouted, knee-deep in the surf as another wave almost overtook her. Miranda was the perfect California girl, radiant with happiness, natural beauty, and long blond hair that she often wore in a low ponytail. Miranda was also one of the nicest people Amy had ever met. It was no wonder they had been best friends since freshman year in college.

Megan exploded in giggles, standing nearby with a camera in hand, determined to capture Miranda in a yoga pose before the waves crashed around her.

"I just want to finish this chapter and then I'll be right in," Amy responded, holding up her book.

"I can't believe this. Our little Miss prim and proper is reading a steamy romance," Miranda said, squinting from the sun.

"Wait ... what? You're actually reading The Back Nine. I never thought you'd listen to our recommendation. Do you love it? I can't get enough of Gia Stone and hope she's fast at work on her next novel," Megan said, turning to snap a picture of Amy with the book.

"All right, all right … enough with the teasing. Let me finish this chapter and I'll join you. Maybe we can grab a little lunch. I'm getting hungry." Amy buried her nose in the book again.

Megan had an artistic eye for photography and had a promising career in the photo department at Diva. In a very short time, they'd become good friends, and Amy often accompanied Megan to Central Park for her shoots, even during the dreaded humid days when clothes plastered to your skin. The scenes captured on Megan's camera were mesmerizing.

Amy had guessed at Megan's privileged background the first time she'd been to her apartment on the Upper East Side. From the polished marble lobby floor to the spacious art deco one bedroom with a high ceiling and a breathtaking view, Megan had a killer place. However, until this trip, Amy didn't realize the extent of wealth that Megan came from or the socialite lifestyle that had influenced her upbringing since childhood. Instead of using her connections and financial standing to climb the corporate ladder, like Amy's previous shrew boss, Megan paid her dues like everyone else by accepting a position working as an assistant to Jane Callaghan, an all-around great woman and one of the most respected and adored executives at Weisman Publishing. Jane managed the marketing division with absolute precision and profession-alism.

Amy breezed through the chapter, the rumbling in her stomach fighting for her attention. Twenty minutes later, she tucked the book inside her beach bag. She'd finish reading tonight after everyone went to bed.

The last day and a half had felt luxurious and indulgent. Her body had become one with the sleek Adirondack chair. She couldn't imagine a better way to experience the Hamptons than this. Every one of their whims was immediately answered, every craving satisfied, and every request fulfilled in record time. "A girl could get used to this fairly quickly," Amy mused.

Only a few days into their beach vacation, and Amy already felt renewed; the ocean air did wonders for her spirit. She wobbled beside Megan and Miranda as the threesome walked the short distance from the private beach to Megan's backyard, her legs feeling like limp noodles from lounging all day. Life couldn't get better than this.

Chapter Two

A FTER A MOUTHWATERING lunch of grilled fish and an assortment of salads, Jeffrey, the house manager and butler, blended a fresh batch of strawberry margaritas for them, urging them to relax by the Olympic-size pool, lined with potted ferns and flowering shrubs.

"You don't want to crisp up on your second day of vacation. Pace yourselves so you're not beat by dinner time," he advised, his voice taking on an authoritative tone. His silver-streaked blond hair and bright blue eyes with soft creases around the corners marked him in his forties, and he spoke often of Megan and her family with an air of respect and devotion.

He floated around them methodically as he opened the umbrellas, reclined the lounge chairs, and placed a few water bottles and fresh fruit in ice buckets on the side tables between each chair. Amy found Jeffrey delightful and she went out of her way to chat with him. Earlier that morning while he was making their coffee, Jeffrey had mentioned that he was going away with James, his partner, to celebrate their five-year anniversary. The smile radiating from his face lit up the room and melted Amy's heart.

"What do you guys want to do this afternoon?" Megan asked, lying on the reclined Adirondack chair, her eyes closed against the blaring sun. Despite Jeffrey's urging, she closed her umbrella, basking in the sweltering heat.

"I would love a little nap. I feel so relaxed, the thought of moving is daunting," Miranda said.

"A nap does sound nice, actually." Amy stretched lazily and wiggled her toes. A flock of seagulls circled above, pulling her deeper into total relaxation. *I wish this feeling lasted forever.*

"All right, it's 12:30 p.m. now, let's meet back in the kitchen at 3:30 and head into town for a walk and ice cream. We'll come back here for dinner and drinks on the beach." Megan grabbed her water bottle and cover-up, leaving her towel on the chair.

"Fine by me," Amy agreed. Miranda nodded, scurrying to gather her belongings while Megan waited for her. The two of them headed in for a nap, leaving Amy to follow. Having just endured a long gray winter, Amy hated to think of wasting a sunny day napping, so she decided to take a short walk on the beach. The glistening water and crashing waves called her name. Birds tweeted, circling overhead. Inhaling deeply, Amy let the salty air work its magic to relieve the tension between her shoulder blades. "Just a short walk," she promised herself.

As soon as her feet sank into the warm sand, she couldn't contain her excitement and started running without a specific course in mind. She ran faster than she imagined she could, especially while still in her red bikini and see-through cover-up, but somehow, her state of dress felt inconsequential as her feet carried her farther. The breeze in her hair propelled her forward, uncontrollable giggles erupted from her throat, and Amy felt more like herself than she had in a while.

She was finally truly and unmistakably happy. She raised her arms high above her head as she slowed her steps, pretending to cross an imaginary finish line at a marathon. The euphoria from the beach, running with complete abandon, and finally being content in every aspect of her life felt exhilarating. "Woohoo," she screamed, vowing to remember this feeling during the next anxiety riddled moment in her life. A task easier said than done, especially for her.

She doubled over to catch her raspy breath, still giggling. Without much thought, she adjusted her red bikini bottom and pulled at the top to ensure all her bits were covered up without any peekaboo action. She shook her head with amusement at her own spontaneous shenanigans.

At the sound of clapping, Amy jerked her head up, fully expecting Miranda and Megan on the sidelines applauding her and teasing her. At first, she didn't see anyone and thought she'd imagined it. And then she spotted him. The god-like hottie stood a few feet away in his backyard wearing shorts and nothing else. Oh-my-God. Amy gasped, mortified that he'd witnessed her most likely looking completely disheveled and deranged.

Amy's tongue practically rolled out of her mouth as she ogled him, unsure of what to do or say. Get it together, Amy. He was tall, with a broad muscular chest, tousled light brown hair, and a dazzling smile that turned her knees into jelly. Was he applauding her? Breathe, Amy.

"Ah… Hi," she said, waving awkwardly.

"That was impressive. I don't think I've seen anyone attempt that kind of speed on the beach—in a bathing suit," he teased.

"It wasn't planned," she said and immediately felt like a fool for saying something so lame.

"I'm Richard, but my friends call me Richie." He opened the small wooden gate separating the yard from the beach and walked over to her.

The thought of him coming close gave her hot flashes.

"I'm Amy." Face-to-face, he was even hotter. Richie was at least a foot taller than her and much fitter than he'd looked from a distance. He extended his hand to shake hers and she took it, staring down at her feet. At his touch, electric waves vibrated through her body, and she quickly pulled her hand back. Did he feel it too? A fresh prickle of heat crept up her neck to her cheeks.

"Are you staying around here?" Richie asked, running his fingers through his hair.

Somewhere between the handshake and his question, he removed his Ray Bans to reveal a pair of stunning hazel eyes that paralyzed her and tied her tongue. All coherent thoughts fled.

"I'm sorry, did you say something?" Amy asked, mortified by her own behavior.

"Are you staying here?" Richie said again, smiling.

Damn him, did his smile have to be so sexy?

"I'm staying with a girlfriend at her parents' house for the week. They're in Europe, and Megan thought it would be fun for us to spend the week here and the timing of my best friend Miranda coming from Los Angeles worked out perfectly."

Stop rambling, Amy!

"That's great. You picked a perfect week for a calm beach. Not so great for surfing but perfect for sailing," he said, glancing quickly toward the water.

"Is that your house?" Amy shifted on her feet, overwhelmed by his closeness. Why did he have to smell so good?

"It's my parents' house, actually. They're away in St. Martin and asked me to dog sit for them. I love it here, so I didn't mind escaping the city to have a week to myself by the beach."

"Me too. I mean, I love the beach too," she said, her heart quickening with each passing minute. She needed to get a grip before she made an utter ass of herself. "Well, it was nice meeting you. I gotta go. The girls will be waiting for me to head into town," she said, trying not to sound reluctant about ending their conversation.

"Wait. I'd like to see you again if that's okay?" Richie said, searching her face for a response.

"Really?"

"Yes, I would." He shoved his hands into the pockets of his shorts and offered her a shy, barely-there grin.

After he'd entered her number in his phone and promised to call later, he watched as she turned to head back to Megan's house.

Out of curiosity, or maybe because it always looked so romantic in movies, Amy turned around and found him still staring after her, grinning from ear to ear.

Chapter Three

A MY PRACTICALLY SKIPPED back to the house, bubbling with excitement. She was grinning like a fool and didn't care. A really hot guy had noticed her. Better yet, he talked to her and wanted to see her again. This kind of stuff just didn't happen to her. Suffering from low self-esteem wasn't part of her repertoire but chatting up a really hot guy wasn't either. In high school, she was a book nerd, hardly a guy magnet, and in college, she was often Miranda's wingman, a role she felt comfortable in because it deflected attention from her. Being the center of attention wasn't her thing and truthfully, casually dating wasn't either. Especially after her painful break-up with Adam, the cheating bastard, dating fell off the docket altogether.

But somehow, the thought of seeing Richie again felt—nice.

Upstairs in her bedroom, the clock on the nightstand indicated 1:45 p.m., leaving little time to get ready. Amy dashed to the bathroom. Discarding her clothes in a pile by the sink, she climbed into the shower, too impatient to wait for the water to warm up. She yelped loudly as the prickling cold water hit her overheated skin. Luckily, piping hot water flowed at record speed, making her shiver at the sudden change of temperature. Twenty minutes later, Amy stood on the bath mat wrapped in a fluffy white towel, her limbs feeling like rubber from the combination of being in the sun all morning and the hot steamy shower.

As she dried off, a few scenarios played out in her mind ranging from never hearing from Richie—not an unlikely scenario—to being on a date. The latter was enticing, a little nerve-racking. Amy pictured their first date. Maybe a nice walk on the beach followed by a romantic candlelit dinner on the patio overlooking the ocean. Smiling, she pictured him reaching for her hand as they ate leisurely, sipping ice-cold Pinot Grigio.

Stop it, Amy.

Sighing loudly, she padded into the bedroom toward the dresser.

A soft knock on the door startled her.

"Who is it?" Amy asked.

"It's me, Miranda."

"Come in." Amy pulled the towel tighter around her.

Miranda floated in, relaxed from what Amy assumed was her afternoon nap. She was wearing a flowery yellow sundress with spaghetti straps that crisscrossed behind her shoulders. Her long blond hair was tied in a low ponytail down her slim back. Effortlessly stunning, as usual.

"How was the nap? Good?" Amy withdrew clean underwear and a bra from the antique white drawers. The room was airy, the light yellow walls reflecting the natural light beautifully.

"It was delicious and relaxing and I don't ever want to go home kinda good," Miranda replied, jumping onto the unmade double bed, not wasting much time in making herself comfortable by burrowing her red manicured toes under the duvet.

"I'm so happy you're having a good time. I love it here too. I had no idea Megan grew up like this," Amy whispered. "She's never once mentioned anything to hint at this house or lifestyle or staff service around the clock. Holy cow!"

"I like her, and she keeps a good head on her shoulders. You probably wouldn't be friends with her otherwise. Your personalities would never have meshed, you know?"

"I do know. But this mansion?" Amy said, motioning with her hands to the estate. Miranda rolled her eyes, not too invested in the conversation and clearly ready to move on to a different topic.

"So did you nap or read more of the smut we recommended?" Miranda teased.

"Ha ha … I actually went for a little walk along the beach and just got back a little while ago," Amy said, a grin spreading across her face.

"And … what? What happened?" Miranda said, sitting up.

"I kinda met a guy … his name is Richie … he lives a few houses down from here. Or his parents do, and he lives in the city," Amy said.

Then she fell silent, shifting uncomfortably between her feet, unsure whether the encounter warranted a conversation. It was just a random moment with a hot stranger on the beach. For all she knew, he wouldn't call her, imagining his type to be tall, leggy with model good looks. She was short, could lose a few pounds, and was hardly model beautiful. Unwelcome doubt crept in, her mind summoning memories of meeting Adam at a work function. He was charming, sweet, and so flirtatious. All the signs were there. And look at how that turned out. Complete disaster.

"You met a guy? What did he look like? What did he say? Did you give him your number?" Miranda fired back questions, her eyes sparkling with excitement.

"Well … it wasn't like that … maybe it was … I don't know … I was running down the beach, feeling kinda good until I was practically wheezing. I bent over to catch my breath and heard someone clapping. I thought it was you and Megan making fun of me but when I looked up, it was Richie, cheering me on. I was horrified but then I couldn't think straight. He was hot. Like sex-on-legs hot. We only spoke for a couple of minutes, tops. He seemed really nice or maybe he's a psychopath, I don't know," Amy rambled on.

"Wait … so you met a hot guy who seemed nice, but you think he's a psychopath?"

"Maybe. I mean, he was really hot. Guys like that don't date girls like me."

"What are you talking about?"

"Because hot guys date equally hot girls. Girls like you. It's a fact. And anyway, what are the chances of this going anywhere?"

"What the hell are you talking about? You're gorgeous and smart and accomplished and braver than anyone I know. I mean, you moved cross-country for a dream job in a city where you knew no one. You're fearless, Amy."

"I know … but … this is different."

"Why? Cut the crap, this isn't about hot guy. Oh wait – let me guess, it's about that shithead, Adam?"

"Well no … maybe, okay. I made such a bad judgment call with him.

What if this is another one? Besides, I'm not ready to date. The timing is all wrong. I just moved here, and I really should focus on work and get my bearings in the city."

"Listen to yourself. 'Get your bearings in the city. The timing is all wrong.' Amy, you moved to Manhattan, not Mars. And timing, shmining. If you allow bullshit from your past to dictate what happens next in your life, then you're not the person I thought you were. Haven't the last few months taught you anything about yourself?

"No … I don't know, okay?"

"You had a bad run in your last job and a bad run with Adam, but those are two distinct periods in your life, and not only did you overcome those bad times, you've shone because of them. Look at where you landed. You need to move on and embrace the future and the unknown that comes with that. Manhattan is a fresh start, even you admit that, so enjoy it."

"You're right. It's just that I'm cautious, you know?"

"I know, and you should be, but you should also cut yourself some slack. Any guy would be lucky to date you. Now tell me what else happened."

"Nothing else happened. I mean he asked for my number," Amy said, exhaling loudly.

"Wow, some afternoon you had. Sounds like he's totally not interested in you." Miranda smiled with approval.

"Don't look at me like that. He'll probably never call, and that's okay. On some level, it felt good to know I still had it. You know? Anyway, I need to finish getting ready if we're leaving in a bit," Amy said, ready to change the conversation. She didn't want to give the encounter too much energy. Nothing had happened and most likely, nothing would.

To Amy's relief, Miranda dropped the subject, hugged her tightly, and slunk out of the room without another word on the matter. Although Miranda's unwavering loyalty and support came with a healthy dose of tough love, Amy couldn't love her more and, not for the first time, she felt grateful for their friendship. She hurried to the large closet along the wall and began looking through the dresses she'd brought along. She settled on a white eyelet sundress and platform sandals and rushed into the bathroom to dry her hair and apply the sheer sunscreen she bought for her face and neck. Her fair Irish skin freckled by just looking at the sun. She didn't need to push her luck this week by avoiding the sunscreen altogether. Red angry-looking skin wasn't a good look. Besides, she might run into Richie and she … Stop it, Amy!

A fresh, bare face and lip-gloss completed her signature look. Amy bounced downstairs feeling the happiest and most relaxed she'd ever been, Miranda's words still swirling in her head. She found Miranda and Megan already at the kitchen counter, heads together whispering and drinking some juice concoction that Jeffrey had no doubt squeezed for them. The conversation ended abruptly as soon as they saw her.

"Hey, how was your afternoon?" Megan asked, taking a sip from her glass.

"Fine, it's so relaxing here. How do you ever leave all this and live in Manhattan?" Amy asked, plucking a red apple from the fruit bowl on the counter and indulging in a big bite.

"Easy. The Hamptons become lifeless in the winter," Megan said.

"I guess you're right. So what's the plan?" Amy said, taking another bite of the apple.

"Well, I thought I could drive us to the East Hampton village and we could walk around a little. Maybe get a coffee and poke around the stores. Jeffrey has an elaborate dinner prepared for us, otherwise I would have suggested dinner out," Megan said, standing up to grab her white Kate Spade purse hanging on the back of her chair.

"Sounds great, let's go," Amy replied as she finished the last bite of the apple. Just as they were about to leave the kitchen, Jeffrey walked in with a huge bouquet of flowers and an even bigger smile on his face.

"Are they from James?" the girls asked in unison, hovering around him to get a closer look. Despite having known him a very short amount of time, Amy and Miranda felt comfortable with him, and he wasn't too shy about sharing tidbits of his life with them.

"Nope, not for me. They're for a beautiful brunette who seems to have made quite the impression on someone," he teased. Amy flushed a deep red from hairline to toes. It couldn't be.

Megan and Miranda turned to stare at Amy, confirming that Miranda had told Megan every detail of their earlier conversation about Richie. She wouldn't be surprised if Jeffrey was in on the secret too.

"Well … don't you want the card?" Jeffrey asked her.

"Yes, thank you," she mumbled, feeling her cheeks burn with embarrassment.

Amy slowly pulled the card from its envelope. Was it necessary to have an audience? Giving up on any privacy, she held the card up and read out loud:

Hi Amy,
I really enjoyed chatting with you. And to think I almost ran errands this morning. I would have missed our encounter and that would have been a bummer. I would love to finish our conversation. How about sailing tomorrow? Pick you up at nine?
And pack that red bikini.
Richie xo

Amy flushed a deep shade of crimson at his request. She wanted to die, except then she would miss sailing and that would be tragic.

"Well, well, well," Megan teased.

"I like him already," Miranda chimed in.

"I also approve. Good breeding, manners, and a flair for romance. Nicely done, Miss Amy." Jeffrey set the bouquet on the kitchen table and left the girls to gossip.

"I don't want to make a big deal out of this. It's just sailing. It doesn't mean anything. It will be a fun day out and that's it," Amy said, trying to suppress the wide grin already splitting her face. "Come on, aren't we still going into town before dinner?"

"You're not getting out of this conversation that easily. We want details," Megan probed, hands on hips in an exaggerated authoritative stance.

Rolling her eyes, Amy turned around, heading for the front door. Megan and Miranda followed behind, giggling like schoolgirls.

During their scenic drive through the neighborhood, Amy filled them in on her short conversation with Richie. There was no point fighting them and there was nothing to tell anyway.

The East Hampton village was quaint and charming and reminded Amy of the Pacific Palisades, her hometown in Southern California. The tree-lined street added to the appeal of the shops and outdoor cafes adorning every corner. Vacationers and locals meandered in and out of the stores and enjoyed the delicacies from the local shops. It was a lifestyle of leisure, and Amy couldn't help but feel like she was floating on a cloud. She snuck a peek at Miranda and found her grinning as she took in the sights and scents of this enchanting small beach haven so close in proximity to the busiest and most hectic city in the world.

Chapter Four

ARLY THE NEXT morning, Amy crept down to the kitchen to avoid waking anyone up. Living in a busy city overcrowded with high rises didn't make it easy or feasible to watch the sunrise or sunset. She was almost certain she would experience a brilliant sunset over the water with Richie tonight and she wanted to start the day with an equally beautiful sunrise.

Tiptoeing barefoot to the poolside deck, she grabbed a large beach towel, walked the short distance to the beach, and plopped down in the sand, the vast ocean ahead of her. "Sometimes life can't be more beautiful," she mused, in awe of the incredible changes in her life. She was still in her pajamas and didn't have a care in the world about who saw her. Amy pulled her knees to her chest and wrapped her arms protectively over her legs. This beautiful moment of silence and serenity was exactly what she wanted. Since moving to New York, she'd gotten into the habit of meditation and yoga. She could never thank Miranda enough for introducing her to this practice.

With the bright yellow sun inching its way above the horizon, Amy stood up and stretched her arms high overhead. "Now I'm ready for the day," she said. She grabbed the towel, shook it to dislodge the sand, and walked back to the house. Amy had already set aside the red bikini as requested by Hot Stuff and chose her outfit for the day and a sundress for afterwards in case the date extended to dinner. Either way, she was prepared for whatever the Universe tossed at her.

In the kitchen, she found Jeffrey at the sink washing and drying grapes and apples with some Tupperware containers already filled and stacked to the side.

"Good morning. You're up early. I hope I didn't wake you," Amy said sheepishly.

"Not at all. I'm an early riser. James and I went to yoga this morning, so I've been up for some time. Besides, I wanted to be here to see you off with Mr. Hottie," he replied, glancing over his shoulder to look at her.

"Jeffrey, I know I haven't known you very long … but I adore you. Thank you," she said, walking over and hugging him from behind.

"I love you too. Now go get ready and we'll have coffee when you come back down," he chuckled, giving the arm still wrapped around his chest an affectionate pat. Smiling, Amy nodded and headed upstairs.

Thirty minutes later, Amy returned to the kitchen, showered and dressed in a frilly white blouse and red shorts with a beach bag over her shoulder containing her red bikini, sunglasses, sunscreen, and a change of clothes for later.

"Well, how do I look?" she asked Jeffrey. He sat at the kitchen table with two filled coffee cups, the steam still floating from them. He always managed to time everything to perfection. How did he do that?

"You look beautiful, but you might want to start with your hair down. You're going on a date, not a school trip. You can do without the ponytail until you're on the sailboat," he advised.

Silently, she pulled the rubber band out of her hair, grateful for his honesty, and stashed it in her pocket, beaming at him. He really was the best. The two chatted quietly for a while, sharing their favorite memories and stories of past relationships. Amy discovered that she shared his birthday month of August and she was almost ten years his junior.

At 8:45, Megan and Miranda sauntered into the kitchen in their swimsuits and cover-ups ready to soak up the hot sun, their early morning yoga ritual already abandoned for more indulgent activities.

"Are you ready?" Miranda asked, suppressing a yawn. Amy smiled, knowing her best friend had woken up early this morning just to support her and meet Richie. Otherwise, it was safe to assume Miranda would have slept till noon.

"Yup, ready as I'll ever be," she replied, feeling grateful for the out-pouring of love and support that surrounded her.

"Oh, before I forget, I packed you a picnic basket. It's just some nibbles to get you through until lunch," Jeffrey said, springing up from his chair to retrieve the basket. Amy was flabbergasted by the thoughtful gesture, and knowing him, it was a lot more than nibbles. Without even surveying the goodies packed inside, Amy threw her arms around him and held on tight.

"It's just a picnic basket. Geez," he said.

The doorbell rang, and they all turned to look at Amy with anticipation, eager to meet Richie. Amy stalled briefly to straighten out her clothes and run her fingers through her long brown hair. Miranda gave her a little shove towards the door, motioning for her to hurry up. Giggles erupted from Megan, and, in spite of trying to maintain her composure, Amy giggled as well.

Motioning for Jeffrey to stay put, Amy walked towards the door. She didn't want unnecessary formalities to start the date.

"Good morning," she said, opening the door wide.

"Good morning. You look beautiful. Are you ready?" Richie asked, leaning in to kiss her cheek. He wore a red Polo shirt, navy shorts, and flip-flops. Amy surveyed him from head to toe, noticing his muscular thighs for the first time. Damn!

She swallowed hard and hoped she didn't make a fool of herself by gawking at him.

"I'm ready. Come in for a second. I just need to grab my bag and the picnic basket for us," she said, stepping aside to let him in.

"Wow, you packed a picnic basket? Thank you."

"Well, it wasn't—" she began.

"It's very nice to meet you, Richie. I'm Jeffrey, the house manager. I wrote down the house phone number and my mobile number for you in case of an emergency." A subtle shake of Jeffrey's head told Amy to zip it about the picnic basket.

After pleasantries were exchanged, with Miranda and Megan practically drooling over Richie, the two set out on their sailing adventure. But not before Megan and Miranda gave Amy the thumbs up. Richie carried both the picnic basket and Amy's beach bag and stowed them on the backseat of the Jeep Wrangler. The chivalry was noted, especially by

Amy.

"The dock isn't too far from here. I took the liberty of buying some bagels, coffee, and wine for later. I hope that's all right with you," he said, turning to look at her.

"That's perfect. Thank you." Meeting his gaze, she smiled broadly to mask the bundle of nerves pulsing in her stomach.

A short drive later, they parked the Jeep and walked the wooden dock to the sailboat, surprisingly very modest in shape and size although it looked brand new and wasn't small by any stretch.

After a quick tour, Richie unpacked their food and stashed everything in the cabinets and fridge while Amy used the small bathroom to change into her bathing suit.

"Wow," Richie said, his eyes roaming every inch of her.

"I'm glad you approve," she retorted, feeling more confident, and headed upstairs, giggling. He was on her heels within seconds and helped her settle down on the deck while he talked to someone on the dock, waved, and then set sail on the open ocean.

"You're so good at this," Amy said as he untied ropes and expertly shifted the direction of the sail, catching wind just at the right time to propel them forward.

"I've been sailing since I was ten. My Dad taught me, and his Dad taught him. There's nothing like the open sea to set your mind straight. Puts things in perspective."

"I can tell how much you love it. I love the beach too. I feel so happy when I'm near water. After my first winter in New York—although I moved here at the tail end of it—I began to wonder if I could survive an entire winter every year. But then I got into yoga, and that seemed to take the edge off a little. But I still miss the beach and sunny skies year-round," she said.

"What made you decide to move here?" he asked, sitting behind the steering wheel on the deck, looking so at ease, his brilliant hazel eyes fixated on her.

"I was ready for a change with work. My boss was a complete nightmare. She enjoyed humiliating me for fun, so I decided I'd had enough and began job hunting. A position I had been dying for at Weisman Publishing was available, and the stars aligned in the most perfect way. Within two weeks, I had packed my apartment in Brentwood, found an apartment in the city, moved, and started a new job."

After an hour on the open waters, Richie untied the mast, allowing the sailboat to drift in the ocean so they could relax side-by-side in the beach chairs he had set up earlier. Amy reclined her chair slightly and propped her legs on the side of the boat while Richie disappeared downstairs.

A short while later, he came up with a plate of bagels smeared with cream cheese and slices of tomatoes on the side. Along with the container of fresh fruit Jeffrey had packed in the picnic basket. A bottle of sparkling juice was tucked in each pocket on the side of his shorts. Amy was in heaven. Maybe Miranda was right about embracing the unknown.

"I could have helped. Why didn't you tell me?" Amy asked, reaching to take a plate from him. "Thank you."

"You're welcome," he said, handing her a plate, her drink, and a linen napkin he'd stowed in his back pocket before sitting down to help himself to the same.

"Richie, you're amazing. I feel so spoiled. Thank you," she said again.

"Stop thanking me. I haven't done anything. It's just some bagels and a drink. Hardly warrants all this gratitude," he said.

"Why are you single?" they both asked at the same time and then both chuckled.

"Until I moved to New York, I didn't have time to date. I was always in the office," she said.

"Hmmm. Well, I must send a thank you note to your former employer because it obviously had a hand in leading you here." He took her hand in his.

"Thank you. It wasn't all work at first. I was dating someone for two years until I found out that he was cheating on me. That was a year ago. So after I broke up with him, I buried myself in work. It was easier than beating myself up for allowing him to lie to me for all those months."

"I'm so sorry, Amy," he said, looking down at his feet. "We have more in common than we thought. I was in a relationship that ended two years ago. I found out she was cheating on me with a coworker of hers, so I ended things. Just this week I started to feel ready to open up to someone new. Then I saw you running on the beach with your hair blowing everywhere and you didn't have a care in the world. I knew I needed to meet you," he said. "And that red bikini…I was hooked."

They both laughed, swept up in the moment. Amy inhaled deeply, the sea air filling her lungs, and she smiled, relieved that she told him about Adam. Before she realized what was happening, he leaned in and kissed her gently on the cheek. Her body relaxed, her guard sliding down. Could he be any more perfect?

They spent the rest of the afternoon soaking up the sun with Richie bare chested, occasionally running below deck to fetch them a snack or a drink, always thoughtful, always the perfect gentleman. She caught him looking at her a few times, and each time, she felt breathless.

They chatted easily about their jobs and apartments. Richie was a senior vice president at his father's investment firm, had just turned thirty-two, and had a younger sister about to turn thirty, the same age as Amy. His sister, Abigail, worked for the firm as well. His place in the West Village was a hike from her apartment on the Upper East Side. She was bummed that they lived so far away and then chastised herself. This might be just a vacation fling. Get a hold of yourself, Amy.

At the end of the day, Richie surprised her for the millionth time. He disappeared below deck and returned with two glasses of delicious, crisp Pinot Grigio that they enjoyed while watching the most breathtaking sunset as streaks of purple, pink, and orange hues intermingled across the horizon. It was the stuff love stories were made of, and Amy was caught in the moment, unable to resist the euphoric feeling of floating with joy.

"We should head back in before it gets too dark. We still have an hour's worth of sailing ahead of us," he said, standing up and surveying the water around them.

"Okay. I'll clean up while you do the sailing stuff," she offered, shrugging sheepishly at her lack of knowledge about the workings of the boat.

The combination of the wine and the motion of the sea had a magical effect on her. Facing him, she reached for his hands, "Richie...in case I forget to say it later...thank you for this amazing day. I loved every minute of it and really enjoyed getting to know you."

"The feeling is mutual. I want to see you again...while you're here and when we get back to the city," he said.

"You do?" she asked, grinning from ear to ear.

"Yes, I do." He took her hand and pulled her against him. Amy's breath hitched at the intense contact. One hand snaked around her waist while the other cradled the back of her head and he was leaning in for a kiss. At the touch of his lips against hers, she shivered. Tingles vibrated through her as their kiss deepened, her body betraying her will to stay grounded.

"I haven't been able to stop thinking about you since we met," he said, bending to kiss her again. Pressing against him, she lost herself in his kiss, unable to form a single thought. When they finally parted, he took her hands in his and kissed each one tenderly. "I need to see you again."

"Me too. This is nuts because we just met, and this sort of thing doesn't happen," she said, snuggling closer to him.

"It does, and it has."

Richie kissed her again briefly before releasing her to set sail for home. Amy cleaned up their plates and glasses and hurried back upstairs, not bothering to change into the sundress she packed earlier. She slipped the sheer cover-up over her swimsuit and joined Richie at the steering wheel. He extended his hand to her, and she happily accepted it, wrapped in his embrace most of the ride home. An internal conflict brewed between the romantic and guarded side of her.

As promised by her private and very sexy captain, they docked back in East Hampton exactly an hour later to a starry sky with a full moon lighting their way. It was the most romantic day and evening she'd ever experienced.

When Amy finally walked into the house, well past midnight, she was relieved to find everyone already in bed and Jeffrey gone home for the night. Richie had surprised her with a candlelit dinner on the deck of his parents' house overlooking the ocean. Just like she had imagined. He had pre-ordered a platter of fresh seafood and salads and had a bottle of wine chilling in the fridge. The enchanted evening didn't end there. After their meal, they took a dip in the heated pool with the soothing sounds of the ocean serenading them. With each passing minute, Amy fell harder for Richie and she knew fighting her feelings was a lost cause.

By the time he walked her to Megan's house, they were both spent and exhausted. They said their goodbyes with promises of seeing each other the next day and every day after that.

Amy tiptoed in through the kitchen patio door and made her way through the quite house to her room upstairs, grateful to be spared from sharing every detail of her day with Megan and Miranda. She wanted to hold on to the magic just a little while longer.

Chapter Five

THE MORNING SUNLIGHT shone bright in Amy's room. She tossed and turned for a few minutes, willing herself to fall back asleep but to no avail. Her eyes remained wide open in spite of feeling groggy from her late night. She was an early to bed, early to rise kind of girl. Turning to face the window, she sighed happily, highlights of the day before coming back to her. She lay in bed smiling and daydreaming until a soft knock on the door jarred her back to reality.

"Come in," she said, sitting up.

"Good morning, sunshine. How did you sleep?" Miranda said, still groggy. She stumbled to the bed and crawled in with Amy, forcing her to scoot over. "Well, how was yesterday? We waited up but we could barely keep our eyes open. We spent the entire day at the beach. I was wrecked by the time we came in for dinner. I'm taking it easy today and, by that, I mean laying low and out of the sun for a few hours."

"That sounds like a perfect day actually," Amy said, turning to face Miranda. "We had a great time. We went sailing, and he thought of everything…like every sweet romantic detail. And then we went back to his parents' house for dinner. I felt so pampered and spoiled the entire day," Amy said, unable to contain the grin slowly spreading across her face.

"Oh wow! You got it bad," Miranda said.

"Nope, it's all under control. It was just a perfect first date, that's all." Amy chewed her bottom lip.

"Don't worry, things will work out," Miranda said, wrapping an arm around Amy's waist. Another knock at the door and Megan walked right in, not waiting for a response.

"Oh, there is a juicy story to tell. I see Miranda beat me to the details." Megan jumped on the bed, positioning herself at the foot.

Amy shared the delicious details from the previous day, keeping some special moments with Richie to herself, both of her friends listening without interruption.

"Can we go down for breakfast now? I'm starving," Amy said. Just as they began to scramble from the bed, her iPhone vibrated with a new text message and her heart skipped a beat.

Miss you already. Call me when you're up and ready to hang out.

No rush. Sleep in. I hope I'm not waking you. Richie xo

When Amy finished reading the text out loud, Miranda and Megan were beaming with approval, delighted for her.

"So he passes the first test," Miranda announced, winking at Amy.

"Well done, Richie," Megan said, following Miranda out of the room to give Amy privacy to respond. Which of course she did. Plans were made, and she skipped down the stairs, counting the minutes till eleven when Richie would come over to hang out with them.

At breakfast, Amy recounted every detail of the previous day to Jeffrey who nodded his approval.

"I really like him, and not just because he's hot—because he is," Jeffrey said.

Showered and dressed in a yellow bikini with small red polka dots, Amy waited by the pool for Richie, trying not to look too eager. At the first sign of him walking up the beach towards the house, Amy hurried down the narrow pathway, jumping into his arms for hugs and kisses. Richie seemed just as excited to see her and he kissed her back, only releasing her to walk up to the house.

Looking up, Amy saw her two friends staring at her, jaws on the floor. She waved, smiled and pulled Richie by the hand up the few steps leading to the deck and pool. This wasn't typical behavior for her, and she wasn't surprised by her friends' shock. Miranda had known her for over a decade and not once had Amy acted this way about any guy, not even Adam during the best times in their relationship.

This felt different in every way.

"Hi Richie, nice to see you again," Miranda said, hugging him. She met them at the top of the stairs with Megan on her heels.

"Hey, you two." Richie hugged Megan.

The foursome toddled onto the deck with Miranda and Megan leading Richie to the picnic table already set up with snacks, beer, soft drinks, and a fresh batch of mango margaritas. "Jeffrey rocks!" Amy thought for the millionth time since meeting him.

Megan, being the perfect hostess, asked Richie about his choice of beverage and, as requested, offered him a beer, then she poured the chilled margaritas for the rest of them. Miranda and Megan drilled him with questions about his past, the sailboat, his job, and his apartment, leaving no skeleton undiscovered. Amy felt bad for him and on a couple of occasions mouthed, "I'm sorry."

To Richie's credit, he was a good sport about it. By the time they were satisfied, the foursome were laughing and chatting easily. They were having so much fun talking and swimming, they didn't realize it was dinnertime until Jeffrey came out to set the table. A handsome man with fair skin, red hair, and bright blue eyes followed closely behind carrying an oversized ceramic platter filled with fresh shellfish and other delicacies that he placed in the center of the table.

"All right mermaids and merman, dinner is ready. Come eat," Jeffrey said. "Besides, I want you to meet someone before we head out."

Amy and Miranda raced each other to the edge of the pool, practically running up the pool stairs and hurrying for their towels. Richie followed, and Megan giggled, swimming towards the ledge of the pool to greet James.

James was easy going and very laid back. He owned a holistic spa in town that offered everything from massages to Pilates and sunset yoga on the beach. Jeffrey was happy and in turn, Amy felt happy for him. He was living with a Zen master. Miranda had loads to talk about with James and the two of them fell into deep conversation, almost oblivious to everyone around them. A short while later, Jeffrey and James headed out, leaving them to their dinner of a mouthwatering platter of lobster tails, crab legs, and other delicacies.

A persistent ringing interrupted the flow of conversation and Richie reached for his backpack to retrieve his phone. Apologizing, he walked towards the far side of the backyard to take the call. Everyone carried on with their conversations, and the warm summer breeze blew, carrying with it the scent of blossoms from the garden. The evening couldn't be more perfect.

A few minutes later, Richie returned to the table visibly upset, his handsome face glum.

"Are you all right?" Amy asked, grabbing his hand.

"Can I talk to you privately for a minute?" He pulled her up with him. She nodded, following him down the narrow wooden bridge to the beach ahead.

When they reached the sand a few minutes later, Amy's stomach was in knots. Without even knowing what had happened, she felt tears begin to prickle her eyes. Whatever the news, it wasn't good. That much she knew.

"Amy…I'm so sorry to do this but I need to leave for London tomorrow night. My Dad just called and needs me to meet with a business associate first thing the day after tomorrow. I'm not sure how long I'll be gone…it could be a couple of days or a couple of weeks. I'm so sorry. I didn't anticipate this." He sounded as broken up as Amy felt.

Why am I so bummed? Spending time with Richie in a dream beach house was more than nice, it was almost like one of those fantasy dates from The Bachelor where everything was perfect. Perfect wasn't real life, she chastised herself.

"Why so sudden?" she asked.

"I can't give you the details. It's all very confidential. The financial implications are huge, but what I can tell you is that I hate going and I couldn't be more miserable about it. I'm sorry, Amy. Can I call you from London?"

"Yeah … sure … that would be wonderful," she said, forcing herself to sound cheerful and upbeat despite the lump in her throat. Get a grip, Amy. He's traveling for work, not leaving for Siberia.

"I had every intention of spending the rest of your vacation with you. I'm sorry. I need to return to the city tonight so I can pop into the office tomorrow morning and be on a flight by tomorrow evening. I'll call you as soon as I can."

He leaned in and kissed her deeply before returning to the backyard to bid everyone goodbye.

The rest of the evening was a blur, and Amy hung in there, carrying on with the banter as if her world hadn't been rocked in a very unhappy way. She tried not to focus on the fact that she might not see Richie again for weeks. By then, he might not have the same feelings for her.

To her credit, she faked it well by willing herself to focus on their beach vacation, savoring every moment with friends. All questions and conversations about Richie were off limits and, surprisingly, that made coping easier.

In the days that followed, she took to crying herself to sleep. Richie never called, and she couldn't believe he'd sounded so genuinely interested in her but hadn't bothered to contact her once. Had she misread his intentions?

On their last day at the beach, Jeffrey surprised them with a decadent brunch by the pool with all their favorites from waffles to eggs Benedict and even packed them a to-go basket with snacks for the long drive back to Manhattan.

They hugged Jeffrey goodbye, thanking him for everything, and climbed into the Land Rover with Megan behind the wheel, Amy in the passenger seat, and Miranda in the backseat guarding their snacks and drinks.

Halfway home, Amy's iPhone buzzed loudly in her purse. Almost afraid to hope for a message from Richie, she retrieved the phone.

Hi Amy.
I'm so sorry for not getting in touch sooner. I left my mobile in the car service in New York and it's taken this long to sort it out and have it returned to me. Miss you like crazy. I'll be home tomorrow mid-morning. I need to see you. I'll call as soon as I land. Richie xo

Amy smiled, the day brightening up once more. She wasn't wrong about him. Richie was everything she thought. Amy beamed at the prospect of another chapter in her life unfolding…with Richie.

Chapter Six

THE MONTHS BREEZED by with the seasons easily transitioning from one to the other, the only constant being Amy and Richie's blossoming romance. White icicle lights dripped from the trees as ribbons of red and green hung from store windows. This was New York City at its finest. The sun barely warmed Amy's face, but it didn't matter. No chill from Jack Frost could dampen her spirits. "This would be the best Christmas of her life." She wanted to swing from one of the light poles and shout out to the shoppers as they passed by. But explaining her blissful outburst to NYC cops was not on her To Do list for today.

The Union Square Christmas Market buzzed with holiday cheer as she weaved her way through the crowd to join the shopping frenzy. The usually open courtyard surrounding the entrance to the subway station had been transformed into Santa's village. Tent after tent in red and white stripes lined the perimeter. Inside the enclave, vendors from near and far displayed their wares—some homemade, everything unique. The holly-lined aisles transported shoppers to a slower pace of holiday bliss. Time stood still here—in a good way. She couldn't hide her smile, so giddy she flashed her pearly whites at every booth she passed. She actually lived here, in the greatest city in the world.

Stopping by a candle-maker's stall, Amy picked up a handmade candle for Miranda's yoga studio in the quaint city of Brentwood in Southern California. The candle smelled of sandalwood and vanilla. She imagined Miranda lighting it before class and smiled. She missed her best friend dearly, and even missed her hometown, but she couldn't imagine living anywhere but NYC. She browsed the racks of bath salts, silk scarves, and sticks of incense. A tall blonde with bright blue eyes lined with black kohl, busied herself wrapping Amy's candle. The colorful beads in her hair clicked with every movement. She hummed to herself, oblivious to being watched with fascination. Amy felt like bursting into a song herself but refrained. She moved deeper into the booth, browsing through the endless possibilities, and she picked up a pale pink silk scarf imported from India. Her mom would love it. With the Fair Trade sticker on the other side of the price tag, it was a done deal.

Beaming at her great progress with her Christmas list, she strolled to the next vendor—handmade jewelry galore. The delicious aroma of hot apple cider wafted around her. She inhaled deeply, relishing the sweet smell of the holidays. She scanned the booths ahead trying to locate the apple cider stand. Bingo! A few feet away, Amy spotted an older woman dressed like Mrs. Claus selling the holiday concoction. Done!

She hurried her steps and purchased the largest size cup, topped with extra whipped cream and a dash of cinnamon. Mrs. Claus wished her a very Merry Christmas.

"This is the season for wishes to come true. Make it good," Mrs. Claus said out of the blue, waving away the money in Amy's hand. "It's on the house, my dear girl." Mrs. Clause's uncanny resemblance to her beloved grandmother had Amy starring at her in disbelief.

"Merry Christmas," Amy replied, feeling like a character in a Hallmark Christmas movie. She looked over her shoulder for a cameraman but only saw jolly shoppers. She waved at Mrs. Claus and resumed her shopping, her mind still mulling over the older woman's words. A Christmas wish, huh?

Her purse vibrated.

Hi, baby. Where are you? Lunch? I already know what I want for dessert.

Richie xx

Hi back, baby. I'm at Union Square Christmas Market. Taralucci for lunch? Maybe some Christmas shopping afterwards? PS: I like your idea for dessert.

Amy xx

Ms. McKinsey, I'm a little surprised that your shopping isn't
done yet. Christmas is less than a month away. I will be delighted
to help you finish your shopping so we can focus on much more
important matters … i.e. dessert. See you at noon.

Richie xx

Amy giggled out loud at Richie's one-track mind. Not that she cared.
"All I Want For Christmas Is You" by Mariah Carey blared on the
overhead speakers. And all she wanted for Christmas was Richie. The last
six months with him had been incredible, and she loved everything about
him—although she hadn't uttered those exact words out loud yet. Not
that he'd said them either. They'd both said a bunch of other words that
implied love though. Amy was ready for more but was afraid to even
think about what it really meant. She hadn't been this happy in a long
time. She didn't want to do anything to ruin an already great thing. She
sighed, and the ornaments hanging on a miniature Christmas tree in the
booth across the way swayed in the wind, twinkling every time the sun
touched them. The glow was like a promise of something yet to come.

At noon, Amy walked the short distance to Tarallucci E Vino, scan-
ning the Santa and reindeer-clad retail windows along the way.
Christmas cheer filled the air. The wind danced playfully around her,
blowing her long brown hair. She hoped she wouldn't look disheveled by
the time she arrived. The thought of seeing Richie created a flurry of
butterflies swarming joyously inside her stomach, almost distracting her
from the tangled mess on top of her head.

The overly chipper hostess greeted her at the door. Tarallucci was
one of her favorite eateries in Union Square, and their wine list wasn't
too shabby either. She loved the low-key atmosphere and mouthwatering
dishes. Megan had introduced her to the hidden gem last summer when
they met there for brunch before shopping for the Hamptons vacation.
That seemed so long ago now, but it was only six months. Amy smiled
thinking about the Hamptons, falling asleep to the sound of waves
crashing, grilling parties on the deck and leisurely swims in the afternoon. And of course, meeting Richie was the best part of the vacation. It

was kismet, pure and simple. Things like this didn't ever happen to her. But then again, since moving to NYC, the world seemed to be her oyster.

"Will you be joining us for lunch or do you prefer the espresso bar?" the perky hostess asked, flipping her red hair to the side.

"Lunch for two, please." The words were barely out of her mouth when, from the corner of her eye, Amy caught sight of Richie getting out of the taxi. He was by far the sexiest man she had ever laid eyes on. Tall, muscular, with dimples that spoke directly to her heart, Amy smiled proudly as she watched a few by passersby gawking in his direction. She was used to women becoming hypnotized in his presence.

"Hands off, he's mine, ladies," Amy wanted to call out. She quickly ran her fingers through her hair, praying it didn't resemble Medusa's. The wind didn't spare Richie either, tousling his light brown locks, blowing them in every direction. On him, wind-blown hair looked sexy, somehow managing to be even more gorgeous. He wore dark washed jeans, a heavy cable knit sweater in a dark tan, and a knee-length navy wool coat. He looked like a model from a Ralph Lauren ad.

Amy rushed to the door, greeting Richie with a hug and a kiss as soon as he was over the threshold. His arms wrapped her waist, lifting her against him, and his aftershave filled her nostrils. Instinctively, she inhaled deeply, breathing him in. His cheek felt cool against her warm one, and she snuggled a little closer, nuzzling her nose into his neck for another whiff before she shyly slid down, flushed with embarrassment. Richie seemed oblivious to the patrons watching them. Beaming brightly, he bent his face towards hers, his six-foot three frame towering over her, and showered her with feathery kisses that started at her jawline and ended in a deeper kiss at her mouth.

"Richie, people are watching," she mumbled against his persistent warm lips.

In response, Richie playfully nuzzled her neck, tugging at her earlobe with his teeth. Somewhere from inside the restaurant, Amy heard a whistle, and heat blazed up her neck and face. This level of PDA was new territory for her. Richie was a damn good kisser, and if it weren't for old-fashioned modesty, she would have nixed lunch and headed straight home for dessert. Chuckling, she pulled him by the hand, lacing her fingers through his warm ones, and followed the hostess to their table. Amy's high-heeled black boots clicked lightly on the shiny dark wood floor. She stole a glance in Richie's direction and found him devouring her with his eyes. Another host of butterflies took flight inside her. They were seated at a farmhouse-style table, made of the same dark wood as the floor, right in the center of the restaurant. "So much for privacy," Amy thought, slacking in her seat. A few empty booths lined the perimeter, and Amy couldn't help but wonder why they weren't seated in one of them. The hostess lingered at the table for a few minutes too long, ogling Richie before she sashayed back to her post at the front of the restaurant. Amy shook her head with disbelief, clamping her lips together to keep from bursting with laughter at the amount of effort some women would go through for a hot man's attention.

The restaurant itself wasn't big, but it was cozy and warm and always inviting. Everything Amy loved. A Christmas wreath twinkling with a string of lights hung in the reception area by the espresso bar. A large Christmas tree decorated with tinsel and ornaments stood next to the staircase leading to the upstairs dining room and was flanked by two red poinsettias. It was the perfect touch to the already festive atmosphere. Soft Christmas music played in the background.

Once their coats were tossed on the empty chair next to Amy and they were comfortably seated, Richie leaned in and kissed her again.

"Hello there." He gave her another kiss for good measure before sitting back in his chair as if to get a better look at her. His eyes twinkled with mischief, and promptly her stomach did a summersault.

Amy caressed his arm, and he reached for her hand, clasping it in his own. Unlike most guys, Richie was the King of Romance, always touching her hands, planting soft kisses on her face and neck, driving her absolutely wild with wanting him. If it were up to Richie, Amy would be secure in his lap as they talked and waited to order their lunch. Good thing he didn't always get his way. Amy smirked, as if she could read his mind. The soft chuckle rippling from his chest confirmed what she was thinking.

The waiter arrived with their water and a basket full of a delicious variety of fresh artisan rolls. Amy's mouth watered. He poured olive oil on a small plate and then took out his notepad to jot down their order before disappearing into the kitchen.

"What are you smiling at? Surely not the menu," Richie teased, playing footsies with her under the table.

"I was actually thinking back to last summer. Megan and I met here for brunch and then went shopping for that red bikini you loved so much." Amy blushed.

"Maybe we should pay the store owner a visit and thank him."

Richie's phone buzzed, rudely interrupting their time together. He eyed the caller ID, his brows furrowed in response before he picked it up.

"I'm sorry, baby. I won't be long, I promise." He kissed her hastily before disappearing to the front of the restaurant to stand by the front door. The hostess was practically drooling as she watched him.

Amy noshed on the bread, generously dipping it in olive oil. She ate more than she intended. She cranked her head toward the door to get a better view of Richie. He was still on the phone, listening intently, his expression withdrawn. Amy wondered if something had happened at work. Her mind drifted to the Hamptons vacation when she had met Richie. The day had started off with morning yoga at the beach, a swim and a spontaneous sprint in her red bikini. Amy giggled remembering how carefree and silly and completely uncoordinated she must have looked as she ran with complete abandon in a bikini. Luckily, all her bits stayed covered.

Fifteen minutes later, Richie returned to the table, somber and slightly agitated. The food had already arrived while he was away. He began shoveling salad into his mouth, lost in thought.

"Are you okay?" Amy regarded him with concern.

Richie nodded. "Let's eat, I'm starved. Okay?"

Lunch was awkward to say the least. Despite Amy's attempt at small talk, Richie was distracted and distant. He almost looked unsettled as he only half listened to her.

"Richie, what is it?" Amy insisted.

"It's nothing. I promise. Are you done? Ready to get back to some Christmas shopping?" He waved to the waiter, handing him his credit card before even seeing the bill.

A knot began to form in the pit of Amy's stomach. Richie had been working long hours without a break. Even the weekends seemed to involve a few hours at the office interfering with their schedules. While she felt bad for him for being the one to miss out on fun weekends, the pity party didn't skip her as she was often left alone mid plans and that sucked. Amy sighed, hoping Richie didn't need to return to the office at some point in the afternoon. By the time they were strolling through the market hand in hand, Richie had snapped out of his mood and was his usual chatty and easy going self. Despite being cocooned in the warmth of Santa's Village, Amy shivered, the December cold air snaking through the booths.

"Is my LA girl cold?" Richie asked, bringing her hand up for a kiss.

Amy tilted her face to gaze at Richie, grateful that whatever had plagued him was taking a back seat to their day together. She snuggled close to his side, allowing his body heat to warm her. "A little, but I'm okay. I love it here and I love being with you." She smiled easily as she took in the Christmas magic around her, making a mental note to address the interruption at lunch at a later time.

Chapter Seven

AFTER A FEW hours of shopping, Richie suggested a break at Joe's, a tiny coffee shop that had quickly gained a cult following for its freshly roasted espresso beans from around the world—Fair Trade, of course. It wasn't unusual to find a line of dedicated patrons wrapped around the block waiting eagerly for a coveted cup of Joe. Thankfully, today wasn't one of those days, and the small shop was surprisingly quiet. Frank Sinatra crooned a Christmas song in the background, completing the already perfect ambience. The twosome weaved through the small square tables toward the back, away from the glacial draft that snuck through the door every time someone walked in.

Amy was delighted that Richie had suggested having coffee together. She had missed him. With his work schedule becoming busier, it was harder to hang out on a regular basis, and she waited with bated breath for the weekends and their alone time together. One of the things she adored about their relationship was their ability to talk for hours about anything. She could be herself around him, something she hadn't felt with a guy in a long time and was almost certain that Richie felt the same way. Secretly, she also hoped for a chance to talk about that pesky phone call that had monopolized their lunch date.

"What's going on with work?" Amy said, sliding into the chair. She didn't want to come right out and ask him about the call, hoping he'd just talk to her about it. It wasn't like Richie to be moody, even on his most stressful days at work. Amy hadn't seen this side of him before and it bothered her.

Amy reached for his hands across the small table. "You can talk to me." She rubbed her thumbs over his fingers, surprised to find them warm in comparison to her frozen ones. "You seem preoccupied."

In the last few months, their time together had dwindled from weekends and spontaneous dinners during the week to seeing each other on the weekend only. And those times were often interrupted by Richie's phone buzzing nonstop with new emails or phone calls. At times, it felt like a long-distance relationship – except Richie lived on the other side of the city, not the country.

Richie exhaled loudly, exhaustion hunching his shoulders. "Work has been overwhelming lately. It feels like there's no light at the end of the tunnel."

The barista placed their drinks on the counter, winked at Amy, and fumbled with something behind the register. Within seconds, the entire coffee shop lit up with Christmas lights—even the small Charlie Brown Christmas tree at the end of the counter. Amy's heart fluttered. First Mrs. Claus at the cider booth—who by the way was gone by the time she returned with Richie—and now the barista. Did NYC have a secret pact to make her Christmas magical?

"Ah … awesome. Thanks, man." Richie grabbed his cappuccino and Amy's hot chocolate, grinning from ear to ear. He placed the mug in front of Amy before settling back down opposite her. The table was so small, barely enough room for their drinks, but neither minded. The cozy coffee shop was a nice change from the whirlwind shopping frenzy taking over Manhattan.

"What were you about to say?" she asked.

"We've signed two large accounts in the last month that my father insists I manage, we're short staffed, and my Dad … I don't know … something is off with him. I can't put my finger on it. I need to hire a new director to oversee existing clients so I can focus on the new ones. HR is bombarding me with resumes every day and I just don't have the time to interview anyone."

Amy listened silently, holding the mug of hot chocolate in both hands to warm up.

"What about your sister?" She set the mug down on the small table and stroked his hand. She knew he was shouldering a lot of responsibility, and being the second-in-command at the investment firm was a tremendous responsibility.

"Abigail's in London, meeting with our oversees clients. Besides, she has a full plate too. We just need to power through the next few months while we find the right person. I don't want to prematurely hire someone who isn't the perfect fit." Richie leaned back in his chair. He looked like he wanted to say more, but then thought better of the idea.

"I'm sorry you're dealing with so much, especially around the holidays. What can I do to help?" Amy leaned into him, kissing his lips. Their gazes locked briefly, a shadow crossing his hazel eyes. Something was going on.

"Nothing, but thank you, baby, for being so supportive and understanding of my schedule. You're the best girlfriend ever." Richie softened a bit, stroking her cheek with his thumb. Despite his sincere effort, he was still wrapped up in private thoughts she wasn't privy to. Conflicted between happy at being referred to as the best girlfriend ever and hurt at being kept in the dark about something that clearly bothered him, Amy looked away, focusing her gaze on the twinkling Christmas tree, swallowing the questions that teetered at the tip of her tongue. Awkwardness settled over them again. Amy wasn't sure what to make of Richie's moods. One minute he seemed genuinely happy to be with her, and the next, he seemed far away. Amy absently picked at her cuticles as she busied herself with people watching while Richie finished his cappuccino. Without even glancing at her hands, she knew she needed a manicure—immediately.

Richie cleared his throat, shifting restlessly on the small wooden chair, visibly uncomfortable. "Should we head home?" he asked, meeting her gaze.

Reluctantly, Amy stood, gathering the packages of Christmas gifts in one hand and her purse with the other. Richie relieved her of the shopping bags, smiling at her. A glimpse of her Richie had returned, but not enough to settle the gnawing worry. She sighed, chewing on her lip, a bad habit since college.

"Lead the way, my lady." Richie waved at the door with an exaggerated sweep of his arm, bending at the waist in a grand gesture. Amy giggled, curtseying in return before she through the door. Perhaps now wasn't the right time to ask about the phone call but she'd probe again later.

The bitter cold outside engulfed her as soon as she stepped onto the street. The clear blue sky was a contradiction to the uninviting wind that whipped at her exposed face and hands. How much colder was it going to get? Amy dreaded the answer. If the last couple of days were any indication of what was to come, she was in for a long, freezing winter. Richie caught her eye, and the concerned look on his face touched her heart. She felt warm and fuzzy inside, the magical Christmas spirit filling her, or maybe it was just Richie burrowing deeper into her soul.

She shivered, tucking her hands deep inside the pockets of her knee-length winter coat.

Richie was at her side, wrapping an arm around her shoulder as he hailed a taxi.

"We can't have my California girl freezing to death before the best parts of winter arrive." He kissed the top of her head, pulling her in tighter against him.

"Oh, don't worry, I'll be fine although I can't promise not to freeze to death. How much colder is it going to get?"

The pinched look on his face told her all she needed to know.

Smiling, she tilted her head to look up at him, searching his face for a clue about his earlier mood.

"Oh I forgot to tell you, my mom called earlier, and she wants you to spend Christmas with us. We'll head over there early Christmas Eve day and return the day after Christmas if that's okay with you." He smiled. "I have to warn you, my mom is over the top with Christmas. She decorates everything. Like-every-single-thing, but she loves it and it's the only time that we all unplug from work—even my dad – for the most part anyway."

"That sounds really nice. Your family has been amazing in making sure I'm okay during the holidays. Thanksgiving was perfect and now Christmas. I'm so touched by your mom's thoughtfulness. I'll give her a call later to thank her for the invitation," she said softly, tucking a long strand of hair behind her ear. "When Peter and I decided to do something nice for our parents by buying them a dream vacation to Bali, we didn't think through the timing or how it would feel to have them away during Christmas. I considered going home anyway and spending it with Peter, but he seems to have made his own plans with his buddies so I decided to stay put."

"Well I'm glad you decided to stay here. I would hate to think of spending the holidays apart." Thankfully a taxi pulled up, and Richie held the door for her as she scooted in and waited for him to slide in next to her. "Lexington and 72nd Street, but drive up 5th Avenue, please," Richie told the taxi driver before turning his full attention to Amy, taking her hands. He leaned in toward her, brushing her lips with his and then pulled her into his side, his body hard and muscular against hers.

Pulling back slightly to look at her, Richie was about say something before his pocket vibrated, interrupting the moment. "I'm sorry, baby, hold on."

"It's okay," Amy mouthed as thoughts of spending the Christmas holiday in its entirety with Richie's family played in her mind, a to-do list forming. She needed to shop for a few outfits, and she needed to add a Christmas presents for her gracious hostess, Abigail, and Andrew, Richie's father. What did you buy the woman who had everything and who happened to be the mother of your gorgeous boyfriend? Amy chewed on her lip as she stared out the window, her mind reeling.

She pulled her phone from her purse and texted Miranda and Megan to tell them about the Christmas invitation and ask for gift ideas. Richie was still talking to whomever had called him, his tone tight and slightly tense as he responded. This was work-mode Richie in full swing as he asked pointed questions and gave precise direction about a client's financial portfolio. She studied him for a few minutes, admiring his focus and knowledge. He was born into privilege but that didn't change his admirable work ethic. He was the hardest working man she knew. While Richie was preoccupied, Amy took the opportunity to exchange a few more text messages with her girlfriends before tucking the phone back into her purse.

The holidays in New York were truly magical. It was no wonder

Richie had asked the taxi driver to take 5th Avenue to her apartment. She stared out the window, strings of Christmas lights and wreaths in all shapes and sizes transforming the city into a dazzling sight. Even the high-end retail shops participated by turning their window fronts typically adorned with mannequins wearing the latest fashions into vignettes from famous Christmas movie scenes ranging from The Nutcracker to Miracle On 34th Street. The scene reminded her of Rodeo Drive during the holidays, except that it wasn't eighty degrees in Manhattan.

Richie's phone call seemed to take forever, and she felt a mixture of annoyance that work was cutting into their private time together, her patience was wearing thin. Promise of an uninterrupted holiday break soothed her impatience and she bit her lip to keep from mumbling her agitation. But then she noted that if it wasn't for Richie asking to drive up 5th Avenue, she wouldn't have experienced Manhattan's holiday splendor during their drive home. Her tendency was to stay away from 5th Avenue because it was always congested with taxis and cars and during the weekdays, she relied on the subway to get to and from everywhere. Her irritation deflated by a few measures and tenderness for Richie overruled annoyance at his work schedule. Her hand slipped into his and squeezed it.

Finally, the taxi pulled up in front of her brownstone three-story walk up apartment building and Richie hung up the phone.

"Is everything okay?" she asked.

"Yes, I'm sorry. Francine at the office is having a problem with a transaction and I needed to guide her through it. I can't ignore their calls when I know the team is working during the weekend too."

"I'm trying really hard to understand, but sometimes it's a bit much."

"I know and I'm so sorry, Amy. It's a phase and it will pass. I promise."

Nodding, she decided to drop the subject for now and reached for her wallet only to be met with a glare from Richie and a wave of his hand to put her money away as he paid the fare himself.

Shaking her head at him, she walked ahead of him up the stoop to unlock the main door. It was full of charm, and Amy had fallen in love with it right away. Falling in love with her actual apartment was another matter. In fact, when she first laid eyes on her studio, she practically had a heart attack at the filth that greeted her. At the time, the interim landlord apologized profusely at the condition of the apartment and practically moved mountains to get it into a livable condition. Thankfully, it all worked out, and over time, she'd learned to appreciate her spacious-by-Manhattan-standards studio and refused the one-bedroom apartment that later became available downstairs. The studio was a far stretch from being sprawling and certainly no comparison to the airy two-bedroom, high ceiling apartment she had left behind in Brentwood. But it was home.

Richie playfully swatted her bottom, walking closely behind her, eager for dessert.

"It's not the end of the world if I pay the taxi fare," she pointed out. "You don't have to pay for everything we do together." Amy peeked over her shoulder at Richie as he nuzzled her neck, one arm wrapped around her waist while the other held the Christmas packages.

"I know, but I enjoy treating you, and it makes me happy to spoil you, although paying the taxi fare is hardly spoiling. Besides, you pay for the groceries for our Sunday dinners so that makes us even."

Upstairs, snuggled in the oversized armchair together, they talked a little more about Richie's work, the tension finally leaving his body. Amy was happy at the thought that she might have something to do with alleviating his stress.

"What are you thinking about?" Richie had some sort of radar for catching her lost in thought.

"I'm a little worried about you. You're shouldering a lot of responsibility and you're working all the time," she confessed.

"I know, and it will pass. We're in the thick of it now and we're understaffed so its impacting everything."

"What can I do?"

"Baby, you're already doing it. You're my stress relief. Knowing you care about me and you're understanding of what's going on takes the pressure off." They kissed deeply. "I'm so sorry about earlier." He held her face in both hands, gazing intently into her eyes.

"It's okay. It's just been hard lately seeing so little of you, but I'll try and be more understanding." Amy pressed her forehead to Richie's. She loved the closeness and intimacy between them. "Who was it that called during lunch? You seemed so upset." Turning her head slightly, she kissed the palm cradling her face.

The jarring buzz of his phone interrupted their conversation for the third time. Amy fumed. His work had practically taken over their entire weekend. Granted, the call sounded important, and from Richie's response, it was an urgent matter. She certainly didn't want to be the unsupportive girlfriend during a critical time in his career, but this was getting ridiculous.

Richie managed financial portfolios for many high-profile clients, working late nights and at times, traveling abroad. The chaotic and unconventional schedule hadn't been a problem for them so far. Talking on the phone every day and exchanging sweet and sometimes sexy text messages lessened the loneliness.

Knowing that Richie loved his job was consoling on some level. It made the sacrifice bearable. She remembered the first time Richie told her about the ins and outs of his work. She had found it fascinating and complicated and intimidating. There was something sexy about the way his eyes lit up. He loved going to work every day. The long-term plan was for Richie and Abigail to take over the firm. Amy knew that and understood the logic. It was her heart that struggled. Selfishly, she wished the timing skewed in their favor a little more.

Until work settled down, they would have to make the most of what little time on the weekends they had together. Richie made her so happy that even on the loneliest days she would rather deal with his undesirable schedule than be with anyone else. The phone calls today were irritating, but nagging him about it was like beating a dead horse. When she'd first met Richie, he'd prided himself on managing a healthy work-life balance, but lately, the scale seemed to be tipping dangerously to the work side.

A white Christmas with Richie and his family in Greenwich, Connecticut sounded heavenly. Until then, she needed to have faith that they'd overcome the limited time together.

Chapter Eight

BRIGHT WHITE BEAMS flooded the apartment through the airy and borderline sheer off-white drapery. The see-through fabric had been purposefully selected to allow for as much light in as possible during dreary winter days when getting a glimpse of the sun felt like an unattainable luxury. That was something she would have to get used to living in New York. On the flip side, a white Christmas was something Angelinos only dreamed of. Amy stirred in bed, pulling the duvet higher around her ears, instinctively burrowing in the warmth. A slow smile split her face as her eyes focused on the sexy man sleeping next to her. Even in sleep, he was irresistible.

To Amy's dismay, they hadn't had a chance to finish their conversation yesterday. Richie's phone rang and buzzed nonstop with calls and messages and he barely picked at the spaghetti and meatballs Amy had prepared. She felt bad for him. Giving up hope for an uninterrupted conversation, Amy went to bed and left Richie to his work. At some point in the night, she'd woken to the vibrating phone, still tucked in the pocket of his pants, thrown over the footboard of the bed. The knot that had started to throb during lunch was practically punching her now. She debated over waking Richie but decided against it. The clock on her nightstand had said 2:00 a.m. Who in the hell was calling him at two o'clock in the morning? It's not that she doubted Richie or thought that he was cheating. Everything about Richie was different than Adam. Richie was honest and loving and transparent with his feelings. With Adam, he was flirtatious at first, but as soon as they settled into the relationship, the affection stopped. He was almost never at the place he said he was, and his job certainly didn't require him to be on call around the clock, yet his phone buzzed with text messages at all hours. Richie and Adam couldn't be more different, and yet she was often alone in both relationships.

She was the common thread.

She stretched her arms from under the duvet, pointing her toes and elongating every muscle from her head to her toes, her body feeling heavy with sleep. Being a devoted yogi for the last nine months, Amy had learned a trick or two about being tuned into her body, and this morning her body was grateful it was Sunday. Turning her head slightly to glance at the clock on her nightstand, she groaned loudly. It was only seven thirty. She blew air out of her mouth and sat up. No point in fighting being awake or rousing Richie. He must be wiped out. She might as well get up and put the kettle on for tea. Amy had given up coffee months ago and hardly missed it, although walking past coffee shops in the morning was nostalgic. It was tough to resist the aroma of espresso beans brewing.

She padded to the kitchenette, filled the red kettle with water, and set it on the stove to boil. Within minutes, she was back on the oversized chair with a steamy mug of tea, the scent of Jasmine wafting through the studio apartment, and Amy inhaled deeply. She didn't want to wake Richie by turning on the TV, so she settled for looking through the stack of magazines she'd brought home from work.

She stole a glance at him still sleeping soundly, and her heart squeezed, the frustration of the persistent work interruptions momentarily tempered. She sagged a little deeper into the armchair, her mind still cloudy from lack of sleep. Rare moments like these, she missed the boost from coffee in the morning.

A phone buzzed, and she knew before looking that it was Richie's phone. She was used to every sound and bell coming from that horrid device. The sleep deprivation, frustration, and annoyance collided as she debated hurling the phone out the window. With tea cup still in hand, she stomped to the nightstand and peeked at the phone screen, ashamed for falling prey to old habits of checking Adam's phone and then calling him out on his lies. Not surprisingly, the text messages on Richie's phone were all work. She even recognized some of the names from conversations with Richie about the London office. Ugh!

She set the tea cup down and rubbed her temples, hating herself a little and knowing she needed to address her feelings with Richie in a way that didn't pile on to his already stressful days and nights. She was his stress relief, he'd said so himself. And she loved being that for him. She wanted to make their moments together fun and easy, but it was becoming hard to do that when they couldn't finish a sentence without the phone ringing.

From the moment she'd met Richie, she'd felt attracted to him. He had materialized out of nowhere on the beach applauding her, a smirk tugging at the corners of his mouth, his tousled blond hair giving him a boyish charm. He was confident, and funny, and he didn't waste any time in asking Amy on a date. Amy was completely smitten by the man who looked like a model from a Ralph Lauren ad. But there was more to Richie than his good looks. He had substance. During the first few months, they would spend hours talking about everything, no topic off limits. He had a calm disposition and a compassionate way of looking at things that resonated with her. His privileged background didn't blind him from seeing both sides of a situation. The more time they spent together, the harder she fell for him, trepidations about taking a risk by putting her heart on the line forgotten. His thoughtfulness toward her and loyalty to the people he cared about made it damn near impossible to be mad at him for not setting boundaries with work. But that lack of boundaries was seeping into their every moment together, fueling her resentment toward his work and his dad.

With the stack of magazines in her lap, Amy flipped through the pages with more force than she intended. Taking a deep breath, she set the magazines aside, lit the giant candle on the coffee table, walked toward the round pillows lining the far wall by the window, plopped down, crossing her ankles over her thighs, and closed her eyes. Calm down Amy.

A half hour later and in a much better state of mind, she sat back with her magazines leafing through the pages, occasionally pausing to earmark a recipe she wanted to try. The last recipe she'd clipped was Jambalaya with fresh seafood that she had made from scratch for Richie.

Going to the fish market at the South Side Seaport in lower Manhattan was a hassle, but worth the effort. Seeing Richie's face light up at the home-cooked meal prepared especially for him was all the incentive she needed. Maybe she'd surprise him with dinner tonight, giving them another chance at a romantic evening before the hectic workweek began. The last few Sundays, Richie had been staying the night and leaving early on Monday to get ready for work at his place. For that reason alone, Amy loved Sunday nights.

She smiled, tapping her finger on her chin as she contemplated what dish he would enjoy. The temperature had been dropping at record speed, almost begging for comfort food. A meal of roast chicken, mashed potatoes, sautéed mushrooms, and roasted green beans seemed to be in order. Amy jumped up from the armchair and dashed to the freezer and then the pantry cabinet to take stock of her grocery inventory, delighted at finding everything she needed. Since meeting Richie, she'd kept a semi-stocked freezer in case they decided to cook, a complete separation from her days of microwaving frozen prepared meals. Her kitchen in Brentwood was twice the size, but she barely used it. When she'd told Miranda about it during their weekly call, she teased Amy mercilessly and sent a text deeming her "The Domestic Goddess."

A couple of hours later, showered and dressed for the day in gray corduroy pants, knee-high Ugg boots and a pale yellow sweater, Amy returned to the armchair with another cup of tea. Richie stirred and sat up, looking for her. She suppressed a giggle.

"Amy?"

"Good morning." She climbed onto the bed, snuggling next to him. Bedhead and stubble had never looked sexier than it did on Richie. She wanted to devour him, unshowered and all.

He wrapped an arm around her, pulling her against him, heat radiating from his body. "What time is it?" he mumbled against her hair as his hands roamed her body, sliding under her sweater. Amy wiggled against him, fumbling with his T-shirt and managing to pull it off, then turning her attention to his boxers, sliding them down without protest. She kissed his cheek, dragging her lips to his mouth, the stubble prickling her lips. But she didn't allow that to hinder her plans. Her hands roamed his bare skin, exploring his broad chest, loving the taut muscles beneath her fingers. She didn't want this moment to end.

"Amy, it's nearly ten o'clock." He sat up abruptly, throwing the covers off, nearly knocking her off the bed. Was he late for something?

"What are you doing?" she protested, disappointment in her voice as Richie rushed past her.

"I want to spend the day with you doing something fun. I feel horrible about yesterday's endless work calls. That's not how I wanted Saturday to go."

She sighed, her shoulders relaxing. "And I love that idea. I was just hoping for a little more of this before I shared you with the world." Amy motioned to the bed, mortified at her own brazenness and request for sex.

Richie stood in the doorway of the bathroom, stark naked, as he watched her with an arched eyebrow. "I believe that's completely and absolutely doable."

Sauntering back toward her, all strong lean muscles, Richie climbed into bed next to her, grinning from ear to ear. He wasted no time ridding her of her clothes, kissing every inch of her until she was on the verge of exploding.

A little while later, ravished and spent beyond imagination, they took turns showering and getting ready, Richie determined to keep work at bay so they could enjoy the day together. She hurried to tidy up a bit, not wanting to waste a minute with Richie on boring household chores. The armchair and coffee table—that also served as a dining table and sometimes desk—were placed at the foot of the double bed and in front of the flat screen TV. The small studio meant that the bed was part of the sitting area and eating area and sometimes office area. Leaving the bed unmade made the space look messy. So she hurried to straighten the bed with all the frilly pillows that were included with the duvet set.

A half hour later, Richie was dressed in dark washed jeans, a green sweater and loafers. His usual bright hazel eyes were dull this morning, smeared with dark circles from exhaustion and lack of sleep.

"I need a coffee in the worst way," he said, rubbing his hands over his face.

"Okay. We'll grab some across the street. You must be exhausted. What time did you get to bed last night?" She said, coming to stand in front of him.

"I think sometime after 1:00 a.m."

Richie went on to tell her about the uncompromising client who hired them to manage his portfolio but wanted to micromanage every detail.

"So what happened?" she asked.

"Things came to head last night because he crossed the line with Abby's team. He was screaming at her assistant over some report that he's not due to get for another few days. The guy is a lunatic."

"How did you leave things?"

"We're going to part ways with him on Monday. Managing someone's financial portfolio is hard enough, we don't need the verbal abuse on top of it."

Running her hands over his arms, she said, "I'm glad that's over now."

"Almost over. Can you believe my dad fought to keep this jerk as a client?"

"What? Why?"

Andrew was a smart and savvy businessman, and from the short time she'd known him and what she'd learned about him from Richie, she knew that she didn't like to pass on new business deals. But fighting his children over a no-brainer situation seemed out of character for him.

Last night was rougher than she imagined for Richie.

She wrapped her arms around his neck, breathing in the D&G aftershave, letting it settle into her lungs. Amy brushed her fingers through his still damp hair, pulling herself up to her tippy toes to kiss his lips.

"I'm sorry, Richie. Your dad seems intent on expanding the business at record speed and maybe it's time you and Abby asked him to tap the brakes a little."

"I know. We're trying, but he's very stubborn and lately, he's unreasonable."

"You seemed very upset and distant after the call during lunch yesterday. Was this client the reason behind it?"

He sighed, shifting uncomfortably on his feet and then headed to the oversized chair, pulling her along to sit on his lap. She could have sworn she detected a hint of sadness in his eyes, but he quickly composed himself, clearing his throat before speaking.

"I'm sorry, Amy." Richie's fingers burrowed in her hair, twirled the silky strands and then unraveled them before starting over again. Twirl and unravel. It was almost hypnotic. Anxiety pulsed inside her in anticipation of his words. He swallowed hard, his Adam's apple bobbing up and down before he continued. "It was my dad who called during lunch. He's acting very strange. He follows up constantly about the same thing, over and over again. It's making me feel like he doesn't have faith in my abilities. Either that or he's becoming a micromanager. And I'm drowning with work so his calls only aggravate me because I'm stopping what I'm doing to give him the same update over and over again." Richie shifted beneath her again, but his hands remained in her hair, methodically twirling and unraveling.

"I'm so sorry, Richie. Have you tried talking to him?"

"No – I should. I will. I just need to figure out the right time and right words. Maybe during the holiday break when we're all relaxed." He tilted his head to look at her, two faint dimples piercing his cheeks as he smiled at her. "I know the phone calls have gotten in the way of our time together and I don't want to waste another minute with you talking about this stuff." His hands slid down to her back, fingers splayed across her shoulder blades, and he pulled her towards him, burying his face in her hair.

Amy wrapped her arms around his neck but remained silent for a minute, processing the new information. "I'm glad we talked. I had a nagging feeling that something was off yesterday. I didn't realize it was your dad calling and texting." His shoulder felt solid underneath her cheek, the cashmere sweater soft against her skin. Her heart ached thinking about Richie at odds with his own dad about the exhaustive work schedule. Surely Richie's dad knew how hard Richie and Abby worked. Driving them to work harder would only burn them out. "Don't worry, baby. Everything will sort itself out." She wished there was something she could do to help or at the very least, alleviate Richie of some stress.

"Have I told you that you're the best girlfriend ever?"

"Yes, but feel free to tell me again."

"You're the best girlfriend in the world, Amy. Thank you for being so understanding."

At his proclamation, Amy lifted her head from his shoulder to face him, pressing her forehead against his. "You're welcome. We'll just have to make the most of our time together."

"Deal." Richie brushed his lips to hers, lingering for a minute before he stood, then pulled her up with him, swatting her bottom playfully. While Richie gathered his belongings, Amy chuckled as she picked up keys, purse, and coat on the way to the front door, relieved they'd had a chance to talk. Her old self would have skirted around an uncomfortable conversation, waiting for the other person to bring it up. She hated confrontation and the icky feelings that typically came along with it. But all things considering, the conversation with Richie felt great.

"Let's go. I'm excited for us to spend the day together." Amy pressed against Richie, holding his face with her hands before she returned his kiss with every ounce of passion she could muster.

A couple of hours later, after fresh bagels, coffee for Richie, and a seltzer for her from the diner near the apartment, Amy stood gawking at the ice rink in Central Park filled with squealing kids, couples, and friends, delighted to join in the winter activity.

"You ready?" Richie stood next to her holding two pairs of skates and a smile that could melt glaciers. Amy's eyes widened with excitement, a grin spreading across her face. Ice skating in Central Park was a favorite scene in Christmas movies, and now, she would experience it first-hand. Blond wisps of hair brushed over Richie's forehead and Amy reached over and combed her fingers through his locks, relishing in the intimacy of the moment.

"Yes." Beaming with delight, they quickly laced up their skates and walked down to the ice rink to join the jolly crowd. Round and round they went, giggling like school children. Amy was laughing so hard at Richie's funny impersonation of a figure skater; she lost her balance and landed right on her backside with a thud.

Richie played ice hockey growing up, so being on the ice was second nature to him. She, on the other hand, was a completely different story and this was anything but natural.

"Are you all right?" Richie was at her side in an instant with his hands extended to pull her up.

"Yes, never better. I almost forgot how cold it is out here." Amy accepted Richie's help, pulling herself up with effort as her sliding feet refused to cooperate. Feeling giddy and carefree, Amy threw her arms around his neck for a kiss and instead, ended up pulling him off balance. Their feet were slip-sliding across the sleek ice, arms flailing as they tried to regain balance but to no avail. They lost the fight with gravity and landed in a heap, entangled on the ice, laughing hysterically while skaters around them pointed and smiled.

"I'm sorry I made you fall," she said once they were both standing again, somewhat composed, and slightly wet from the ice.

"It's quite all right. Some things are worth falling for."

Whoosh! Amy's heart burst from her chest with the intensity of the moment. Small beads of sweat pearled along her hairline as her eyes locked with Richie's.

"I couldn't agree more," she said.

"I'm glad we're on the same page. I have to admit I was a little worried you were turned off by the million work calls lately. I know it's draining for me and I can only imagine how annoying it is for you."

"Knowing that your feelings for me are deepening, it makes it easier to deal with the small stuff because now it is small stuff when looking at the big picture."

"There's definitely a big picture, Amy, and I'm grateful you're being a good sport about the last few weeks." He leaned in and kissed her chastely, aware of the clusters of families skating around them.

Richie's face flushed a deep pink, and Amy doubted it was a result of the cold temperatures. Love was in the air, even if the actual words weren't verbalized. Amy's hands rested on Richie's chest, his heart thumping erratically beneath her fingers, and she was suddenly hyper aware of their bodies pressed together. Heat rushed to her face as she took a step back and turned to stand next to him, looping her arms through his as they skated off the ice.

Still floating from the exhilarating excursion, they hailed a taxi and headed to Serendipity 3. Richie had promised it was the best hot chocolate on earth. Amy was looking forward to finding out if he was right.

Within fifteen minutes, they walked into the boutique coffee shop oozing with charm, seeing waitresses balancing massive trays of mouth-watering food and, of course, their specialty frozen hot chocolate. Amy was in heaven.

Over burgers and the signature drink topped with a generous serving of thick whipped cream and chocolate shavings, Amy told Richie the gory details about Adam, the details she had kept to herself until now. She shuddered remembering the perfume that clung to his work shirts and the text alerts that persisted throughout all hours of the night. She shook her head from side to side to clear the painful reel of memories. Today was a huge step for their relationship.

"I'm so sorry, Amy. That jackass didn't deserve you." Richie reached for her hand, planting a kiss to her palm as she wiped at the tears clinging to the corners of her eyes. Talking about Adam wasn't as hard as it used to be and owning her part in it helped with healing. She couldn't move forward with any relationship without confronting the ugly truths of her past, mainly her role in all of it. Looking back, she had turned a blind eye to Adam's lies, convincing herself to believe him when every instinct told her to run like hell. And while she'd forgiven him a while ago, until recently, she hadn't forgiven herself. After the initial trepidation of allowing herself to be vulnerable again by being open to another relationship and letting Richie in, she decided to make peace with her naivety and mistakes where Adam was concerned. It was liberating.

"What made you stay in the relationship for so long?"

"I guess a part of me didn't want to believe that someone I cared about would intentionally hurt me. And I didn't have the courage to stand up for myself. I don't know why. I thinking the timing was rough all around. I was dealing with Adam at home and battling with Sarah at the office. It all seemed like too much."

"I hate that he did that to you. On some level, I do understand the feelings of denial that someone you love, someone you think loves you back, is capable of hurting you. When I found out that Joanne was cheating on me, it knocked the wind out of me. I couldn't believe that someone who swore she loved me would hurt me in that way. Did I ever tell you how I found out?"

"No, you didn't."

"She had given me a key to her apartment and on that day, I had used it wanting to surprise her with a home cooked meal for when she came home from work. I walked in on her with a co-worker who was also my friend – on the couch, naked. She thought I was in Connecticut for the day. It was awful. For weeks I couldn't sleep, I barely had an appetite. It really messed with me because I didn't see it coming."

"What did you do?"

"Well, I beat the crap out of him, cussed her out and then I left. I haven't seen either of them since. They both reached out in the beginning to apologize and meet in person, but I didn't see the point. After that, I threw myself into work until that weekend I went to the Hamptons and met you."

She studied him attentively, an unexplainable inner peace flooding through her. There was something to be said for sharing your deepest and darkest memories and knowing it was emotionally safe. "Thank you for telling me. I don't want to run from you, Richie. I'm excited to see where our relationship goes."

"I don't want you to run either, and I promise to never give you reason to. I've fallen for you, Amy, and I can't imagine my life without you in it."

Amy wiped at the tear that trickled from the corner of her eye. She really didn't want to cry and ruin this near perfect day. Richie slid his thumb across her cheek, holding her gaze for a moment.

"He really didn't deserve you."

She nodded in agreement, grateful for every curve ball that had led her to this moment.

Later that afternoon, Amy put the final touches on their dinner, occasionally stealing a glance at Richie as he lay on her bed with the paper. A sweet magical vibe hovered around them, and Amy found herself silently mouthing words of thanks to the universe for the abundance of goodness in her life. Despite the slew of work calls from Richie's dad, their relationship was solid, their bond stronger. Richie had said all the right things today, starting with sharing his deepest wounds with her and declaring his feelings toward her and about their future. Richie's dad was a minor wrinkle in their relationship, but not one they couldn't overcome.

Chapter Nine

AFTER A SUCCULENT dinner of roast chicken and all the trimmings, which neither had any business consuming after eating their body weight in burgers, fries, and frozen hot chocolate at Serendipity 3, the two of them collapsed on the bed, too tired to move. Every muscle in Amy's body ached from the hours on the ice rink. She had so much fun racing Richie in circles she'd lost track of time until the burn in her thighs slowed her down. And now, she paid the ultimate price as her muscles throbbed in complaint. But she didn't mind. It was all worth it.

"I think I need a hot shower. I'm feeling like the Tin Man," Amy joked. Slowly rolling off the bed, she hobbled to the bathroom without waiting for Richie to respond. Knowing him—and she did—he would follow. Of course, she was barely surprised when he joined her a few minutes later, the steam wrapping them in a romantic bubble. Richie focused his undivided attention on her, lathering every inch of her before giving her an impromptu massage starting at her shoulders and ending at her ankles.

Turning to face him, she returned the favor by lathering his broad shoulders and working her way down his washboard stomach, pausing briefly to look up at him from under her lashes. His eyes smoldered, their usual hazel color turning liquid with desire for her. Every inch of him responded to her touch, begging for more physical contact. Amy's breath hitched at his visible reaction to her, giving her the confidence to do more. She had never felt such a strong connection to any man before Richie. He was the complete package.

"That was one hell of a shower, Ms. McKinsey." Richie snuggled Amy as they both lay in bed, him in boxer briefs and a white T-shirt and Amy in a burgundy lace camisole and matching boy shorts.

"Hmmm … it was. You're very talented, Mr. Hendricks." Amy kissed him softly, her eyes half closed, sleep creeping closer.

"Good night, baby."

Amy was awakened abruptly from deep sleep by the raging wind outside. If she didn't know better, she would have guessed a tornado had overtaken Manhattan. But she was practically a New Yorker now and was used to the volatile winter weather. Turning to look at the clock on the nightstand, Amy exhaled with frustration at being awake at three o'clock. Sleep evaded her, and the exhaustion from earlier was replaced with restlessness and thoughts of Richie's dad, pushing his son to the breaking point with work. She couldn't help but wonder about the dynamic of Richie's family. Surely, Richie's dad realized the amount of stress he was placing on his children, and yet, he continued to push as if their entire purpose for living was to run the family business. Didn't he want them to have a happy and healthy balanced life?

Thoughts of her parents occupied her mind, and given Richie's stressful work situation, she appreciated her parents that much more. Amy's parents were always perceptive of her and Peter's needs—reading their moods and tuning in to their wellbeing. Amy knew without doubt that her parents' sole concern was her and Peter. And as unfair as Amy knew it was, she couldn't help but judge Richie's dad for not having the same protective instinct for his children.

Amy rolled over to face Richie, seeing his features relaxed and peaceful with sleep. His breathing was shallow, rhythmic, a contradiction to the storm brewing outside. She knew the talk with his dad wouldn't be as easy as Richie hoped. Stories of Andrew working through the weekends didn't give her comfort that he'd expect less from his children. Outside, the wind picked up momentum, angry and destructive. Amy burrowed deeper under the covers, missing the warm California sun spoiling her year-round. She closed her eyes, willing sleep to overtake her restless body, but instead she tossed and turned, unable to fall back asleep.

Opening up about Adam had released some of the memories buried deep in the dimmest part of her past. The cheating bastard! Thanks to him, a seed of self loathing and mistrust had forever been planted in every relationship she had because she hadn't listened to her instincts and confronted him. Not until the relationship nearly destroyed her.

At first, Adam was nice and flirtatious. He was the life of the party and he had his finger on the pulse of every social event worth attending. Quiet the opposite of Amy who preferred an evening at home to large crowds. At first, Amy gladly obliged by joining him at this bar or that house party, but as time went on, long hours at the office and her desire for a peaceful weekend drove a wedge between them, their differences more glaring than before when Amy was more accommodating to Adam's whims. Slowly, he became distant, almost aloof, insisting that work deadlines kept him at the office when his position didn't require him to be there. In fact, no one at his office ever worked late. The affairs didn't happen overnight. In the beginning, there hadn't been big red flags waving in front of her, however, there were plenty of subtle signs that Amy had chosen to discredit, believing him over her intuition. It wasn't until Adam's phone rang and buzzed with text messages from female friends and colleagues at all hours of the night, constantly, that Amy became suspicious. With every call and text, Adam created an excuse to take the call in private, disappearing for long stretches of time while he talked to "work." When she'd ask him about the call, he never had anything of substance to say about the big emergency that required his undivided attention. That's when Amy's antennae shot up with alarm, and she started to question him.

He shamed Amy by making her feel paranoid, accusing her of creating problems where there weren't any. So Amy believed him for as long as she could. But it became more and more difficult to trust Adam as evidence of his deceit stacked up, smacking her in the face. The faintest smell of women's perfume clung to his shirts. He bought new underwear, different clothes, changed his haircut. All for work, of course.

One night after an evening of one too many cocktails, Adam passed out drunk, face down on her bed, leaving his mobile phone on the dining table. When the phone blared loudly at 3 a.m., Amy rushed to the phone to silence it only to find a text from a woman named Cynthia. Needless to say, it was the beginning of the end, the feeling of betrayal gutting.

Now, lying in bed with Richie, she was grateful that at the very least, she was dating an honest man who valued trust as much as she did. Her relationship wasn't perfect, and her frustration with his unreasonable dad was a thorn in her side but she wasn't lying awake worrying about Richie's whereabouts or extracurricular activities in someone else's bed. Fatigue finally took over, and she fell into a deep sleep.

When the alarm blared, jarring her awake at five forty-five, Richie was already gone. Her heart sank a little. If this week was anything like previous weeks, she wouldn't see him again till the weekend, and that just sucked. His scent lingered on the pillow next to her, and it was divine. Instinctively, she scooted to his side of the bed, hugging the pillow against her cheek, inhaling the faint aftershave clinging to the pillowcase. A handwritten note fell off the bed, and Amy caught it before it landed on the floor. Her ninja reflexes were impressive, especially considering her lack of sleep. Richie was by far the most romantic man she had ever met. Delicious little vibrations flowed through her body as she scanned the note.

Good morning, baby. Have a great day at work today. I miss you already. I'll call you later. Richie xx

Chapter Ten

T HE SHORT WALK from the subway station to the office was blustery, gray, and typical of an east coast winter, the complete opposite of what she'd left behind in Los Angeles. But this morning, her numb toes—clad in completely impracticable high heel boots—were barely a bother as she pushed her way through the overcrowded throng of people beelining for their warm destinations. Amy was preoccupied with the vivid dream from the night before. A part of her felt like a magical creature still traipsing in Santa's village, looking for him. Her mind recounted the details: gigantic glittery red and green bells dangled from lamp posts, occasionally swaying in the winter breeze. In the dream, she leaped from her office window into a Christmas wreath hanging on a lamp post below, becoming miniature in the process. Once inside the greenery, she realized the wreaths were brilliant portals to Santa's village in the North Pole. She quickened her pace, eager to see Santa, to tell him her Christmas wish. Wide lanes, surrounded on both sides with enormous candy canes, curved and twisted, leading into a forest of Christmas trees. Feeling like Dorothy in The Wizard of Oz, Amy followed the path, her heart racing with anticipation. The forest was enchanted, each brilliant color adding to the beauty of her surroundings. Every sound was strangely familiar. Beautiful birds of different colors and species perched high on the tree branches, watching her with amusement. Some chirped greetings; others tweeted among themselves, somehow understandable to her. Smiling like a fool, she continued, walking briskly now, the light beyond the forest visible through the dense trees.

"Are you lost?"

She turned. Looking around, she didn't see anyone.

"Woohoo, down here," the voice said.

Amy jumped back with alarm at the elf standing a few feet away from her, a basket filled with holly hung on his tiny arm.

"I'm … I'm … looking for Santa." Amy's voice was merely a whisper as she quickly sized him up. He was dressed in green pants, a red jacket, and the cutest little red elf hat.

"I see … and why are you looking for him?" The little elf was clearly protective of his boss.

"Well … it's really important that I see him before Christmas so I can tell him about my Christmas wish," Amy explained, pulling herself taller. Then realizing that she already towered over the elf, her body slacked slightly. There was no need to intimidate him.

"Ahhh … yes. Just follow the path and you'll find yourself at Santa's workshop. One of the elves there will help you locate him."

"Thank you, thank you." Amy leaned down and gave the elf a hug before running as fast as her feet would go, choosing to ignore the little facts that she'd spoken to an elf and that he knew her name.

"Merry Christmas, Amy," the elf called from the distance.

Just as he promised, within a few short minutes Santa's workshop was in full view in front of her. Panting from the spontaneous run, Amy stood at the red front door decorated with a handmade wreath of holly, candy canes, and shiny ornaments. She breathed deeply, rehearsing her request in her head. Just as she raised her hand to knock, the door swung open, and Amy found herself face to face with Mrs. Claus. Strangely enough, Mrs. Claus was a dead ringer for the Mrs. Claus from the Union Square Christmas Market and even more bizarre, the resemblance to Amy's grandmother was uncanny. Her grandmother's spirited energy seemed to surround her lately as if trying to telepathically tell her something. But what? This was all too weird.

"Come in, dear. You must be freezing."

"It's you." Amy couldn't hide her shock.

"Come on in. I just made the most delicious apple cider. Come have a cup. Mr. Claus will be here soon." Her grandmother's look-alike dressed as Mrs. Claus stepped aside, opening the door wider to let Amy in.

The workshop was beyond anything she had ever imagined in her wildest dreams. Dozens of workstations filled the large open space, some covered in toys, while others had toy parts ready to be assembled.

The elves hummed and sang happily as they worked in the most magical place on Earth. Mouth gaping open, she stood frozen as elves moved around her, some smiling sweetly at her, others not taking much notice, too consumed with their tasks.

The deep voice of a man startled her, and she turned, eyes searching for him, his familiar laughter echoing through the workshop.

"Santa … Santa, I really need to speak with you." Amy zigzagged her way through the tables, desperate to reach the man capable of making Christmas wishes come true. A loud buzz sliced through the air, monotonous, almost rhythmic, overpowering all other sounds in the large room, including her own voice calling Santa. The workshop became fuzzy, out of focus, as if a sheer white veil had been cast over everyone. And then they faded, the buzzing sound dragging her from dreamland into Monday morning. It was five forty-five. With a groan, she rolled to her side facing the window, her body heavy and uncooperative, images of the North Pole still vivid in her mind.

By the time she stepped out of the elevator on the 24th floor of the Weisman Publishing building, she felt more grounded in reality, the dream taking a back seat. Except the bit about seeing her grandmother. That didn't feel like a dream. That felt very real. She shook her head to clear her mind as she continued towards her office, brown heels clicking softly on the hard wood floors, freshly polished over the weekend. The office was festively decorated for Christmas, the scent of fresh pines and cinnamon wafted throughout the hallway. Ornaments of all shapes and sizes adorned the plush Christmas tree just right of the elevator by the set of floor-to-ceiling windows overlooking Times Square. Weisman Publishing was home to many household publications, including Diva magazine, where perfectly touched-up celebrities graced the glossy covers once a month. At the urging of Jane Callaghan, the creative and advertising departments had moved to the same floor as the marketing team to work closer.

In Amy's humble opinion, the 24th floor was the best floor in the building. From late nights working together before a deadline to happy hour with the team, Amy felt like she'd won the lottery by being part of Jane's team. Not to mention Jane's implicit support and mentorship. It was such a different experience from her previous job. Actually, there was no comparison. Amy's previous boss, Sarah Mitchell, was handed the role of Head of Marketing because of her family connections and nothing more. Sarah was a socialite who circulated with the elite and wealthy and certainly knew nothing about marketing, magazine publishing, or managing a team.

During last week's staff meeting, Jane had urged the team to provide constructive but positive feedback and then made a point to mention some of her favorite things about the marketing campaign from photography to team collaboration. She even had the team applaud the creative director for his work on the storyboards that ultimately informed how the campaign would look in ads all over the country. Jane was what every boss should aspire to be, period.

Since starting at Diva, Amy pinched herself at least once a week to make sure the dream of living in Manhattan and working for the most popular lifestyle magazine in the country was real. Amy sauntered towards her office at the end of the hall, the light bouncing off the twinkling wreaths on office doors. The scent of hot chocolate wafted through the air, filling her nostrils with sweet childhood memories. She swallowed the nostalgic lump in her throat that manifested out of nowhere, feeling more homesick than she imagined possible. Her older brother, Peter, had a way of making her feel better, and she made a mental note to call him once she got settled at her desk. As excited as she was to experience a white Christmas with Richie, a Pacific Palisades Christmas by the beach wasn't too shabby either. Christmas morning at her parents' started with opening gifts, a leisurely, mouthwatering breakfast on the veranda overlooking the Pacific, surfing, naps, and for dinner, a feast fit for royalty prepared by her mom. Christmas at the McKinseys was perfect in every way. When she closed her eyes, she could almost smell the salty ocean air. Almost.

Her phone buzzed in her purse, and Amy quickly fished it out. It was a text from Richie sending her a heart emoji. Her heart skipped a beat, the homesickness momentarily forgotten. She had to suppress the squeal of joy erupting from her throat. A white Christmas in picturesque Greenwich, Connecticut was just a week away, and experiencing a true New England Christmas with Richie's family was everything she wanted.

Smiling, despite the lack of sleep from the previous night, Amy ambled toward her office at the end of the hall. It wasn't even nine o'clock, and a palpable buzz vibrated from the cluster of colleagues gathered at Megan's desk outside of Jane's office. Megan was Jane's executive assistant, with a promising career in photography. Megan had submitted a few photographs to the photography department and a couple had been selected and published in previous issues. Amy couldn't be more thrilled for her friend.

"Have you heard?" Megan asked, rushing toward Amy.

"Good morning to you too, Megs. Heard what?" Amy took a sip from her to-go teacup, a giant heart circling planet earth printed on one side.

"Jane is leaving Diva. She's been promoted to Head of Marketing for Weisman corporate overseeing the entire publishing company." Megan's eyes twinkled with a mixture of sadness and excitement.

Amy's mouth dropped open at the news, shock and disbelief slowly registering. The timing couldn't be worse. They had a massive marketing campaign a couple of months away. A swarm of ants scurried across her skin, and she shuddered with shame at feeling bummed instead of happy for her mentor. The thought of Jane ever leaving the magazine she helped build was unfathomable. With so much change underway already, losing Jane perpetuated panic, especially in Amy who benefited from Jane's guidance. The buzz she'd felt a few minutes earlier slowly seeped out, leaving Amy feeling deflated. Jane's leadership and focused vision was what kept the team motivated and excited to push forward, and now, they'd have to get used to new boss, and possibly a new vision. Losing Jane had personal implications for Amy as well, because she would be losing her strongest advocate and mentor. Of course she was glad for Jane's success and recognition, but she mourned her own good fortune.

The weekend with Richie had ended on a high note, but it had been far from a blissful weekend, and now this. Amy began to wonder whether her charmed life in Manhattan was coming to an end. Somewhere in the distance, Christmas music played festively, a contradiction to her mood.

"It sucks for the team to lose her," Megan rattled on.

"I need to go settle in before our staff meeting, okay?" Amy was a horrible liar and she knew her friend sensed the shift in her usual chipper personality.

"Let's grab lunch today."

Amy nodded absently in Megan's direction. In the privacy of her own office, Amy sank into her chair and glumly powered on her computer. Working for Sarah Mitchell had taught her one thing—crying at work was a big fat no-no. Amy breathed deeply, swallowing the misery gnawing at her. This was the first time she'd felt truly unhappy since setting foot on the magical island of Manhattan. She reached for her phone and called Richie with the news.

"Hi, handsome. Thanks for the note and text. I'm already counting down the hours until I see you again."

"Me too. Did you just get in?"

"Yup and the office is buzzing with news of Jane's promotion to corporate. She's leaving the magazine."

"Aw, man. That sucks. I know how much you love working with her. Now what?"

"I don't know. I imagine they're already working on her replacement." She cradled the phone between her shoulder and neck as she peeked out the window, overlooking the bustling city below, crawling with tourists year-round. If she pressed her forehead against the window and looked right, she could see a sliver of Times Square.

"Hang in there. This could be a good thing."

"How's that?"

"Career growth, my young Jedi." Richie loved Stars Wars and sometimes referenced lines from the movies, adding to his boyish charm. Today, she felt like the Grinch, grumpy with a dose of irritated at the unexpected change.

"Hmmm, maybe."

"Amy, use this as an opportunity to think about what's next for you. With Jane leaving, you now have an advocate at the most senior level in the company, plus she's still supporting you in your current role. It sounds like a win-win to me."

"I know you're right. I'm just really bummed to lose the daily interaction with her. Once she's in her new role, she won't have as much time to oversee the marketing team or time for me."

"Maybe on some level she won't be as involved with the department at large but she'll make time for you. Get ahead of the ball and schedule one-on-one bi-weekly meetings with her and go in with an agenda of things you want to discuss or get guidance on."

"You think so?" She waffled, biting her nail.

"Absolutely. One hundred percent."

The ping every time an email arrived had her ending the call with Richie to focus on work. She freshened her lip gloss, determined to overcome the new wrinkle in her happiness, and plowed through the emails. Change was good, she reminded herself. Change had led her to Manhattan, and in turn, had led her to Richie. With a notebook, a pen, and her phone in hand, she meandered towards the marketing conference room.

The conference room was overcrowded this morning, with the marketing and creative team chatting loudly among themselves as they waited for the staff meeting to begin. Amy paused in the doorway, searching for Jane or Megan, but neither was there. A few people nodded in her direction, and she smiled back. She decisively walked across the enormous conference room to the empty seat by the window.

Scribbling in her notebook in a feeble attempt to look busy, she crossed and uncrossed her legs, fidgeting restlessly in the chair; a smile plastered on her freshly glossed lips. The idea of Jane leaving the department was more than upsetting but Richie was right, it also presented a great career opportunity and a chance for mentorship with a senior leader. It was refreshing to work for a woman of Jane's caliber— both professionally and personally. Jane was a rare gem who was driven by group success rather than individual glory. Not to mention, Jane took pleasure in mentoring the team and took the time to understand each person's strengths and weaknesses, helping them overcome challenges to reach their fullest potential. Amy couldn't help but have a side by side comparison list in her head with Jane in one column and Sarah in the other, the difference jarring.

A few moments later, Jane and Megan arrived together, deep in conversation, stopping abruptly when they walked over the threshold of the conference room. There was nothing Amy could say to ease her misery about the situation but at the very least, she decided to be supportive. It wasn't Jane's fault for getting a well-deserved promotion. She sat up taller, her spine pressed firmly into the back of the chair, making a conscious effort to stop chewing her bottom lip as she often did when she was upset about something. Having a poker face wasn't her strong suit. Deliberately relaxing her face muscles, she tried to look serene and not the wreck she felt inside. Shifting in her seat, she reminded herself of how far she'd come from the jittery and reactive person she once was. Amy swallowed hard, channeling inner calm as she forced herself to sit still. A small part of her felt the last nine months had been too good to be true, and every now and again, her stomach summersaulted at the lucky streak coming to an end. Of course she had no reason to believe that it would, but Jane's promotion stirred emotions and anxiety that had been bottled up since leaving Los Angeles. Had she confronted Sarah about her unprofessional behavior and filed a complaint with Human Resources, maybe she would have a better sense of closure. But she never did. She was so happy to part ways with Glitz and any interaction with Sarah, she couldn't be bothered. Now she wished she had, because months later, Sarah still had a negative hold on her, and she hated herself for it.

"Good morning, everyone. I know news travels fast so let's talk about that first and then we'll catch up properly." Even in the most uncomfortable circumstances, Jane was a class act, exuding confidence and poise. Dressed in a black pencil skirt, green blouse, and black Chanel heels, Jane was the vision of elegance.

"So … as you may have heard, I will be beginning my new position as Head of Marketing for corporate on January 1st. I'm very excited by this new opportunity, although it's bittersweet, as I hate to leave all of you. I've been leading this team for the last eight years and it's with great difficulty that I hand the reins to someone new." Her voice wavered. "Until we find a replacement for this role, I'll be juggling both positions. I ask for your patience and I promise you, HR is doing everything in their power to find the absolute best fit for our department. Now, can I answer any questions?"

"Do you have someone in mind for your role or are you looking to fill the position from outside the organization?" Jeff, one of the senior designers asked. He had taken a liking to Amy's marketing ideas and over time, the two of them had become friends.

"We are open to promoting from within but it's more important to me to hire the right person than force a fit with someone internally." With that said, Jane inhaled deeply as she glanced around the room, her eyes resting on Amy, holding her gaze for a few seconds before resuming the meeting. Amy sat tall pushing her back against the hard cushion of her chair, a smile pasted in place for good measure. Why was Jane looking at her that way?

She couldn't possibly be considered for Jane's role, but maybe Richie was right about change being the catalyst for career growth.

After a few more questions from the staff about logistics and deadlines, the meeting was adjourned with Jane running out to another meeting before Amy could speak to her or congratulate her. She shuffled back to her office without any more information than she walked in with and lots more questions. The phone vibrated, still cradled in her hand. It was her brother, Peter, confirming her feelings about Christmas, although he hadn't wasted any time making plans with his buddies.

Megan stepped in front of her, startling her. "Hey, what did you think?" she asked, her eyes searching Amy's face.

Amy made a face, "I have mixed feelings. Let's catch up during lunch." Amy walked around Megan, hurrying to the safety of her office. The last thing Amy wanted was to air her concerns in the hallway. No thanks!

Back in the security of her office, Amy sat heavily in her chair, swiveling it to face the large window behind her desk. Absently, she stared outside, reminding herself that despite the unexpected shake up with Jane moving to another department, Amy was still damn lucky to be working at Diva, call the vibrant city of Manhattan home and be living her dream. Besides, she had a white Christmas to be excited about with Richie.

"Hi Amy, do you have a minute?" Jane poked her head into Amy's office.

"Yes, of course." Amy sat tall, brushing her fingers through her long hair.

"I'm sorry we haven't had a chance to catch up. Everything happened so fast with the promotion, and I've been moving a million miles a minute." Jane sat back in Amy's guest chair, crossing her legs.

Amy's shoulders relaxed. Jane's presence had a calming effect on her. She adored Jane, as a boss and mentor.

"Listen, I don't want you to think that I've abandoned you," Jane went on. "I'm still here and will be watching your career. I've actually wanted to talk to you about the next step for you here, and with me eventually fully transitioning out, this is a good opportunity for you to take on stretch assignments." She leaned onto Amy's desk as if wanting to whisper a secret to a close girlfriend. "I'm promoting you to Senior Director effective immediately, and if you continue to show us the same promise we've seen these past eleven months, you'll be Assistant Vice President by this time next year. I know it's an accelerated timeline, but if anyone can do it, it's you. Someday, this will be your department, Amy." She glanced at her wristwatch and stood abruptly. Jane's calendar was always jam-packed with meetings, often double booked and yet she managed the department so meticulously well.

Amy thanked Jane profusely and congratulated her on the promotion as she rushed to her meeting, leaving Amy feeling humbled and grateful to have Jane in her corner. So maybe her world didn't turn upside down, just slightly tilted to the side. Pressing a hand to her mouth to keep from screaming with joy, she sent Richie a quick text telling him about the promotion and Jane's plans for her.

A couple of hours later, Megan and Amy sat at Haru Sushi, ravenous and grateful for the quiet restaurant.

"I've seen some of the resumes for Jane's job," said Megan over a pot of green tea. "Jane asked me to be the liaison between her and Joan at Human Resources. I'm told they're being very selective about who they're considering for the role."

Megan took a sip of tea, rubbing her hands together to warm up. The only downside to eating at a sushi place in the winter was the cool temperature in the restaurant.

"Considering the big shoes they're looking to fill, I would hope they take their time finding the perfect fit."

"True. You're taking the news in stride. What's up?"

She told her dear friend about the conversation with Jane.

"Amy, that's incredible news. Congratulations. You must be so excited."

"I am but it's more than that. Working with Jane has restored my faith in women at work. Jane has been a true mentor and guide and I've learned so much from her."

"She really is amazing and she continues to surprise me. I thought I'd be transitioning with her but instead, she's added a headcount to the photo department for me. I nearly fell out of my chair when she told me."

"Wow"

"She said I have great potential and there's no time like the present to spread my wings. Can you believe that? She'd rather go through the pain of hiring a new assistant and training her than hold me back."

"It doesn't surprise me one bit. For a long time, I didn't think women like her existed at work, especially at senior levels." Amy picked at her cuticles, a terrible habit she needed to break.

Megan nodded in agreement, taking another sip of tea.

"So I heard through the grapevine that Glitz magazine is struggling and there's been a major reshuffle in management, again. To be honest, when I heard that, my biggest fear was that Sarah would somehow worm her way back into my life. Publishing is a small world and magazine publishing is even smaller."

"It must be nice to hop from one big position to the next one without any consequences for the mess she leaves behind." Megan craned her look to look for the waitress, anxious for lunch.

"Right? Megan, she was awful to everyone but she loved torturing me the most."

"I'm so sorry, Amy. I had no idea it was that bad. Don't give her any thought. You've moved on, just got an awesome promotion, and you're dating a great guy. It's safe to say that life is good. So cheers to that." They clinked tea cups, giggling.

"I'm grateful for all of it, especially yoga. It keeps my head clear of negative nonsense," Amy half joked, pulling herself taller in her seat. Both girls fell into a fit of laughter. "Seriously though, we know Jane wouldn't settle for a mediocre replacement and neither will human resources. I'm so bummed to lose Jane, but she won't be truly gone."

Their conversation was halted while the waitress returned with their sushi and miso soup, then disappeared again.

"You're right. So how was your weekend with Richie?"

"It was nice. Like really nice. Aside from him working over the weekend again. But at least we were together. And we talked about Christmas again."

"Wow. That's a huge deal. Things must be getting serious. First you spent Thanksgiving with them and now Christmas. That's awesome. I'm so happy for you and so damn jealous. Everything is falling into place perfectly for you guys. Are you sure Richie doesn't have any brothers or cousins?"

Amy chuckled softly before she expertly picked up a piece of sushi with her chopsticks and quickly popped it into her mouth.

"Things are great, but I'll have you know they're not perfect."

"What do you mean?"

"Well … based on the number of work calls Richie got this weekend, my gut is telling me that his dad is not a fan of anyone or anything distracting Richie from work."

"Oh, Amy. I'm sorry. What does he call about?"

Megan chewed thoughtfully while Amy gave her the abbreviated version of the weekend. "Don't worry. Things will settle down," Megan offered.

The twosome chatted easily for the reminder of lunch. They never lacked for conversation. Megan started telling Amy about the latest drama at her gym. Apparently, a particular gym goer preferred skimpy workout gear to practical workout clothes and had no shame flaunting her half-naked body on every machine.

"So I took your advice and took a yoga class, and of course the skimpy outfit was in the class too. First downward dog and her boob actually fell out of the flimsy top and she didn't have a care in the world. She just moved on to the next pose like nothing happened. Can you even imagine?" Megan asked between bites.

They laughed so hard Amy's sides hurt and Megan snorted loudly. A few disapproving looks were tossed their way, but the two girlfriends were unfazed.

Back at the office, grateful for the girl time, she chuckled to herself at the lunchtime conversation. Megan was a great storyteller and had a knack for witty description of a scene. She was also a magnet for the bizarre. It was the norm for Megan to have a funny and yet completely outlandish story to share at least a couple of times a week. Only Megan would be on a yoga mat next to someone whose body parts fell out of their clothes. Amy shook her head with amusement. After refilling her water bottle from the kitchen, she settled in her chair, tackling out the pile of creative mock-ups for approval, carefully reviewing each layout and suggested image. She loved her job. Her phone buzzed, cutting through the silence. In her haste to delve into work, she had forgotten to turn on music. She picked up the phone, glancing at the screen. It was Miranda.

"Hey babe. Sorry about Jane. Bummer! Chat tonight my time?" Miranda asked.

Amy quickly responded and agreed to a phone date, excited to chat with her best friend. The day was almost over and not a peep from Richie. Amy chewed her bottom lip, contemplating whether to call him.

Chapter Eleven

AMY HURRIED TO yoga class, grateful her work day was over, her body humming with anticipation at being stretched like a pretzel. Yoga was one of her favorite escapes, and since moving to Manhattan and taking a job with reasonable work hours, she managed to attend a few classes a week. Ironically, it took moving to the busiest city in the world to find work/life balance. When she worked at Glitz, late nights were a guarantee, and Amy often ate dinner at her desk. Life was miserable, and socializing on weekdays was nonexistent. At first, Amy didn't mind the rigor until she realized there was no end in sight. Sarah expected her staff to arrive early and stay late. However, she never held herself to the same standard.

After yoga, Amy practically bounced home, eager to decompress with a glass of wine while doing laundry. Thankfully, her building had brand-new washers and dryers, sparing her the trip to the Laundromat. Hanging out with Richie over the weekend meant doing laundry during the week, but it was an inconvenience she gladly put up with if it meant seeing him.

Later that night, Amy wasn't sure whether to feel concern or upset at not hearing from Richie as she settled into bed to read, her mind everywhere but on the book in her hand. Tidbits of the dream intercepted her thoughts.

She rolled her eyes at her own silliness, glancing down at the book again in another attempt to read. Her phone vibrated next to her, and Amy practically fell off the bed in her hasty attempt to answer it. Richie's face lit up the screen. She had taken a picture of him sitting on her bed smiling at her and saved it as her screensaver for his number. She had been waiting all day for his handsome face to appear.

"I miss you, I miss you, I miss you and congratulations," Richie crooned into the phone.

"Miss you baby and thank you. I didn't hear from you all day. Is everything okay?" Amy held her breath for his response.

"I know, I'm sorry. I've been on back-to-back calls all day. I'm still in the office. But the good news is that Abby is back from London tomorrow and can help with managing our new portfolios."

Amy's heart twisted at the sound of exhaustion in his voice. "It's almost nine. I can't believe you're still there."

"It's alright. It's just a short phase and it will pass. As long as this schedule doesn't interfere with Christmas with you, I'll gladly do the long hours now. But on a happier note, I'm so proud of you. We'll celebrate your promotion this weekend"

Richie's voice sounded subdued, tired. Amy toyed with the idea of spilling every detail of the day but decided against it, giving him the highlights only. Richie had enough to deal with.

"So basically, HR is working overtime to find Jane's replacement," said Amy. "Until they do, Jane will continue to oversee two busy departments at the same time. I don't know how she's going to juggle it all." Amy's said levelly.

"Wow, it sounds like Jane will have her work cut out for her. Her promoting you before leaving is great though and confirms her plans for you."

Amy's heart melted. He remembered everything they ever talked about.

"Anyway, let's not talk about work. The strangest thing happened today. I had the most vivid dream last night or maybe it was early morning. I dreamt that I was in the North Pole looking for Santa and I met Mrs. Claus." In spite of herself, Amy began giggling, unable to control herself.

"That's one heck of a dream. Oh … hold on," Richie said, returning to the phone a few seconds later. "I'm sorry, baby, my Dad just walked in. I'll call you tomorrow."

Richie hung up before they said a proper goodbye with their usual, 'I miss you and can't wait to see you.' She had to remind herself that Richie's insane schedule was just a phase.

Amy dialed Miranda knowing chatting with her best friend always cheered her up.

Miranda picked up after the first ring. "Hey."

"Hey yourself. How's your day going?"

"I'm just leaving the studio now. My class was at capacity again. I spoke with Sean and he's adding a couple more classes for me to teach. I'm really excited."

"Miranda, that's awesome. Congratulations. I know how much you love working for Sean."

"Yeah, things are working out nicely. So tell me, what's happening with you? It sounds like you had a magical weekend with Richie."

"We did, sort of. His Dad called a few times about work but overall, it was really nice. We skated at Central Park. Can you believe it?"

"Sounds amazing. I'm sorry about Jane?"

"Me too but she promoted me to Sr. Director today and then let me know I can go to her for anything. It meant a lot to me that she did that."

"Wow! Congratulations. See good things happen to good people. Keep the positive energy flowing."

"Thanks Miranda. I promise, I will. I'm actually really looking forward to spending the holidays with Richie's family. I feel like our relationship is moving to the next level and I'm so happy."

"You deserve all the good things happening Amy. You're a great girl and Richie knows it."

"Thanks Miranda. You always say what I need to hear. I love you."

"Love you too Amy. I gotta run but we'll talk over the weekend."

Amy briefly debated about calling her Mom, but it was getting so late and she had another packed agenda the following day. She'll call tomorrow, she decided.

Grabbing the book again, she stared at the same paragraph for over twenty minutes before deciding to put it away and get a good night's sleep, not bothering to put away the folded stacks of laundry on the oversized chair in front of her bed. She went through her bedtime ritual of washing her face, brushing her teeth and putting a glass of water on the nightstand. In the darkness of her apartment, Amy reflected on the day, images of Santa's workshop played in front of her. As strange as the dream was, Amy decided to hold on to the euphoric carefree feeling it gave her. Amy climbed into bed and pulled the duvet around her shoulders, thoughts of the last year replaying in her mind. Miranda was right about keeping the positive vibes flowing. Besides, unexpected change led her to Manhattan.

A year ago, Amy was a shell of herself working for Sarah, defeated and voiceless. Truthfully, it was pointless to fight the unshakable force of Sarah because Sarah's family money saved the magazine from financially collapsing. Investors seemed to flock from every corner of the world, all connections of Sarah's father. Had Sarah not come onboard, Glitz would have shut down and Amy would have been jobless. With Sarah there, Amy was nearly jobless because Sarah had every intention of firing her and callously broadcasted it to e.v.e.r.y.o.n.e. at Glitz. At the end, Amy was meant to leave Glitz and when she did, the world seemed to open up to her from landing a dream job to living in the city of her dreams. Amy no longer fought change and instead, she embraced it – even when the meantime sucked, like Jane leaving.

The next morning, Amy woke up at five o'clock, feeling surprisingly rested despite the early hour. When she first moved to Manhattan, she used to attend early yoga class before work every morning. She felt and looked her absolute best during that time. Something about connecting with her higher, wiser self did wonders for her mental health. A few years ago, the thought of connecting to a higher self felt hokey and weird. Now she couldn't imagine a day without some form of meditation to feel and remain grounded. Waking up early this morning was a sign to be more diligent with her yoga practice. God knows she needed inner peace now more than ever.

Without hesitation, Amy dashed to the bathroom to wash up and get ready for yoga. With hot tea in her to-go thermal cup and her yoga mat slung over her shoulder, Amy practically skipped out the door of the building and into the frigid air outside. The soothing effects of yoga were already affecting her positively and she hadn't even done a single downward dog yet. Now that's magic!

At the yoga studio, she was greeted with smiles and hugs by classmates she hadn't seen in months since switching to the evening class. The positive vibration was like a drug and right then and there, on her yoga mat during the first set of sun salutation, Amy decided to return to morning yoga, every day or until her life settled back down.

A series of sun salutations, back bends and chest openers later, Amy's body pulsated with an inner strength beyond explanation. Something about the morning class suited her more and she was glad she'd listened to her body's internal alarm and got out of bed. She practically floated from the yoga studio back to her apartment to shower and get ready for work. The Christmas decorations around her looked brighter, bigger, and so much more festive. Amy was seeing her world with new eyes. She felt alive and her body hummed with excitement at the thought of spending a white Christmas in Greenwich with Richie and his family.

Just a little before nine, Amy walked through the jolly halls of Diva as she hummed "Santa Claus Is Coming to Town". Her cheeks were flushed pink from being windswept during the brisk walk.

"Someone is chipper this morning?" Megan teased from behind her desk, coffee cup in hand.

Amy shrugged her shoulders and strolled to Megan's desk for a quick catch up before the day officially began.

"I went to yoga this morning and last night. I feel so good. And I talked to Richie last night. He's been working around the clock. He was still at the office when he called me at nine. Can you believe it?" Amy said.

"Poor guy. Come on, I'll walk you to your office."

Amy eyed her friend suspiciously. Once inside her office, Megan shut the door and made herself comfortable in the plush chair across from her desk. She clearly had something important and confidential to share, most likely about Jane's replacement. Amy raised an eyebrow, eager for the news.

"So I found out that Joan and Jane have been interviewing candidates for the last few weeks. Jane doesn't seem to be happy with anyone and Joan hired another recruiting firm to help with finding qualified candidates."

Megan rattled on so fast, Amy couldn't help but wonder at the amount of coffee she'd consumed this morning. She was practically bouncing in the chair.

"So are they close to finding a replacement?"

"I don't know. They seem to have a short list but they're keeping that information under lock and key. Jane wouldn't even tell me. All I know is that a new person will start Monday, and HR will send a company-wide email to welcome them."

Megan sat back in the chair with a loud exhale, and Amy regarded her quietly, a million thoughts whirling in her head.

"Wow, poor Jane. The pressure must be overwhelming. So is the person starting Monday her replacement?" Amy froze in her seat, her eyes glued to Megan's face as if the candidates' names were etched on her friend's forehead. She inhaled deeply through her nose, determined to hold on to any shred of inner calm from yoga. Her reaction to Jane's departure was slightly irrational, Amy knew, but she couldn't ignore the dreadful feeling that her streak of good luck was about to expire. Success at Diva wasn't hinged on hard work alone. Amy had worked her tail off at Glitz and that didn't pay off. The only difference between her soaring career at Diva and mediocre career at Glitz was plain and simple. Jane admired Amy while Sarah had hated her.

"I don't know, I guess it could be." Amy felt Megan's warm hand touch her frozen one and she jumped. Amy's mind was going off on tangents and she was working overtime to stay in the moment and maintain a positive outlook. Negativity attracts negativity—something Amy had learned early on during her yoga retreat with Miranda one summer after college graduation.

They had spent two weeks in Big Bear Mountain at a lake house. They started each day with sunrise yoga and ended it with sunset yoga and meditation, with other classes in between. The evenings were free, and Amy always opted to stay in and curl up with a book on the porch overlooking the lake. There was something so serene about the silence of the nights. The sky looked so different than the sky in Los Angeles, just a couple of hours west. Every night before she turned in, Amy gazed at the inky sky, magnificent and filled with a million twinkling lights ranging in brilliance and size. During that retreat, Amy heard her own voice for the first time. She understood the true meaning of being connected to your higher self. She exuded confidence, inner strength and calm. The following week she had interviewed at Glitz and landed the job. Dozens of candidates had been interviewed—some multiple times, she found out later—but she was offered the job on the spot. It wasn't until Sarah joined the company several years later that Amy's world began to crash miserably around her.

Relax, Amy, and don't feed the situation negative energy.

"I guess the lucky candidate will be announced soon enough," Amy said now as she plugged her phone into the small desk speakers and pushed play. Christmas music piped through the office. Ah, Frank Sinatra! His voice could cure anything.

"That's the spirit, my friend," said Megan. "I have to run, Jane will be returning from Joan's office any minute now."

Amy saluted Megan, suppressing a laugh as Megan saluted back before turning on her heel and marching out of the office.

Her phone chirped loudly, rudely interrupting Mr. Sinatra's rendition of "Silent Night". Richie's picture popped up on the screen and Amy yelped with excitement, nearly knocking over her teacup. She wasn't expecting a call from him this morning.

"Hi. This is a pleasant surprise." Amy gushed, smiling through the phone.

"Good morning, gorgeous. We didn't get to say a proper goodbye last night. Besides, I needed to hear your voice before the day got away from me. How are you? Any other developments with Jane?"

"I'm so glad you called. And yes, some developments I guess with a new hire starting on Monday."

"As in Jane's replacement new hire?"

"I don't know. Possibly. I wish we could pause all the insanity with work and run away." Cringing at her own admission, Amy stilled, hoping she wasn't putting more pressure on him. But her heart ached at the thought of not seeing him all week, again. Hopefully with Abby returning to Manhattan today, Richie's workload would ease up a bit and they'd have some weeknights together.

"I wish we could run away too. Come over after work." His voice drove her wild, especially when he spoke to her in a hushed tone, like he was doing now.

Amy's breath hitched at his request, fanning her face to cool down. "Uh … yes, if you promise to come home at a decent hour," she leaned into the desk, imagining Richie across from her.

Feeling like a schoolgirl being asked to her first dance, Amy giggled and twirled her hair around her finger until she remembered she was at work. She straightened in her chair and turned her attention to her laptop. At the very least, if someone walked by, they wouldn't necessarily guess she was swooning and consumed with a personal call.

"Deal. I'll see you at mine tonight around seven thirty. I can't wait to see you. Text me when you find out more about the new hire. Bye, baby."

"Ok. Bye." Amy blew kisses into the phone before hanging up. She felt her body elevate from her chair and floated midair with happiness. Frank Sinatra's voice filled the office again. This time Amy joined him, her Christmas spirit soaring despite being tone deaf.

"Amy, I didn't realize you're a fan of Frank Sinatra." Jane popped her head in the door. "I grew up listening to his voice." She seemed to hesitate for a brief second before walking in and shutting the door behind her.

Amy's stomach lurched. What could Jane possibly need to say to her behind closed doors?

"Yes, I'm a sucker for Sinatra. Sometimes I think I was born in the wrong decade." She motioned for Jane to sit down.

"Amy, I wanted to tell you myself about some new developments. We have a new hire and you'll be working very closely with her on the campaign. We're hired Sarah Mitchell as Sr. Director in marketing. She'll be your counterpart and projects will be split between the two of you.

Just between us, she doesn't have the breadth of experience we typically want in this role, but she comes with a lot of contacts in the industry, and with the right coaching and shadowing from me, I think she'll grow nicely at Diva."

Whatever Joan said after Sarah's name, Amy didn't hear it. The world had gone dark around her and the dormant knot in her stomach was now revolting with a vengeance. Amy prayed she wouldn't vomit all over her desk or worse, all over Jane.

"So you've changed your mind about finding a replacement?"

"For now, yes. We didn't come across the right candidates so instead of replacing me, we'll staff up and divvy the projects. What is it? I thought you would be thrilled to work with an old colleague." Jane regarded her with concern.

Amy was utterly speechless and in a desperate state. How could this be happening?

"I … I … I don't know what to say." She managed to mumble, torn about telling Jane the truth about Sarah or pretending everything was fine.

"We mentioned your name to Sarah since you both came from Glitz and she seemed genuinely thrilled to be working with you again."

Jane's soft voice did very little to soothe Amy's rattled nerves. She was convinced that Sarah knew exactly what she was doing when she applied for the position in the first place. Everyone at Glitz including Sarah knew that Amy had moved to Manhattan to work at Diva.

"I don't know what to say …." Amy gulped air, feeling her chest compress tightly.

Amy twisted her hands under her desk, her palms clammy with sweat, the walls closing in on her. She prayed Jane didn't probe into Amy's hesitation about working with Sarah. She watched her for a reaction, keeping her eyes steady and focused. The tears were threatening to spill any second now and Amy wasn't sure she could control herself any longer. Her good luck had officially crashed with a screeching halt. The persistent knot in her stomach was convulsing painfully now.

"I see …" Jane regarded Amy apprehensively. "Is there something I should know about your working relationship with Sarah?" she asked pressing her lips together.

Amy shook her head, misery enfolding her. Deciding there wasn't a professional way of telling Jane about the sadistic behavior of her previous boss, Amy bit her tongue and choked back tears. As far as she was concerned, the writing was already on the wall—her career at Diva was coming to a sad end.

"I appreciate your diligence and commitment to the projects underway, Amy. I really do. I assure you, I'll continue to be heavily involved in the department until we find my replacement. So for the meantime, can you please help onboard Sarah into the department?" Jane smiled reassuringly.

Amy nodded in agreement. If only Jane realized the doom about to befall her beloved department. Although the fact that Sarah was brought in as Senior Director and not a senior leadership role spoke volumes and wasn't wasted on Amy. She still hated the idea of Sarah at Diva, but Sarah's wasn't her boss. She was a colleague.

After Jane left, Amy stood on shaky legs, feeling achy all over. She walked around her desk, shut the door, and cried bitterly at the unfair turn of events.

Chapter Twelve

PRACTICALLY SPRINTING TO yoga class after work followed by an hour meditation, Amy headed home, limp from the intense class. Her eyes were still puffy from sobbing uncontrollably on the subway ride home. The hot shower did wonders for her achy muscles, but her eyes were still bloodshot, and she felt mentally drained.

Amy couldn't understand what could possibly have happened to lead Sarah to Manhattan. She guessed the rumblings about a change of management at Glitz included rotating Sarah out. But why Diva? Surely Sarah's parents had other contacts in Los Angeles.

Going to yoga class had helped put things in perspective, a little. Amy was glad she didn't fall into her old ways by folding into herself and wallowing in misery. Less than a year ago, she'd been jaded about relationships thanks to Adam's heartless cheating, victimized at work by Sarah, and overall emotionally and mentally depleted. So much had happened since. She'd met an incredible guy who adored her and wanted her to spend Christmas with his family, she worked for a wonderful boss who believed in her, and she was living in the best city in the world. Crying was a good release from the built-up anxiety about Sarah joining the team. It was all too much, but Amy was determined to stay strong throughout all of it even if it meant taking two yoga classes a day and meditating during her lunch hour.

Dressed in jeans, knee-length Ugg boots, a pink turtleneck sweater and winter coat, Amy packed an overnight bag and headed to the West Village to Richie's apartment. She debated briefly about hailing a taxi but decided against it. Traffic was always tough in the city and Amy didn't have the stamina to sit in a taxi while it weaved its way in bumper-to-bumper traffic. She took the subway instead, making the necessary subway transfers to head to the trendy West Village where Richie lived. Passengers were packed like sardines into the subway car, shuffling in and out. Amy winced in pain as something heavy pressed on her feet. She quickly located the culprit – a middle age man with a suitcase in tow was shoving his way out of the subway car. Amy forced deliberate meditative breaths. Nothing further was going to rattle her tonight. She was about to see Richie and that was all the incentive she needed to float to her happy place. With her soon-to-be nightmare work life, they needed to figure out a better way to see more of each other.

Within a half hour, Amy was unlocking Richie's door with the key he had given her a couple of months ago. Richie had put the key inside a Tiffany heart-shaped jewelry box, placed the whole thing in the Tiffany signature blue box, and wrapped it with pink and white ribbon. It was such a thoughtful and romantic gesture. Amy had taken a picture of it and sent it to Miranda and Megan who had gushed with approval.

Richie's apartment was in a pre-war brownstone building in the heart of the West Village. The building only had three apartments, each spanning an entire floor. Richie was on the third floor, with sole access to the rooftop deck. During the summer months, Amy felt spoiled rotten when Richie insisted on grilling their meals while she lounged with wine and a book on the chaise chair. When the sun got too hot, Amy scooted to the plush patio furniture under the large canopy with misters and fans clipped around the frame. Richie was meticulous about his comfort and downtime and didn't miss a detail in making the rooftop a true escape from the bustling city below. Evenings there were Amy's favorite times, with the only light, apart from the moon and the stars, emanating from tiny accent lights strung around the canopy and transforming the rooftop into an enchanted hideaway.

Amy reveled in the memories, feeling toasty inside despite the chill in the apartment. Richie liked to keep the thermostat on low when he wasn't home, something about doing his part in conserving the planet. He was a man after Amy's own heart in every way. She walked to the stereo system and inserted a Christmas CD—a compilation by multiple artists from Bing Crosby to Harry Connick Jr.—desperately hoping their silky voices would fill the apartment with Christmas magic.

Richie wasn't home yet even though it was nearly eight. Amy's heart squeezed with longing for him. She wanted to be a supportive girlfriend during this stressful time for him, and yet she questioned the amount of strain the time apart put on the relationship. She couldn't help but wonder if Richie was having the same internal dialogue. And yet, when they saw each other it was like no time had passed. He was always attentive, thoughtful and very romantic. Maybe Amy was creating an issue out of nothing, like Megan had suggested during lunch.

Groaning loudly, she combed her fingers through her hair, grabbing her purse from the floor by the front door to dig for a rubber band or a clip to pull her hair back, away from her face. Standing in front of the decorative mirror above the stereo, Amy examined her tired features, sallow from the emotional stress. Immediately, she changed her mind about tying her hair back. She needed to hide her puffy eyes tonight, not put them on full display. Negative forces were swarming around her, tugging at her in every direction. She needed for something to work in her favor.

Amy sauntered to the kitchen to open a bottle of Mondavi Pinot Noir, and left it to breathe on the counter. A good bottle of red needed time to breathe before being enjoyed to its fullest potential. She learned that from a wine-tasting tour in Santa Barbara with Miranda. Amy chuckled thinking back on that road trip, trunk filled to the gills with the cases of wine they spontaneously purchased and lugged down the boardwalk to the car.

Amy wished she had been in a better state of mind earlier to buy a few snacks, or an assortment of cheeses to nosh on while they drank. Better yet, maybe they'd order in when Richie finally came home. Emotionally drained, she curled on the couch with a book and blanket, hoping Richie wouldn't be too long. Her body molded to the soft cushions and, for the first time since her conversation with Jane, she felt relaxed and happy in her safe bubble at Richie's place. She was still miserable at the prospect of working with Sarah but being here lessened the angst. With Richie in her corner, and the two of them continuing to move forward in their relationship, she felt that despite the challenges at work, she still had happiness in her life that Sarah couldn't poison. For that, Amy was grateful. Now if only she could maintain that levelheaded thinking.

The key turned in the door and Amy bolted up, running to the door to greet Richie. She pulled the door as Richie was pushing in causing Amy to tumble backwards with her arms flailing ungracefully. Richie caught her before she actually hit the floor and pulled her into his arms.

"This is the best homecoming ever. I've never actually had someone fall backwards for me before," he teased, planting a wet kiss on her lips. He kicked the door shut behind him as he carried her to the couch, dropping a large paper bag on the floor by the door. His mouth was on hers immediately, ravishing her with his kisses. She was breathless.

"I missed you so much." He moaned between kisses.

Amy's head swam as Harry Connick Jr. crooned in the far distance and she drifted deeper into Richie's embrace.

"I missed you too. I'm so glad you're home." Amy held on to his broad shoulders, running her hands hungrily over his back and arms. He was so strong and muscular, years of playing rugby and ice hockey in college contributed to his swoon-worthy physique. He was at least a foot taller than her and Amy loved every inch of him.

"How was your day?"

He planted soft kisses along Amy's jawline, landing at her lips and staying there, her insides turning to mush. Amy was grateful for the delay in responding because she couldn't form a single coherent thought with his lips on her tingling skin.

"My day sucked, but its much better now that we're together." Her hands were in his hair, pulling him back to her.

"What happened?" Richie held her face tenderly with both hands, searching her eyes.

Still panting, she said, "they hired a new person in marketing to help with losing Jane." Amy inhaled deeply determined to keep her emotions under control.

"That's great, baby. It's a good sign they're not rushing to replace her.

It means they're committed to finding the right person."

Richie's thumb was caressing her cheek and Amy wanted to push away thoughts of work and focus on the delicious moment with Richie. Besides she didn't trust her unstable emotions. Tears were just under the composed surface.

"It's actually all bitter without the sweetness. The new hire is Sarah Mitchell." Her eyes cast downward before she squeezed them shut. She didn't want Richie to see how gutted she was. But he had a knack for knowing exactly what she felt, even when she plastered a smile on her face and tried to pretend otherwise.

"Oh no. Oh god Amy, I'm so sorry, baby. How could this happen? I thought your HR was more diligent than that. Surely, they have a file filled with qualified candidates. The irony of landing on Sarah of all people."

Richie's words touched her more than he'd ever know. Amy wrapped her arms tightly around his neck, a hint of aftershave clung to his warm skin, intoxicating her, reminding her to focus on the present moment, determined to enjoy the alone time with Richie. She rested her cheek on his chest, savoring the feeling of security and happiness in his arms.

"Let's talk about something else, okay?" Amy kissed his cheek and reluctantly slid from his lap to get the wine and glasses. With unsteady hands, she poured a generous amount of the Pinot Noir into their glasses and moseyed back to Richie.

"Listen, for what it's worth," he said, "you're a different person now and you don't have to take her crap. She's not your boss or anyone else's boss for that matter. If things get out of hand, quit. I'll help you find another job, and in the meantime, you could freelance for us. Abby and I would be thrilled for the extra help." He pulled her back into his lap, careful not to spill the wine.

"Thanks, Richie. That means so much to me. I'll figure something out." Even though she wasn't prepared to say the L word, Amy felt it in spades. And that scared the heck out of her. She was madly and hopelessly in love with Richie and his support of her meant a great deal more than she knew how to express. He was right, she had options, and she was a different person now. The sad, meek punching bag that silently took every one of Sarah's blows was gone. In her place was a strong, accomplished and respected professional who didn't slink away from challenges.

"So I figured you didn't eat before coming over and I'm starving," said Richie. "My last meeting was in SoHo, so I popped by Pompeii and picked up a few things. I hope it's still your favorite restaurant after we try their take-out."

Richie leaned over, kissing her nose before he settled her on the couch while he went to get the bag of food. He took out containers and arranged them on the coffee table. His thoughtfulness and sweet demeanor weren't wasted on Amy. The hell with work, she had Richie.

After feasting on eggplant rollatini with a generous amount of sauce and cheese on the top, just the way Amy liked it, they also had fresh caprese salad and lemon chicken. They ate in comfortable silence—yet another trait that she loved about Richie. They didn't always need to fill the space with banter and yet they remained tuned to one another.

Afterwards they sat back on the couch with their heads reclined and their hands intertwined in Richie's lap.

"Dinner was delicious. I think they pass the take-out test. Thank you for picking it up," Amy said, turning her head to look at Richie.

He grinned, his eyes still closed as Amy stared at his handsome features, strong jawline, full lips and hair that seemed to do its own sexy wild thing by the end of the day. It was a little spiky tonight and Amy debated about grabbing a handful before hopping into his lap. He looked so relaxed and peaceful; she didn't want to disturb him.

Richie eventually broke the silence.

"How about a hot bath?" He raised an eyebrow at her and Amy's stomach did an Olympic summersault.

She grinned, nodding enthusiastically. A hot bath with Richie was exactly what she needed to release the pent-up anxiety.

Richie's apartment was completely renovated, every detail of the charming apartment restored to its original state from crown molding to wainscoting in the bathroom. The finished job was meticulous and was even featured in an architecture magazine highlighting old world charm dwellings in Manhattan. The deep tub with jet streams was one of her favorite new additions to the projects and Amy looked forward to a relaxing soak with Richie. She'll sleep well tonight, she mused.

Forty-five minutes later, relaxed and pleasured beyond words, Amy padded to the king size bed and crawled inside the cool crisp sheets with Richie on her heels.

"That was amazing." He nuzzled her neck, nibbling on the sensitive spot below her earlobe.

"Hmmmm." Amy tilted her head back against his smooth lean chest; she was still hazy from the bath. Richie was an expert at giving pleasure and the euphoric sensation hummed in her veins.

"I love you, Amy." Richie was asleep as soon as he uttered the three simple words that catapulted their relationship to the next level. His breathing was even and shallow, he was already in dreamland.

Amy drifted to peaceful sleep in the arms of the man who loved her, the man who she loved back with her whole heart.

Chapter Thirteen

AMY FLOATED TO work on a big white fluffy cloud that twinkled with Christmas lights. Richie's declaration of love filled her with bliss. The previous night had confirmed Richie's feelings for her. She didn't realize how much she'd needed those three earth-shattering words to feel secure in their relationship. And now she had them, safely tucked in her heart.

Richie and Amy were early risers who loved to squeeze in a good workout before going to work. But this morning they both skipped the workout, opting to enjoy a leisurely cup of cappuccino for him and tea for her, along with fresh scones that Amy bought from the café across the street. They sat cross-legged on the couch talking, their voices filling the morning silence, a welcome change from the blaring horns and bumper-to-bumper traffic of her neighborhood. Before getting dressed, Richie read the horoscope section out loud, adding his own two cents to the daily predictions that had Amy clutching her sides with laughter. She could start every morning like this without a single complaint.

She sauntered happily down the hall to her office, feeling as bright and sunny as the color of her yellow sweater. From somewhere down the hall, Sarah Mitchell's loud cackle pierced the serene atmosphere. Amy's happy bubble deflated a little. Just a little. She gulped air, straightening her back in anticipation. Tiny beads of sweat formed along her hairline and in her palms. She briefly debated slinking to her office, postponing the unnecessary introductions and welcome, or tackling it head on. The old Amy would have struck a deal with the devil if it meant bypassing Sarah. But this wasn't the old Amy. The new Amy was confident in her accomplishments and skills, happy, and had a hot boyfriend who wasn't afraid to profess his love for her.

"Amy, Amy ... wait ..."

Megan ran toward her, panting, pale, and panic-stricken. "Great, Sarah has been in the building for less than an hour and the team is already on edge," she thought bitterly. Stop it, Amy.

Flicking her long brown hair to the side, Amy turned to face Megan. "Hey ... what's wrong?"

"The new hire ... the senior marketing director, as in your counter-part ...is ... Sarah Mitchell ... your old boss. Oh Amy, I'm so sorry." Megan's chocolate brown eyes watered with unshed tears. Amy loved her friend's unwavering loyalty and appreciated Megan's concern for her.

"I already know ... Jane told me. It's okay. I promise," she reassured Megan. "Things are different now. I know what she's really like and I can handle her while protecting my career here. Besides, she's not my boss, she's a colleague and it's a whole new playing field."

Guilt seeped in as Amy watched Megan fidget. Perhaps some of the gory details of her previous job should have been left in the past. Besides, it wasn't out of the realm of possibility that Sarah would have evolved into a kinder and more thoughtful individual. She'd accepted a lesser title, and that had to mean something. Either way, feeding energy into optimism beat wallowing in misery worrying about something that hadn't happened. In an attempt to alleviate Megan's anxiety, a direct result of her doing, Amy leaned in and hugged her friend, whispering, "All will be okay, young Jedi."

Megan giggled, and Amy's shoulders relaxed, the tension deflating. Now if only she could maintain that light-hearted feeling as she carried on the rest of the day. Either way, she needed to fake having a solid grip. No signs of weakness or she might as well pack up her office immediately. The Sarah she'd known took no prisoners.

"Okay, if you say so," Megan said. "You seem especially chipper given the news. What's going on?" she asked, looking around to make sure the coast was clear.

"Hmm ... nothing really. Except one small thing. Richie told me he loved me last night. A small part of me wondered whether he was half asleep and delirious, but this morning, he said it again." Amy shifted on her feet, color rising to her cheeks.

"Oh wow! That's huge. Did you say it back?"

"Yes, both times," Amy said softly, feeling momentarily untouchable. "Listen, I should go and welcome the wicked one to our department. Maybe by some miracle, she's changed," she said. "Let's have lunch."

Megan beamed, nodding before walking back to her desk.

Nervously, Amy combed her fingers through her hair, channeling inner strength to get her through whatever was in store for her. With false confidence, she turned on her heels, straightened her shoulders, and walked into Jane's office to welcome Sarah to the department.

"Good morning, Jane. I thought I'd pop by and welcome you to Diva, Sarah." Amy smiled broadly, her eyes fixed on the woman who'd tortured her for an entire year.

Sarah shifted on the sofa, the same sofa Amy had sat on during her interview with Jane eleven months ago. Amy noted the displeasure in Sarah's demeanor, and the way she sized her up from shoes to hair. The glare penetrating from her icy blue eyes wasn't wasted on Amy but she decided to ignore it. It would take a lot more than that to unsettle her, and she realized in that moment, her old boss hadn't changed one bit.

Sarah wore a cobalt blue sheath dress with a beige pashmina wrapped around her shoulders and tied elegantly to the side. The knee-length black boots were from this season's Jimmy Choo winter collection. They must have cost her a small fortune, not that money was ever an issue for an only child with a trust fund. Long, glossy gold locks cascaded down her back, silky wisps of hair framing her pale, pretty features. Sarah had everything going for her from looks to a sizable bank account. It didn't make any sense why she wasn't traveling the world instead of working at a regular job and tormenting everyone in sight.

"Amy, I'm a little surprised that you're still at Diva," Sarah responded, flicking her hair to the side.

Amy tilted her head, regarding Sarah closely. Her fangs were already out, and it was barely day one on the job.

Just as she was about to respond, Jane stood up, addressing Sarah head on. "Amy is one of our rising stars at Diva, and the executive team has taken a keen interest in her development and growth here. You'll find her marketing ideas to be fresh and innovative, qualities that we harness with great care here," she said coolly.

Amy's mouth gaped. For a split second, she wanted to scream with joy at having someone stand up to Sarah, and better yet, someone of Jane's status. Sarah's pale cheeks turned multiple shades of red, no doubt matching her venomous mood.

Amy stood a little taller, although she couldn't help the disappointment at realizing that Sarah hadn't evolved one bit. "I look forward to working with you again, Sarah. The next few months will be extremely busy for our team, and we're very excited by the marketing campaigns rolling out."

By choosing to gloss over Sarah's nastiness, Amy had won the mini battle that morning. Besides, the shock on Sarah's face at Jane's defense of her was worth biting her tongue. Jane's no-nonsense approach left little room for cattiness, and although Sarah's comment was harmless enough, the meaning was clear.

"Amy, I look forward to reviewing final plans for the Valentine's Day marketing campaign after lunch," Jane said. "Sarah, you should join us. We'll need everyone to hit the ground running after the New Year. I'm sure Amy wouldn't mind walking us through the fine points." Jane sat, dragging her chair closer to her desk, turning to face the computer. The meeting was over.

"I'd be delighted. I'll see you both here at two o'clock." Smiling her brightest smile, Amy practically sprinted out of Jane's office, amusement tugging at the corners of her mouth, an extra zip in her step. Everything was sorting itself out, at least for now.

Sitting behind her desk, which was cluttered with files and design layouts for review and approval, her bottom lip caught between her teeth to suppress a smirk thinking about the look of horror that had crept over Sarah's face when Amy hadn't buckled under her belittling. And yet, Amy felt uneasy. She didn't believe for one second that Sarah had any intentions of backing down. Her silence was merely an attempt to assess the situation further. Knowing that Jane was squarely in Amy's corner only meant Sarah would refrain from showing her true colors in front of Jane, not the rest of the team. What remained a mystery was the real reason Sarah moved her entire life to Manhattan when she had everything going for her in Los Angeles.

The mesh desk chair squeaked under Amy as she pressed her back into the lumbar support panel, the hard edges of the top rim cold against her neck. She groaned at the throbbing pain pounding against her temples.

Not a tension headache, not now. Amy sighed with annoyance, her cold fingers pressing into her clammy temples, massaging in circular motions. She didn't have time for this. Reaching for the top drawer in her desk, she slid it open and retrieved the bottle of Advil, drowning a couple of pills with the water bottle at her desk. Then she texted Megan, asking for a rain check on lunch. Today of all days, she needed to have her ducks in a row for this meeting. Sarah would be looking for any opportunity to zing her. Taking a deep breath, Amy sent a quick text telling Richie she loved him, relishing the fact that she could say it now. She also gave him the highlights from her meeting with Sarah and Jane.

The phone buzzed. Richie immediately responded with heart emoticons and said he was thrilled for her and not surprised by Jane's support. More heart emoticons followed, as well as "I love you."

At least her personal life was in order and wasn't causing her anxiety.

Placing her phone in the dock on her desk, she flipped through her music library, selecting one of her favorite Christmas albums. Within seconds, Christmas bells rung in her office from the mini speakers on her desk, drawing Amy into a Zen-like happy place filled with memories of the strange dream, proclamations of love, and Christmas magic. She sighed, an unexpected calm settling over her, no doubt the fast-acting headache relief pills kicking in. For the first time since finding out about Sarah joining the team, Amy felt confident that everything would work out in the end, even if the meantime sucked. And after this morning's meeting, there was little doubt about Jane's support, and that put Amy's mind at ease.

Deciding the present moment wasn't the optimal time to analyze

Sarah's psychosis, Amy immersed herself in work—fully aware that she needed to be on guard at all times, which meant crossing every T and dotting every i, multiple times if necessary. And it was necessary. She read through emails, reviewed piles of suggested magazine page layouts from the creative department that she needed to approve, and then focused her attention on the meeting with Jane and Sarah. She had been over the schedule a million times already but knowing her archenemy was in the room, eager to pounce given the opportunity, she reviewed every line item with a fine-tooth comb.

At two o'clock, Amy stood in Jane's slightly open door with folders and creative layouts in hand, waiting to be motioned in. Jane was still wrapped up in her previous conference call—not unusual lately. She was juggling a gazillion projects at the same time, and as per her MO, nothing fell through the cracks. HR had their work cut out for them because it wouldn't be easy to fill Jane's shoes. Amy leaned against the wall, trying not to eavesdrop on Jane's call, instead focusing on the upcoming meeting, mentally rehearsing what she was going to say.

Amy found it refreshing that Jane believed and practiced an open-door policy—barring meetings of course. There were no "behind closed doors" gossip sessions or plotting other people's demises under her watchful eye. Amy had little doubt that Sarah, who wasn't anywhere in sight, wouldn't play the role of team player. She just hoped it wouldn't negatively affect the Valentine's campaign.

A few minutes later, Jane called Amy in. At the sound of Sarah's loud cackling, curiosity got the best of Amy and she turned her head, nearly tripping over her feet at the sight of Sarah bouncing her way down the hall, coffee in hand, with none other than her dear friend Megan, both chatting and giggling like old friends. Amy's eyebrows shot towards her hairline, her eyes the size of saucers as she watched them. A small chuckle threatened to erupt, but she quickly pressed her lips together to maintain composure. Sadly, Sarah's antics were predictable. What the hell was she up to? A master manipulator on her worst day, Sarah didn't do anything without purpose and a fully plotted agenda. Conscious of Jane's limited time, Amy marched in and sat at the round table by the window and waited for Jane and Sarah to join her. Sarah had only been at Diva for one day and she was already buddying up to Jane's executive assistant. "Underhanded but very clever," thought Amy. Sarah would not get the best of her. Not this time around.

Inhaling deeply, Amy placed photocopies of the marketing timeline on the table, one in front of Jane.

"I've been meaning to catch up with you. You all right?" Jane whispered, eyeing Amy thoughtfully.

"Yes, I am. And thank you for the heads up yesterday. It meant more to me than you can ever imagine." She met Jane's eyes.

"I told you yesterday, I'll be watching. Your career is of great interest to the company and me. Keep me in the loop."

Jane fell silent as Sarah hurried in, taking a seat across from Amy at the round table.

"Sorry, everyone," said Sarah, placing her to-go coffee cup in front of her. "My spontaneous lunch with Megan ran a little late. We know so many people in common, we lost track of time."

"Should we get started?" Jane nodded in Amy's direction to kick off the meeting.

"I printed a timeline of all the marketing initiatives launching from now through next December. I also highlighted the milestones and critical deadlines for all of them." Amy began detailing the first campaign when Sarah rudely put a hand up to silence her.

"I'm sorry ... this feels a little incomplete to me. Are all the campaigns in here?"

Amy inhaled deeply, fully prepared for Sarah questioning everything in an attempt to make her look unprepared. "Yes, they are. I had each team lead review and approve the timelines last week. Is there something specific you're not seeing?" Amy glared at Sarah without flinching, an invisible cord pulling her spine towards the ceiling. If Sarah wanted war, she was going to get it.

At the mention of team approvals, Sarah shifted uncomfortably in her seat. "Well ... I certainly don't mean to criticize the Diva team. That was never my intention, Jane. I simply wanted to make sure this was a comprehensive timeline to help us all stay on track, and now that I'm looking more closely, I see that Amy has included everything." Sarah was back-pedaling, pathetically.

Amy sat back in her chair, eyeing Sarah thoughtfully. For the first time since meeting Sarah, Amy saw her for what she really was—a fraud. She'd always been under-qualified for the role she left in Los Angeles, but she'd been able to get away with it because her family endorsed the magazine financially – in a big way. Sadly, for Sarah, in spite of the best financial connections in the world, she didn't seem to benefit anyone, especially the magazines she'd joined. In that moment, Amy actually pitied her—but not enough to allow Sarah to diminish her contribution and hard work.

"Right," Amy began. "You'll also note that deadlines are highlighted in yellow, critical meetings in blue, and working days in green," she countered, her eyes burning through Sarah's feeble attempt at belittling her.

"Sarah, you seem a little confused. You have worked with timelines before, yes?" Jane said, almost daring her to disrupt the meeting again.

Sarah opened her mouth and then clamped it shut, daggers shooting from her eyes. A silent war was brewing between the Head of Marketing and the new Senior Director, and Sarah was at a complete disadvantage. The temperature in Jane's office either dropped drastically or the chill between the women had iced Amy over. She actually shivered. Things were going to get a whole lot worse before they got better.

Jane's reputation preceded her, and no person in their right mind would take Sarah's side over hers. As ballsy as Sarah was, Amy was shocked by her snarky behavior on her first day on the job. It was almost as if Sarah accepted the position out of desperation—but that seemed ridiculous.

The next three months were shaping up to be very interesting and treacherous. The one thing Amy hated more than Sarah was drama, and now it was squarely in her office.

Having Jane's support was a tremendous lifeline she hadn't counted on, and apparently neither had Sarah. Amy wanted to leap with joy, except she couldn't because her coworkers would think she had lost it completely. Jane's strong endorsement had changed the playing field in the best of ways.

The remainder of the meeting was uneventful, without as much as a comment from Sarah. Amy was eager to return to the safety of her office. Gathering her notebook and papers, she turned to Jane, silently begging for the meeting to adjourn. On cue, Jane thanked her profusely for her attention to detail and hard work, standing up to escort her to the door, then shutting it behind her.

A meeting between Jane and Sarah following the contentious meeting they'd just had was probably not a great thing, but Amy happily fled to the sanctuary of her Zen office, closing the door behind her before exhaling loudly. She felt somewhat calmer, the tension in her shoulders easing a little as the invisible protective shield she wore around Sarah began to melt away. All things considered, the meeting wasn't nearly as bad as she'd imagined in her head. Or maybe, she'd finally toughened up. Heart still palpitating from the meeting, Amy shut off the noise in her head, the way she often did during yoga class. She pranced lightly around her desk, feeling weightless, and then settled in her swivel chair. The pile of paperwork from earlier awaited her undivided attention, and she gladly obliged, feeling exhilarated and slightly victorious at handling the meeting with poise and confidence. For once, Amy had the upper hand, but she didn't feel the relief she expected to feel. Her nerves were still shredded. She hadn't signed up to play this ridiculous game of chess, but to survive Sarah she needed to master the game.

Her stomach growled loudly, reminding her she hadn't eaten since breakfast with Richie. Groaning, she stood, accidently pushing her chair against the desk, bumping into the water bottle, tipping it, and drenching the loose papers. Amy scrambled to find something to soak it up with, and when she couldn't find anything, she ran at record speed to the kitchen at the end of the hall to grab paper towels. Twenty frenzied minutes later, her desk was wiped down and the files salvaged. Wet printouts were laid out to dry on the windowsill on top of the air vents—probably a fire hazard but Amy didn't care. She needed to get out of the office, now. A change of scenery would do her good. She grabbed her coat from the hook behind her door, slung her purse over her shoulder, and marched purposefully toward the elevators. She managed to avoid Sarah completely.

Soon she was walking down Broadway headed toward the new coffee shop a few blocks away. She'd much prefer a hot apple cider from the Union Square Christmas Marketplace, but this would have to do. Besides, she wanted to leave work right at five today and it was already three-thirty.

The chimes of Christmas bells filled the air as taxi cabs whizzed by and tourists pushed past her to their next shopping destination. Despite all the noise and chaos synonymous with Times Square, the bells rang loudly above everything else. The temperature had dropped drastically, but Amy embraced it. The freezing temperatures outside were much better than those inside, compliments of Blizzard Sarah Mitchell.

She was floating again with Christmas magic, feeling whimsical and almost dreamy. She looked for the source of the bells, hoping for a Santa sighting. But it wasn't Santa that her eyes landed on. It was Mrs. Claus. The same Mrs. Claus who resembled her beloved grandmother and sold apple cider in the Union Square Christmas Market and in her dream.

With childlike excitement, Amy hurried toward Mrs. Claus, her imagination in full force, dreaming up the most elaborate storyline. Admittedly, it was a bit insane, and most certainly naïve, to entertain the thought of a real Santa and Mrs. Claus. Amy knew that. And yet, she couldn't shake the urge to see the plump woman with rosy cheeks, offering Christmas cheer.

Amy crossed the street, barely avoiding the manic traffic. A few angry drivers gestured rudely in a very un-Christmas-like way. No matter, she was almost there.

"Hi ... remember me ... uhmmm ... from Union Square Christmas Market..." Amy panted slightly, the combination of bone-chilling air and the brisk walk winding her. No amount of yoga helped condition her body against the extreme weather. Compared to a Los Angeles winter, this felt like the Ice Age.

"Hi, Amy. It's good to see you. I had a feeling I was going to run into you today." The older woman smiled at Amy, the same apple cider stand perched to her right. "Have an apple cider."

Amy accepted the tall take-away cup and nodded silently when Mrs. Claus offered to top the hot cider with whipped cream and a sprinkle of cinnamon. The sweet scent wafted into her nostrils, filling her with warmth, and for a brief second, Amy forgot she was standing at a busy intersection in Times Square with blaring angry horns leading the mayhem.

"Why did you think you'd see me today? And how did you know my name?" Amy sipped, the hot liquid decadent over her tongue as she peered over the rim of the cup, deciding to play along in this strange but very entertaining charade.

"I figured you were craving a cider, and you told me your name," Mrs. Claus offered casually, clasping her thick hands over her belly.

"When?" Amy questioned, taking in the authenticity of Mrs. Claus's costume, right down to her salt and pepper hair pulled into a loose bun. She wasn't wearing a hat today.

"I think we have more important things to focus on ... the magic of Christmas is highly underestimated. It's a shame, don't you think?"

Amy nodded, the warmth emanating from the cup feeling delightful against her frozen hands. "Does that mean you believe something magical will happen to me?"

"It already has, my dear. We often get so wrapped up in the misery of the moment that we forget to see the big beautiful picture."

The screeching sound of tires diverted Amy's attention to the street behind her. Two yellow taxi cabs had nearly collided, barely missing one another and the scrambling pedestrians crossing the overcrowded street. That could have been a tragic accident.

When Amy turned back, Mrs. Claus was gone. Not a sign of her or the portable cider stand. She had vanished into thin air. The only proof of their encounter was the take-away cup still cradled between Amy's hands. Shivers ran down her body as she stood frozen, staring at the empty spot.

Chapter Fourteen

S INCE THE NEW marketing campaigns had been announced a few weeks ago, days at the office were unbearably long, and since Sarah had joined the team, they were mentally draining as Amy braced for the worse. The latter was a little self-inflicted but justified given the history between the two women. Amy sat on her bed, wrapped in a blanket, and contemplated the unexpected turn of events at work. She had fully expected uncomfortable interactions with Sarah, snide remarks meant to needle and undermine her ability at work. Surprisingly, none of that had happened. Sarah was either channeling the Dalai Lama or she truly was a changed person. Either way, Amy was happy with the way the week had unfolded. Although she was exhausted every night and worked longer hours than she liked, she was happy, with the exception of Sarah's comment the first day in Jane's office. Then again, perhaps Amy had been overly sensitive and had read too much into an innocent comment. Maybe on some level, she was looking for reason to still hate Sarah. And perhaps Sarah was surprised to find Amy still in New York. Sarah had been pleasant to be around, and the team had embraced her, so watchfully, Amy tried to as well.

Darkness crept over the city, the thick clusters of gray clouds veiling the night sky and stars, the only light from the decorated street lamps. She stared sleepily out the window of her apartment, past memories of Sarah's shrewdness not allowing her to move on in spite of her desire for a fresh start. Funny how the mind worked, clutching to unresolved feelings and wounds, ripping them open when triggered. A sharp pain sliced at her shoulder blades and had Amy wincing with discomfort. She was a ball of tension, and the more she analyzed Sarah's every word and behavior, the more drained she felt, the throbbing pain intensifying. An acute reminder that she hadn't healed at all, she had merely put distance between the past and present. Moving to Manhattan had allowed her to reinvent herself, embrace a healthier lifestyle, and find happiness in the present moment, but it didn't heal the past or provide the closure she needed to move on. Yoga and meditation were great, and Amy was grateful for the brief moments of inner calm and clarity, but since Sarah had returned, anxiety had returned as well, coiling painfully in her stomach, reminding her of how quickly things could take a turn. She needed to ramp up meditation and quickly. Rolling her head from side to side to loosen the tight muscles at the base of her neck, Amy decided to give Sarah a second chance, with caution, of course. There was power in forgiveness, and Amy needed to move beyond the painful past because it no longer defined her. Having endured a miserable situation before, Amy knew that eventually, what was meant to happen would happen whether she stewed about it or not. Tormenting herself with what ifs was useless and sapped her of the inner peace she worked so hard to achieve.

Torrential rain pounded on the window as the howling wind twisted the tree branches. Contortionists had nothing on the bendy trees outside. Winter was in full swing on the east coast, and for the first time since moving to New York, Amy felt homesick for the beach, grilling parties in the garden, and sundresses. Flowy, romantic whimsical sundresses. A bright light cracked through the sky as thunder and lightning battled. She groaned, burrowing deeper under the covers, images of Richie on a surfboard teasing her mind into a happy place. She imagined them living together, maybe in Santa Monica, Richie opening a Los Angeles office in Westwood. With Sarah in Manhattan working for Diva, Amy could go back to Glitz. She sighed, the daydream bubble popping loudly with another clap of thunder outside.

By Wednesday, Sarah had nestled comfortably at work and was giggling in the hall with the staff like she had known them for years. When, later in the week, Sarah was overheard offering advice about the benefits of being thin to the chubby advertising coordinator; Amy winced slightly, praying the old Sarah wasn't worming her way in. Thankfully, Sarah's comment seemed to be rooted in concern. "Being overweight has a domino effect, and if you're not careful, it will spiral into every part of your life. You should eat more salads and fewer carbs. I only allow myself to eat carbs once a week, and even then, it's just for one meal. I can help you stay motivated."

Justine had turned multiple shades of red as she tugged at her blouse, stretching the filmy fabric over her curvy hips. Whether Justine appreciated Sarah's unrequested advice or not, she didn't let on. A shy smile had graced her lips and she nodded, squashing perceived tension. It was questionable whether Sarah's comment was meant to be encouraging or mean. The words were laced with just enough concern that it was hard to be angry. Later that day, Amy had heard Sarah cozy up to the vice president in the promotions department, complimenting the well-thought out campaigns from the previous year. All seemed great. Christmas was days away and Amy couldn't wait to spend uninterrupted time with Richie and get to know his family better. She should have been doing cartwheels with joy, but she couldn't shake a nagging feeling that all wasn't as it seemed with Sarah.

As optimistic as she felt about the evolved woman who graced their hallways, there were some eyebrow-raising moments. Overall, nothing worthy of a visit to Human Resources, though. Only a glimmer of the person Amy had lost respect for, who had eventually forced her to bolt to another position clear across the country. Although in fairness, working for Diva was a dream job, and she would have bolted at the chance regardless of her current situation.

Between conference calls and dozens of unanswered emails waiting for her response, Amy remaining in her office for the majority of the morning. Just as she was about to run across the street for a Chai Latte, an invitation for a team pizza lunch from Jane popped into her inbox. Every single person from marketing, advertising, and promotions was invited. Amy's eyebrows shot up to her hairline. She was puzzled by the random and unexpected invite. When she had first joined the department, the team occasionally went out for happy hour or at times ate their lunch together in the large conference room. An official team lunch was odd, but she was quite happy to break up the day with an impromptu midday social gathering. She reached for the phone to call Megan for the scoop but remembered her friend was at a photo shoot. Megan was spending more time in the photography department, and the two barely saw one another. They talked over the phone, but it wasn't the same and she missed Megan dearly.

She couldn't help but shudder at the memory of a similar spontaneous team lunch Sarah had hosted. Her former boss had used the time to criticize the team under the pretense of feedback. "Jim, given your seniority, I guess I'm just disappointed by the article. It's very poorly written and the subject is stale. How many times are we going to cover environmental issues?" Jim had shifted uncomfortably in his seat, retorting it was Earth Week. Sarah was unfazed and quickly moved on to her next prey. "Jessica, if you're going to use this model for the center-fold, she needs to be airbrushed—a lot. She's too fat to be a model. I can't believe we're still hiring her." Jaws dropped open, the tension heavy like a wet blanket, deflating what was left of the team's morale. Jessica, a sassy redhead, had reminded Sarah of the agreement to showcase healthy looking women instead of the underweight ones, given their key audience was filled with high school girls who tended to obsess over their weight. Again, Sarah shrugged and moved on. On the best of days, Sarah lacked decorum and a filter, and her biting remarks were counterproductive. On the worst of days, Sarah was mean. It became impossible to overlook her bad behavior when Sarah offered nothing else. Team recognition didn't exist, and after a while, her team stopped waiting for it and then, they stopped performing and began seeking jobs elsewhere. Amy's departure was the first of many. It was a shame because Glitz was a wonderful magazine and, pre-Sarah; it had been a fun place to work.

Thirty minutes later, Amy sat in the large conference room with a slice of pizza and seltzer water positioned in front of her. A large billboard for Mamma Mia perched outside the window, the perfect representation of Times Square. Her mind drifted, and she remembered her night out with Megan months ago. Front row seats, and singing along with the cast, bellowing out every song like their lives depended on it. That was Amy's first real New York experience. She would always cherish it.

Amy sent Richie a quick text message. She hadn't talked to him since yesterday's mid-morning exchange.

The click-click sound of Sarah's stiletto heels got louder as she approached the jam-packed conference room, chatter escalating in volume and excitement. Being surrounded by everyone, all happy, supportive, and true team players, reminded Amy how far she had come and how much she loved her new job. Sarah's old antics wouldn't work here. Unlike the team at Glitz, this team was seasoned and didn't care for nonsense that took away from the work. It would take the manipulation of a sorcerer to turn them against one another. Not to mention, the magazine's popularity and strong financial standing created stability and security at work. None of the old feelings of desperation and fear over losing their jobs existed here. For that, Amy was eternally grateful. She chatted easily with Jeff, the head of the creative department. She had liked him from day one, and his brilliant creative execution continued to impress her.

In between bites of pizza, Amy met Sarah's gaze as she confidently glided into the conference room, her beautiful features passive, and a complete contradiction to her aggressive nature. Sarah's blue eyes were bright and flickering with mischief as she sauntered towards the long boardroom table and helped herself to pizza. She scanned the large conference room, assessing the team and strategically planning her seat. Knowing Sarah, she wouldn't sit next to anyone who couldn't benefit her in some way, so when she zeroed in on Anna, an accomplished vice president in the promotions department, Amy wasn't surprised one bit.

Amy's heart thumped against her rib cage, in part amused, in part weary of Sarah's hidden agenda. As much as she wanted to believe that Sarah had reformed, her gut told her otherwise, especially when she noticed Sarah glaring at her for no reason at all. Unfazed, Amy smiled coolly, refusing to participate. I'm on to you, Sarah.

Sarah saddled up to Anna, interrupting her conversation with Cindy, the pimply-faced coordinator who worked in Anna's department. Sarah quickly engaged in small talk with Anna, hanging on her every word, completely dismissive of Cindy. Anna was a willowy dark-haired woman in her forties. She had angular features and a boyish figure, and wore pantsuits in every color in the rainbow, but somehow always looked elegant and fashionable. Her heavy Venezuelan accent only added to her charm. Amy watched them off and on, intrigued by the dynamic between Anna's genuine, bubbly nature and Sarah's pretentiousness at feigning to be sincere and easy going.

Ten minutes later, Sarah surprised everyone by standing at the helm of the large boardroom table and addressing the team. Ballsy.

"Hi everyone. I wanted to thank you all for making my first few weeks here so pleasant. I've enjoyed getting to know some of you and look forward to learning more about each of you. To be perfectly candid, I'm a little nervous about being part of such a high-functioning team and I hope you're patient with me as I ease my way into my new role here. I know I'm just one of the senior marketing directors, but I was head of marketing at Glitz, and with my leadership, our small but mighty team accomplished tons to be proud of. I hope I'm able to leverage that experience here when appropriate. Anyway, I'm really excited to be here and I still can't believe I've landed my dream job in the most intimidating but exciting city in the world. I'm still learning my way around the city, so all tips and recommendations are welcome. I can't thank you guys enough for being so warm and welcoming." Sarah slid into the chair, a sweet smile plastered on her glossy lips just as Jane walked into the conference room.

The fact that Sarah had conveniently left out the detail of working with Amy at Glitz wasn't wasted on her.

"Hello, everyone. I'm sorry for being late but I hope everyone enjoyed our first pizza lunch." Jane reached over, grabbed a slice, and sat next to Sarah. "You'll be happy to know this is one of many. With all of us being so busy, I'm hoping we can use this time to catch up and hang out." Jane took a big bite of pizza, somehow managing to look graceful eating it.

"I was just thanking the team for being so welcoming," Sarah chimed in, reaching for another slice of pizza.

"Great. One of the things I love most about our team is the generosity of everyone's spirit. I have no doubt you'll fit right in, Sarah."

Amy nearly choked on her pizza. If only Jane knew.

"Me too, Jane." Sarah was all smiles. "Thank you again for dinner last night. I had a great time getting to know you and learning more about Diva."

"It was my pleasure, Sarah."

Jane gracefully made her way around the conference room, chatting with everyone, stopping by Amy and Jeff for a few minutes. "I'm glad you could make it, Jane and thanks for the lunch. I love the idea," Amy said with Jeff nodding in agreement.

After a few minutes, Jane excused herself and made her way out of the conference room, patting Sarah's shoulder as she passed her.

Perplexed by the exchange between Sarah and Jane, Amy stared out the window, unsure whether to be thrilled by Jane's guidance or petrified that Jane had fallen prey to Sarah's antics. She rubbed her lips together, every now and again darting a gaze towards Sarah, sitting in all of her arrogant glory.

The room began to clear out, a few stragglers welcoming Sarah to the department. Jeff cleared his throat loudly, tossing his plate and empty cup in the trash. "Sarah, we are delighted to have you join the team. We already have one phenomenal senior director, and with you on board, we'll be able to accomplish even more. If you need anything to help you transition into your role here, please don't hesitate to ask." He waved in Amy's direction and scooted out. Sarah was all smiles, of course.

Anna stood, phone in hand as she hurried out waving at everyone, motioning for Sarah to call her. Amy shifted uncomfortably in her seat. She thought she'd known how this charade would play out, but she had been mistaken. Sarah was pleasant and complimentary of the team, catching her off guard. She regarded the poised woman sitting a few feet away from her, the very same one who had made her life miserable only nine months ago, and began to wonder if there was hope for a new beginning with Sarah. This morning she had walked in with full armor, prepared for whatever grenades Sarah tossed in her path, but now, she felt at ease, her guard lowering a little—but just a little. Did she dare hold a bit of optimism about working with Sarah again?

With the last few people clearing the room, Amy followed, her steps faltering slightly as she debated if she should stop and talk to Sarah. Perhaps the jab in Jane's office wasn't a jab at all. She vowed to keep the past at bay. It was clearly not serving her well.

She was almost out of the conference room when Sarah called out, "Amy, do you have a few minutes to talk?"

"Of course," Amy said.

"I know we haven't always gotten along but I'm hoping this is a new beginning for us."

"I ... I would like that."

"Good. I'm glad to hear it. It sounds like your time here has been very valuable."

"Ah ... yes. I love it here, and the team is wonderful."

"I'm really excited to be part of things here. The winters are nothing like we're used to, but we'll reminisce about the sunny skies of Los Angeles together."

Amy smiled brightly. Perhaps Sarah had changed after all.

"I'm glad Diva has been good to you, and I can already see a difference in your work."

"Ah – thanks, Sarah." What the hell?

"Great. To tell you the truth, I was dreading working with you again. It was very difficult and time consuming for me to continue mentoring you without results. I'm glad Jane's had better luck."

"Excuse me?"

"We're both here now and, funny enough, we're both senior directors. Imagine that. Anyway, let's try and grab lunch soon, okay? Enjoy the rest of your day." Sarah patted Amy's arm, like a mother placating a child so a tantrum wouldn't erupt. A cold smile slid across Sarah's placid features, and then she disappeared before Amy could respond.

Rage surged through Amy's veins. She was just as nasty as before, only this time, she was careful about being public about it. Amy stormed out of the conference room and then realized she was playing into whatever bizarre game Sarah was plotting and slowed down. Forcing a deep breath, she sauntered to her office with her head held high, a confident smile masking the storm brewing inside her.

When Mark from advertising called Amy later that day to check in, Amy calmly listened as he raved about Sarah and how excited he was about working with someone who had their finger on the pulse of all things trendy. Amy wanted to vomit. For Mark's sake, she hoped he would never meet the real Sarah.

"I've been meaning to tell you, I love the design mock-ups for the Valentine's marketing campaign. Everyone's been enthusiastic about the fresh new look and direction. I'm excited to see our hard work come to fruition," Amy said evenly, hoping the change in subject was subtle enough.

"Amy, thank you. I appreciate your support. Listen, I have to go. I have another meeting, but we'll catch up later."

Amy cradled the receiver against her chest long after Mark hung up.

The conversation with Mark was just one of many Amy had throughout the week that unnerved her. The list of Sarah fans grew by the day. She'd created quite the following, but Amy wasn't fooled. The off-hand comments, glares, and overly enthusiastic demeanor were all part of the charade. Amy felt confident enough in her own ability and contributions that regardless of Sarah's hidden agenda, she would be just fine. Sarah's fan club wouldn't change that – unless Sarah began building a case against her as she had done at Diva. Amy had been a rising star there too until Sarah arrived and began talking about dead weight in the department, shrewdly pointing at Amy. The magazine was in dire financial straits. No one cared about the loss of a few worker bees. Without Sarah's connections sending huge sums of cash to keep the magazine afloat, Diva would have collapsed.

Anxiety from the past thrummed in her ears, sucking her in, unsettling her and momentarily clouding her judgment. She breathed in and out, shaking with rage. How dare Sarah force her way into my happy place. Calm down, Amy. Everything always works out and just the way it's meant to. An unshed tear clung to the corner of her eye, but she refused to let it fall. With a shaky breath, she blinked it away, reminding herself of the vast difference in situation and circumstance at work, not to mention that she was now equal to Sarah in position. Besides, public endorsement of Amy's work from the two most powerful executives in the company was worth something. She believed that, and she took comfort in that knowledge. Whatever Sarah was up to, it wouldn't last. Jane was a no-nonsense executive, and Joan was no different. Sooner or later, the charade would end—if indeed it were a charade. For the immediate future, Amy would keep her head down and focus on her work. Confrontations and drama were low on her list and engaging with Sarah guaranteed both.

It didn't take long for Sarah to shed a layer of poise and professional decorum. "Old habits die hard," thought Amy. It wasn't unusual to find Sarah in the kitchen gossiping with one of the staff members. Sometimes it seemed inane and other times, when the whispering stopped as soon as someone walked into the kitchen, it was clearly about a fellow employee.

"I just can't believe how inexperienced she is, given her position. That's shocking to me," Sarah said to Mark one afternoon.

Amy was getting printouts from the copy machine located next to the kitchen. The wall was paper-thin, and every conversation was public knowledge. She was surprised Mark would engage in such an exchange. He knew the kitchen area provided zero privacy. She shook her head and quietly returned to her office, making it a point to stay clear of the kitchen for the rest of the day.

Unfortunately, that didn't spare her from enduring Sarah's constant pop-ins into her office. Every time, Sarah pointedly assigned her tasks that clearly were meant for the department's administrative assistant, not the senior marketing director—and Sarah's equal. Sarah was pleasant and polite enough in her requests, but there was an underlying current that left Amy uneasy. Choosing the Zen path of non-confrontation, Amy quietly forwarded the assignments to the administrative assistant. Tasks like ordering lunch for the staff meeting or letting office service know about a dirty bathroom. It was mentally exhausting to remain detached and focus on work as if nothing out of the ordinary was happening.

"Is there a reason you passed off the tasks I needed your help with?" Sarah hissed, her tall, slender frame perched in the doorway, intentionally leaving Amy's office door open.

"Sarah, ordering sandwiches for a team meeting isn't my job and certainly isn't the best use of my time. While I'm thrilled to help you navigate the office and our systems, ordering lunch is a job for the administrative assistant. If you have issue with that, I'd be happy to schedule a meeting with Jane and Joan."

Sounding braver than she felt, Amy stood her ground, staring at Sarah who had both hands propped on her hips in battle mode, no doubt to intimidate.

"That won't be necessary. I know it's not your job to order sandwiches but I hoped you would be a team player by helping me out, that's all. I'm still learning who everyone is and I didn't see the harm in turning to someone I already know. I'm sorry if I've offended you." Sarah shrugged her shoulders apologetically, pivoted on her heel, and left as quickly as she had come in without giving Amy the opportunity to respond. The click clacking of her Jimmy Choos echoed loudly in her wake.

On the surface, Sarah's request could be seen as innocent enough, but Amy knew better. With Sarah, every word and action were carefully calculated and planned and a lunch order should have been given to any of the assistants, not a senior director. Amy wasn't fooled. She was enraged.

That conniving snake. Amy groaned loudly and reached for the phone.

Hey, Miranda. Need your advice. Call me. xx Amy

Once Miranda called, Amy brought her up to speed with the latest run in.

"Amy, you're giving her too much power over you. Ignore her. She's clearly the same insecure manipulative person she was a year ago. Don't play into her games. Take the high road. Besides, she's now your equal. She can't assign you anything. All that negativity isn't good for anyone," Miranda said. "Some people can never be happy, and Sarah might be one of them. Either way, she's not your problem."

"She's been here less than a month and the office is upside down. She's turned the whole place into a cliquish popularity contest. One girl was crying in the bathroom yesterday."

"Don't give her any more energy. Her karma will catch up to her."

Miranda was clearly channeling Oprah with talk of Universal karma.

Sarah's true colors had started to seep through but only subtly, her bad behavior quickly countered by a nice gesture like treating the office to fresh bagels for breakfast, no doubt to deflect attention from the underhanded comments she dolled out.

"Taking the high road means I'm actually subservient to her will," Amy contended.

"No, it means you play the part of team player and continue to shine as you have been. Sooner or later, she'll reveal her intentions, and if they're as crazy as the ones she had at Glitz, she'll get the boot."

"True. I just hate walking on eggshells around her. I know she wasn't sincere in asking for my help. And I hate feeling like she's baiting me."

"So ignore it. Keep your nose to the grindstone and focus on the good stuff. You love your job, you've got Jane and Megan and Richie. Sounds like you've got the upper hand to me."

"You're right, Miranda. Thank you. I'm sorry she brings out the worst in me."

"It's okay, just don't get sucked into the drama. You have more exciting things to think about. How are things with Richie?"

"He's great and still busy as ever with work." Within a few minutes, Miranda was fully briefed.

"How can you waste any energy on nonsense with Sarah when you have bigger and better things to focus on?"

"You're right, and I'm sorry for forgetting the important stuff. Tell me what's happening with you?"

"Remember I told you about the extra classes I was taking on? Well, I got them, and sign-ups are maxed out already. Can you believe that?"

"Miranda, that's incredible. Is it all word of mouth?"

"Yeah ... my students love the class so much, they're telling everyone about it. I'm hoping this gives me a salary bump. I could really use it. I've been saving to buy a condo."

"They'll give it to you. You're their star yoga instructor. If you walk, tons of followers will leave the studio. It's better for them to give you a raise than find a replacement for you."

"I hope you're right. Listen, I need to grab a smoothie before my next class. Love you and please chill out with the Sarah stuff. Everything will work out."

"I know and you're right. Love you and I'm so proud of you. Let me know what happens with the salary increase."

The call calmed her enough to focus on work and plow through her long to-do list. She skipped lunch all week and worked late hours every night, except the Monday she spent with Richie. She ached for him, living for the calls and text messages that barely came. With his equally busy schedule, he worked late too, and their conversations seemed rushed and disconnected. She had come to rely on Richie to be her burst of sunshine and now he wasn't there to help lift her spirits. It was time she found her own joy, independent of anyone else.

Amy couldn't wait till Christmas when she knew their time together would be uninterrupted. In the meantime, she threw herself into work. Every report, timeline, and budget were checked with a fine-tooth comb, leaving nothing to chance. The last thing Amy needed was a silly mistake for Sarah to hang her hat on.

Back at the safe haven of her apartment, she curled up on the bed, still in her office clothes—a black dress and black knee-high boots that she roughly yanked off her feet and tossed on the floor—the perfect outfit to match the somber weather and her mood. She shivered, pulling the blanket tighter around her shoulders. So long great outdoors, she thought, snapshots of warm beaches teasing her playfully. Between the frigid temperatures outside and unpredictable temperament at the office, she needed every ounce of inner strength to pull her through.

Coincidentally, work-life balance had also vanished with the warm temperatures. Up until a few weeks ago, Amy and Megan had been inseparable. They often grabbed dinner or drinks after work. It was an easy friendship that Amy cherished, finding a loyal confidant in Megan and vice versa. It was because of Megan that Amy met Richie, the second-best part of being in Manhattan. With Jane transitioning out of the department, Megan was eager to spread her wings and wanted the coveted role of staff photographer for the magazine. Megan was exceptionally talented, and lately, many of her pictures had been selected for feature articles. Megan's photography career had real potential, which meant long hours in the studio and many hours on location. The two barely had time to text. The loss of that daily interaction was unbearable. They two had been each other's lifelines whenever tough situations arose. Amy missed her dear friend and for the first time since arriving in Manhattan, she felt completely alone. The unsettling environment at work had indirectly isolated the two, their career goals taking precedence over hanging out. Amy kicked herself for allowing work stuff to cloud a slice of happiness she savored. She buried her head under the blanket in an effort to block out the world, her mind racing with thoughts of finding her footing again. No Megan and no Richie.

She contemplated a hot cup of tea or glass of wine to warm up and conjure inner peace, but stayed under the covers, too exhausted to move.

The aftermath of Sarah's presence in her life at Glitz had been suffocating and demoralizing. When Amy wasn't sad, she was mad, and when she wasn't mad, she was swimming upstream desperate to stay afloat. Regardless of how hard she tried to stay one step ahead of Sarah's scheming, somehow, she always ended up in a pitfall.

The pandemonium she thought she'd left in her past had returned and taken residence in her present. Every time she thought she had a handle on the situation and managed to find inner calm, a flashback would surface, dragging her right back to the bottom of the pit. She was spiraling out of control.

A half hour later, Amy stood in the kitchen and poured herself a glass of Pinot Grigio, choosing the wine over hot tea and over self pity, tucked the cordless phone under her arm, and padded back to the oversized chair to dial Megan, needing to hear her friend's voice before they each went their separate ways, Amy to Greenwich and Megan to Aspen for the holidays.

Amy prayed that Megan picked up.

"Hi Megs," Amy chirped into the phone.

"Hi, stranger. I was just thinking of you. How funny that you called at the exact moment. How are you?"

"I'm good and sad and lonely and so happy we're finally catching up. I was afraid you'd leave for the holidays before we had a chance to talk. Playing text catch up doesn't cut it, you know."

"I know and I'm sorry for not calling earlier. I've been at the studio every night until eleven. I'm a walking zombie most days but I'm pretty sure they're going to offer me a permanent position in the department."

"Megan, that's wonderful. Congratulations. It's so well deserved."

"Thank you. Jane is truly is amazing. If it weren't for her, I'm not so sure any of this would have been possible. I even told Sarah in passing, and I gotta say, Amy, I think she's a changed person. She's not the Satan-worshipping boss you described, because she's been super supportive."

Amy paused, weighing her words carefully. "Be careful of her, Megan. She's not changed at all, she's just being more careful."

Amy recounted the incidents in Jane's office, the conference room, and the conversation with Jeff a couple of days earlier. "It's hard to buy she's changed."

"I can see why you'd feel that way. Maybe she's feeling insecure about coming in with a lower title. That would make me insecure and a little catty."

The phone remained cradled between her ear and shoulder as she listened to Megan, wine glass in hand.

"Forget Sarah. Let's talk about more important things like your Aspen trip. Are you packed?"

"Aspen is no big deal. It's an annual trip with my family. Yours, on the other hand, is a huge deal. You're hanging out with Richie's family—over the holidays. If that doesn't scream commitment, I don't know what does. Did you buy his Mom a hostess gift yet?"

"Not yet, but I was thinking of a really nice bottle of wine and maybe chocolate. And I was planning on making the s'mores cake my mom always serves at Christmas. It's a tradition in our family, and I wanted Richie to experience something from our holidays."

"That's really thoughtful and sweet. Yes, do that and don't stress, Amy. Things will work out. They always do. Listen, I gotta run. I still have a pile of laundry to do tonight." Megan blew kisses into the phone before hanging up.

Truthfully, Amy wanted to give Sarah a second chance and, if by doing that, she dodged unnecessary anxiety, then even better. But Sarah was making it nearly impossible to close the door on the past. After the initial calm week, Amy had seen with her own two eyes the conniving and malicious chatter Sarah was brewing. Yes. Sarah was evil to the core.

If only Amy knew the real reason Sarah had abandoned her post at Glitz to relocate to Manhattan to work at Diva with a lesser position.

Chapter Fifteen

C HRISTMAS EVE HAD finally arrived. The wintry gray sky had turned
opaque white, and a calming quiet settled over the busiest city in the
world. Nothing short of Christmas slowed down the city that never slept.
The forecast called for snow today, and Amy was beside herself with
excitement at the first snowfall of the season, the promise of a white
Christmas dancing in her mind.

The buzzing of her phone had her jumping with joy. Richie said he
would text her from the curbside—parking was hell in the city, especially
during the week. Amy combed her fingers through her freshly washed
hair and rubbed her lips together. Glancing down for a final check of her
outfit, she giggled at her own excitement at seeing Richie. She felt like a
teenager on her first date. Amy was glad she opted for the skinny
corduroy navy pants, flat heeled riding boots, and white cashmere
sweater. She felt and looked like a girl headed out on holiday.

Grabbing her overnight bag, coat, and purse, Amy dashed for the
door, swinging it open forcefully.

She yelped, startled out of her wits by the six-foot-two breath of fresh
air standing in her doorway, looking sexier than she remembered. He
grinned his million-dollar smile, perfect white teeth flashing. Her heart
leapt into her throat, stealing her breath.

"I thought I was meeting you downstairs?"

"Did you really think I would let you struggle with your bag down
three flights of stairs?" Leaning in, he kissed both her cheeks before
landing on her mouth, lingering deliciously.

"Hmm … I suppose not … more kissing, please." Standing on tippy
toes, Amy abandoned her purse and coat, letting them drop to the floor,
her arms wrapping around Richie's neck, kissing him deeply, the taste of

mint lingering in her mouth. She loved that he always smelled so minty and woodsy and sexy. It didn't hurt that he was a great kisser either.

"I've missed you, baby." Richie wrapped Amy in his strong arms, lifting her up against him. She breathed him in, savoring him and this sweet moment. "Looks like a white Christmas is in the forecast and, lucky for you, you'll experience it in the magical land of Hendricks."

"Magical land of Hendricks, eh?" Amy laughed, tossing her head back with careless abandon. "I'm ready to be whisked to the magic land, Mr. Hendricks." Amy slid her hands down his broad torso. He groaned in response, his gaze burning through hers. At least some things never changed.

Hand in hand, they walked to the car with her luggage in tow, Richie insisting on carrying everything but her purse. She shook her head in resignation and scooted to the passenger seat while he stowed her stuff in the trunk.

The scenery began to change as soon as they drove out of Manhattan. Concrete and skyscrapers were replaced with a narrow highway that curved through the deeply wooded river towns in Westchester County. A dusting of snow covered everything, the flurries becoming thicker and heavier with each mile. Excitement bubbled within Amy, threatening to pop like a champagne bottle.

"A white Christmas," Amy exclaimed, pushing the button to roll the window down to catch a few snowflakes on her hand. The frosty wind chill smacked her in the face, and she quickly regretted her decision. Feeling frozen to the bone, she rubbed her hands together frantically, the circulation slowly returning to her blue fingertips.

"Why didn't you tell me?"

"Ah – I figured you knew – you know – with snow coming down and all. What did you expect?" Richie teased, suppressing a chuckle.

"Well I didn't – oh never mind." She rolled her eyes. Her happiness with Richie was all the warmth she needed.

From the back seat, the ringing of Richie's mobile filled the car, and Amy twisted in her seat to retrieve it for him.

"I thought you were off for the holidays?" Amy asked.

"I am. It's probably my mom checking in to make sure we're on the road already." He smiled, reaching for the phone.

Amy's gaze landed on the screen. The name didn't belong to his mother. She handed the phone to Richie. "Hmmm. I thought your office was closed today."

"What? It is." Puzzled by Amy's reaction, Richie glanced down, his brows furrowing tightly, the slightest twitch in his strong jaw preceding annoyance creasing his handsome face at Francine's name staring back at him.

Throwing the phone on the console between the two front seats, he grabbed Amy's hand, keeping his other hand on the steering wheel. "I'm afraid my assistant is taking the word ambitious too seriously. She's lobbying for a promotion in the worst way, but she's not ready for one yet. She's dedicated and loyal and driving me batty with the constant emails and calls. But I don't want to crush her spirit."

She felt his thumb caressing her hand tenderly. "Maybe you can talk to her about the importance of work-life balance and tell her that your girlfriend would very much appreciate the balance bit to be uninterrupted with the work bits."

Richie grinned, those delicious dimples piercing his freshly shaved face. He nodded and brought her hand up to his lips for a kiss. "Excellent reasoning, my love. I'll add that to my talking points." Richie's voice was light; clearly, he was amused by their conversation.

"Thank you, Mr. Hendricks, for hearing me." Amy squeezed his hand.

Richie ran his fingers through his hair. "Any other requests, Ms. McKinsey?"

"Well since you asked, I would like a stroll in the snow with you, hot chocolate by the fireplace, and cuddles, unlimited quantity. Oh wait – are we sharing a room? I don't want your mom to think badly of me. We should sleep in separate rooms." Amy's voice rose an octave. A mixture of excitement and anxiety toiled inside her.

"I believe we're sleeping in separate rooms. My parents are old fashioned when it comes to certain things. But I'll come visit if you promise to be quiet."

Amy swatted his arm playfully, laughing out loud at his suggestion. "You'll do no such thing. We'll be respectful while we're under your parents' roof."

"Fine, we'll have to resort to the car then."

"Richie –"

"What? I can't wait a whole week to be with you. I miss you. We'll figure out a way. Leave it to me." He winked.

Amy smoothed out her pants, subtly stealing a glance in Richie's direction. His head rested against the seat, his shoulders relaxed, and the slightest smirk tugging at the corners of his mouth.

"Dare I ask what you're thinking about?"

"Hmmm … I was thinking about you, me, naked in my car, and how fun that would be."

"Richard Hendricks the Third, you have a one-track mind."

"I can't help it. My girlfriend is the hottest woman alive."

Amy rolled her eyes, secretly loving the attention he was dotting on her. She placed her hand on his thigh, squeezing gently, letting him know she was on-board with whatever plans he had for them.

Mrs. Claus's advice resurfaced, and this time, Amy understood its significance. Not that long ago, she was engulfed in worry about work and losing Richie to his career, and today, steady confidence and calm radiated from her. Nothing had changed but her perspective and the ability to stop obsessing over details that were out of her control. The big picture was what mattered. Relationships were complicated, and Amy was no stranger to that notion. She lived in the real world and expected some hiccups along the way. The fear of losing Richie to his career was a legitimate concern and might still happen, although she prayed it wouldn't. They certainly wouldn't be the first or last couple to fall apart because they barely saw each other. Absence didn't always make the heart grow fonder. At times, it made the heart move on.

Turning slowly to face Richie, Amy tucked her hair behind her ears and sat up straight.

"Tell me more about your parents and Abigail," Amy said. She had met his parents over lunch a few months ago at the Boathouse in Central Park, and more recently when they invited her for Thanksgiving dinner. Both times, they were warm and welcoming, their conversation easy and effortless.

"Abigail is amazing and has the ability to make everyone feel important and valuable. She's very smart and can run circles around me with time management and multi-tasking."

Amy's heart danced. Richie's praise of Abigail had resonated with her because she shared the same closeness with her brother, Peter.

"I love that you're so close, and that you work together too. It must make things easier.

"It does. We see things in a similar way which helps when dealing with my dad."

"What do you mean?"

"He can be very set in his ways. He's rigid when it comes to business and how he sees the future."

"Does he still want you to take over the company someday?"

"He does, and that someday might be sooner than I expected."

"Why, what changed?"

"To be honest, I don't know. He seems different lately. He says he's tired and wants more time with Mom."

"And you don't believe him?"

"No, it's not that. I know he loves my mom and God knows she's spent enough time alone. Growing up, he was always at work, traveling to meet clients – I don't remember him being home much. My mom raised us. The holidays were the only time work was on the back burner. Mom insisted. But I know him and I know he'll be bored out of his mind. All he does is work."

"Maybe he is getting tired then. He's in his late sixties, right?"

"Yeah – but he's been acting strange lately. He's always checking and double checking on things."

"Well maybe he's making sure you're ready to take over."

"Yeah, maybe. I just miss him – the old him. We used to joke around at the office. He would stop by to tell me about something he read or saw and now, nothing. I swear there's a permanent furrow on his face."

"I'm sorry Richie. I had no idea."

"It's okay," he said. "I hope being disconnected from work during Christmas will level things out. Tell more about your parents?"

"My dad is an architect, and my mom was a high school English literature teacher. They're easy going. I think us Southern Californians are much more laid back in our attitude towards life. My parents have always worked hard and were smart about savings and money in general. After six o'clock, it was family time. My dad would rather wake up at four to catch up on work than miss dinner with us. And living by the beach has its bonuses. It keeps things in perspective, I think."

"Growing up by the beach sounds amazing. Are you homesick?"

"I am – this is the first time we're spending Christmas apart."

"What made your parents decide on Bali for Christmas?"

"They didn't. Peter and I bought the travel package for them as an anniversary present. Christmas was the most affordable deal."

"I'm honored to be your beach replacement."

Amy leaned over the console and planted a kiss on his cheek.

The rest of the drive was uneventful and pleasant. The scenery around them was breathtaking, the antidote she needed to let go of her own work. Between Richie's overzealous assistant who felt the need to be in touch constantly, and his workaholic dad, she had a feeling Christmas wasn't going to be as relaxing as she had hoped.

After a couple of hours of driving through what felt like a Thomas Kincaid portrait, Richie negotiated the car down a pebble stone driveway that must have measured half a mile long. The Tuscan-style villa was closer to a mansion and it was even more beautiful than she remembered from a few weeks back. From the black shutters against the limestone to the wreaths made of fresh holly and pine on every window, the villa was picture perfect. Even the shrubbery, planted with precision alongside the driveway and bordering the house, was lit with dainty Christmas lights that twinkled delicately. It was beyond Amy's wildest imagination.

"I told you, my mom goes all out for Christmas. You'd think Mr. and Mrs. Claus lived here. Wait till you see what she's done inside the house."

Inspecting her makeup in the visor mirror, Amy applied a fresh coat of lipstick and wiped away the imaginary mascara smudges under her eyes. "It's beautiful, Richie. I can't believe you grew up here."

He shrugged dismissively. His parents' wealth wasn't something he'd ever talked about, she realized now. He climbed out of the car and walked around to the passenger side to help Amy out, his black snow boots slipping a little on the fresh powder of snow. With her hand firmly in his, he pulled her against him, pressing his lips to hers.

"Come on." They walked to the house, the sound of their footsteps muffled by the wet ground beneath their boots.

Amy squeezed his hand, feeling slightly out of place. She had grown up in a beautiful neighborhood in the Pacific Palisades in Southern California. Her mom had inherited the Spanish style bungalow with a red roof from Amy's grandmother. Back then, the Pacific Palisades was affordable, and there had been nothing like the sprawling mansions that surrounded the house now. But even those mansions paled in comparison to this villa yanked from the pages of an architectural design magazine.

Two green shrubs adorned either side of the front door, bright red poinsettia plants positioned in front of each pot. Amy marveled at the size of the lacquered black door with its brass knocker and elegant wreath of pinecones and holly.

Reaching for the doorknob, Richie jumped back as the door swung open. "Hello, Mom. I didn't realize you'd be waiting right by the door," he teased, chuckling.

Mrs. Hendricks beamed, tilting her head back to get a better look at her son before opening her arms wide to hug his large frame. Richie leaned down to kiss her cheeks, and then wrapped his arms around the petite woman. "You can't blame a mother for missing her children."

"I've missed you too, Mom. You look beautiful and the house looks incredible." His hand blindly found Amy's and he threaded his fingers through hers.

A whiff of cinnamon and pine wafted through the Christmas-clad villa. From Amy's vantage point in the doorway, she could see a glimpse of the antique white kitchen at the far end of the hallway. Amy loved everything about the villa, especially the open layout style. On one side of the hallway, family portraits in dark mahogany frames hung at regular intervals. On the opposite wall, two antique-looking crystal candle sconces framed either side of an oil painting of a scenic landscape. Perhaps the oil painting was a family heirloom. Richie stepped aside, releasing Amy's hand again, making room for Amy and his mom to greet each other. He shifted on his feet, sticking both hands in his jacket pockets in an attempt to stand still. His excitement was so endearing. Amy's heart squeezed at being included for the holidays, knowing how much Richie loved her, and desperately tried to let go of the trepidation in her heart about work interfering with their alone time. A little voice in her head assured her that everything would be fine.

"Focus on the big picture. This is part of the big picture," Amy thought. Being part of Richie's private world during the moments that mattered made the loneliness and evenings apart more bearable. Only a little though.

"Thank you, darling," said Mrs. Hendricks, turning her attention to Amy. "Amy, it's so wonderful to see you, dear. I'm thrilled you'll be spending the holidays with us. We'll see if we can make this an extra special Christmas for you since it's your first one on the east coast." She winked at Richie.

Amy wrapped her arms around the slender shoulders of her boyfriend's mom, glad they'd had the chance to bond a few months ago. It made staying with the family over the holidays less awkward. The two of them had a mutual fondness for one another that deepened with each visit.

"Come inside," said Mrs. Hendricks. "I prepared a light lunch for us."

Amy happily followed her down the double wide hallway leading to the kitchen, her boots clicking on the polished dark oak floors, while Richie went to retrieve their bags from the car before the snowfall got heavier.

Elegance oozed from the colonial house. The long hallway felt more like a runway to Santa's shrine. Tall black lanterns with red chunky candles lined the hallway leading to the airy kitchen at the back of the house. A delicate vine of red berries wrapped around the base of the lanterns, giving them a festive effect. So simple and yet eye catching. Richie was right about the house transforming into magic land of sorts. Every surface, empty wall space, and doorway was meticulously decorated with a variety of Christmas ornaments, berry encrusted holly, and fresh mistletoe.

"How was the drive from the city?" Mrs. Hendricks asked, smoothing an invisible wrinkle on her beige knee-length dress, her feet soundless in Ugg slippers. She looked like a modern-day Doris Day right down to her easy smile and sparkling blue-gray eyes. She was beautiful in every way, and Amy was in awe of the woman who had raised such accomplished children.

"It was breathtaking. The Merritt Highway is nothing like any highway we have in Los Angeles, or anywhere, actually. It's so woodsy and beautiful. The best part, it started to snow," Amy added, the corners of her mouth lifting in a small smile. The nervousness lingering in her heart faded a little.

Mrs. Hendricks looked over her shoulder as Richie rushed through the door with their suitcases and shut out the freezing cold air behind him, snowflakes clinging to his hair and coat.

"This is my favorite time of year, I'm sure Richie told you." Mrs. Hendricks winked at her son, who was following closely behind now as she led the way. Richie had inherited his mom's coloring and his dad's looks and build. It was hard to imagine this dainty, petite woman had given birth to the Greek god that towered over them as they entered the large, white French country style kitchen.

Richie tucked the suitcases in the corner of the vast room and walked over to the dark marble counter to peek at the food. "What's for lunch? I'm starving."

"Pressed chicken sandwiches and tomato soup," Mrs. Hendricks said.

"Sounds perfect. Thank you for going to the trouble, Mrs. Hendricks." Amy fidgeted anxiously, hoping no one noticed. She couldn't help but feel a little out of place in the grandeur of the house. It resembled a Pottery Barn catalogue full of Christmas cheer.

"Call me Diane. We're very informal around here. And Richie, don't worry, I'll bake the cookies while we eat lunch so they're warm," Diane added, motioning for them to sit at the oval, honey-colored oak table.

Richie chuckled out loud, sauntering over to Amy and snaking an arm around her waist, pulling her close for a pre-lunch squeeze. Amy's eyes darted across the kitchen, unsure of how her hostess felt about this very public display of affection.

Her anxious eyes were met with a soft, heartwarming smile. "I'm so glad you're here, Amy. I haven't seen Richie this happy in ages."

Warm fuzzy tingles swarmed inside Amy's stomach. Her shoulders relaxed. Maybe things were meant to work out after all?

Diane glided around the marble counter top with two plates that she delicately placed on green placemats. She hurried back for the soup bowls, setting them down carefully next to the plates.

"This looks incredible," Amy commented, her gaze settling on the mouthwatering pressed chicken sandwich, cheese oozing from the sides, begging to be savored. "Aren't you eating with us?"

"I already ate, dear. I tend to get hungry early because I wake up so early. Sit, please. Eat while it's warm."

Diane made Jackie O look belligerent. Feeling Richie's eyes on her, Amy looked up at him from under her lashes. He arched an eyebrow at her, curious about her private thoughts, no doubt. She shook her head, urging him to drop it, but that only encouraged him more as he poked her sides. This was a happy moment that Amy wanted to bottle forever.

Shifting focus back to their mouthwatering lunch, they ate in silence while Diane fussed over them, pouring them each a glass of water, then wine, while carrying on the conversation, filling them in on the latest happenings in town, not that Amy knew what she was talking about. She nodded politely anyway.

"Abby and your Dad will be here later this afternoon," Diane said as she worked methodically, scooping out small portions of dough from the mixing bowl and placing them on a baking sheet. Ten minutes later, she had filled two trays with chocolate chip dough balls and stuck them in the oven.

Stuffed to the gills, the wine working its magic on her limbs and state of mind, Amy gazed dreamily out the large window to the lake past the backyard.

"Richie, why don't you show Amy to her room. I've prepared the guest room across the hall from yours," Diane chimed. "While you two unpack and freshen up, I'll finish up here. Come down when you're ready and we'll have cookies in the family room."

Suppressing a giggle at the guest room comment, Amy slacked in her chair, feeling the most relaxed she's felt in a while. "Thank you so much for lunch, Diane. It was delicious. You'll have to teach me how to make these recipes so I can prepare them for us." Amy carried her plate and Richie's to the sink and ran water over them.

"I would love to teach you all of Richie's favorites, Amy. As you've figured out by now, he's a die-hard foodie, just like his dad." Diane's voice rose an octave with excitement, kindness lacing her words.

"You must have your hands full keeping them on their toes, then."

"I do, and it might sound like I'm betraying the feminist movement, but I absolutely love spoiling my family rotten. It makes me happy to cook something special for Andrew or one of the kids. Their smiles are the best gifts."

"I don't think it's a betrayal to feminism one bit. And I love that you love it. My mom loves it too and she's the biggest champion for feminism."

Diane's face lit up, her eyes shining with contentment.

Richie ushered Amy toward the staircase, just by the entryway to the kitchen, threading his fingers in hers as they walked up to the guest bedroom.

"I'll be right up with the luggage," he said.

Amy took the opportunity to look around the room. It was fit for a princess. The white furniture, plush duvet in crisp white linen, and pink and gray accents around the room exuded happy energy. The queen size four-poster bed was placed perpendicular to the bay window overlooking the garden below. An ornate porcelain white lamp with a pastel pink shade sat on a matching dresser, and a small white writing desk put Amy's imagination into overdrive thinking about love letters written using a feather pen and inkwell on that desk over the years.

The anxiety she'd felt a few days before seemed like a distant memory, and she delighted in feeling more herself again, relaxed and happy. Being on guard at all times at the office, trying to anticipate Sarah's next move, was downright exhausting and she was glad for the break. The physical distance had given her perspective. She needed to maintain inner peace regardless of the chaos erupting around her, otherwise Sarah would win, again. Sinking onto the plush bed, she sat still for a few minutes, pushing away all thoughts but the ones associated with spending the holidays in this magical haven.

Chapter Sixteen

D OWNY SNOWFLAKES THE size of cotton balls floated down to the ground, clinging to tree branches, shrubs, and rooftops, transforming the gardens into a winter wonderland. A luminous white glow settled over the villa.

Amy stood at the French doors overlooking the magical scene outside. The family room was more windows than walls, capturing the beauty of the outdoors with the warmth and comfort of being inside. To say the house was stunning both inside and out was a huge understatement.

"Hi, Amy." Abby hurried towards her, and the two embraced.

"Hey, it's so good to see you. When did you get here?" Amy asked.

"A few minutes ago. How are you?"

"I'm good and couldn't be happier for vacation. I finally get the winter wonderland thing. It's almost magical."

"It is breathtaking, and sadly, we take it for granted sometimes. I'm so glad you're spending the holidays with us." Abby's blue-gray eyes twinkled. She pulled Amy by the hand to join her on the couch.

Tucking her legs under her, Abby sat facing her. "What's been going on with you? Richie mentioned your old boss is now working at Diva. How's that going?"

Amy spared no detail, telling Abby everything that had happened since Sarah walked through the doors of Diva, pausing only occasionally to reel her emotions back in.

"Wow. There's nothing I hate more than vicious women at work going after other women. So much for upholding the sisterhood."

"Exactly. She wouldn't recognize the sisterhood if it punched her in the face. Everything she does and says is with malicious intention. I think the old scheming Sarah is very much alive and well."

"Maybe she'll rub enough people the wrong way and that will be the end of her there."

"Maybe. It's only been a couple of weeks and already she's stirred the pot a few times. Anyway, let's talk about something more pleasant. I'm making a conscious effort to block negativity from my mind, and that's basically all things Sarah. How was London? Did everything go well?" Amy asked.

"It's been tough. Richie and I are both pulling long hours, and I'm drained lately. If I'm not in the office, I'm on a plane or in a meeting. My dad has been different too. I don't know if it's stress or anxiety, but he's been a little... aloof."

Abby was leaning in, resting her elbows on her knees. Amy had only met Abby a couple of times before today, and yet, Amy felt comfortable around her. The two of them had a lot in common from their dedication to yoga and healthy living to loving the outdoors. And they were the same age.

"Funny, Richie said something similar. Do you think he's ready to retire?" Amy didn't have a chance to say anything more as Richie's boisterous laugh erupted from the hallway. He was followed by his dad, and seconds later his mom, who carried a large platter of fruit and cheese that she placed on the coffee table.

Amy stood to greet Richie's dad, an older version of the man she loved.

"It's wonderful to see you again, Amy." Andrew Hendricks embraced her tightly, the frostiness from the outdoors clinging to his coat and making her shiver in response. Andrew chuckled at her reaction.

"I'm sorry. I should have warmed up first before hugging you. The temperatures dropped quite a bit outside. There's a black ice warning for the highways."

"It's all right, Andrew. I'm glad you're here and not still on the road," Amy reassured him, rubbing her palms over her arms for warmth. She was an LA girl through and through, and as much as she loved the magical white Christmas, she could do without the freezing temperatures.

Andrew turned to Abby and planted a tender kiss on top of her head and cupped her face with his hands. Abby squealed like a child, wiggling out of his grasp.

"Oh come on, they're not that cold, are they?" Andrew's playful antics made them all laugh. Amy loved the Hendricks clan, and with each visit, she felt closer to them. In spite of the grandeur that surrounded them, they were easy going and down to earth. Something she appreciated.

"In case I forget to say it, thank you for having me, Andrew. I'm excited to spend the holidays with you guys." Amy blushed, shifting on her feet.

"We're delighted to have you. It's going to be a wonderful Christmas and much needed downtime."

"Andrew, where's the wine?" Diane chimed, waltzing into the family room.

"Oh, sorry, honey. I got distracted catching up with these two beauties." Andrew shrugged half apologetically, angling his head towards Abby and Amy.

Chuckling softly, Diane shook her head, accustomed to Andrew's charm. The two had met freshman year in college, fell in love, and got married three months after graduation. The following June would mark their thirty-fourth wedding anniversary. Diane's face still lit up when Andrew looked in her direction. Their love was evident to anyone within a mile of them. Amy's parents were the same way, and she counted her blessings for being raised in a home full of love with her parents setting the example for a healthy relationship. Their strong marriage served as a mirror for her not-so-healthy relationship with Adam. And it was that kind of love and mutual respect for one another that solidified her decision to end things with her cheating ex.

"Richie, would you mind grabbing a bottle of red from the cellar? I'll get the glasses." Diane dashed out of the room with Richie on her heels.

Diane was back within minutes with five sparkling crystal stem glasses on a silver tray. Orange flames danced seductively in the hearth. Diane and Abby fell into easy conversation as Diane rearranged the pillows on the couch before sinking into the plush cushions next to Abby and Amy. Andrew remained standing, occasionally scrolling through messages on his phone. For the briefest of moments, Amy noticed Andrew fidget uneasily. A shadow passed over Andrew's handsome features, dimming his bright green eyes so quickly and so briefly, had she not been watching him closely, she would have missed it. Amy stole a glance at Abby, but she hadn't noticed. Diane had, however. Sadness tugged at Richie's mom's face, her eyes brimming with tears she quickly blinked away. Something was going on.

Outside, snow drifted steadily, blanketing everything in sight. The winter wonderland she dreamed about was finally here, but the sudden change in atmosphere felt anything but magical. Brushing away the uneasiness that thrummed in her belly, she shushed the little voice in her head and allowed herself to get lost in the scene outside, the shrubs lit by the delicate string of twinkling Christmas lights.

Turning to Abby, she opened her mouth to speak and then clamped it shut again, feeling silly about being so giddy over a white Christmas. She sighed, partially listening to Abby and Diane's banter, partially lost in her own daydream and very curious about what had transpired with Andrew a few minutes ago. Andrew remained on the outskirts of the conversation, safety hidden behind the small screen of his cell phone. Whatever caused his earlier reaction hadn't loosened its grip on him or Diane. With his guard down, his shoulders seemed stooped in comparison to his usual stance that exuded confidence and strength. Diane's eyes never left Andrew, even as she listened to Abby talk animatedly about a family friend who had returned from safari the day before.

"I think we should plan a family vacation to South Africa. That would be an amazing experience." Abby's voice had a chipper tenor that made everything she talked about sound thrilling.

"That would be fun, honey. Let's see how the year shapes up," said Diane.

After what felt like an eternity but in reality, was probably ten minutes, Richie's hurried footsteps echoed on the hardwood floor in the hallway before he appeared in the doorway with a bottle in each hand, grinning from ear to ear. Once over the threshold, he thrust the bottles forward, holding them like they were prized possessions for his mom to choose from. She nodded appreciatively at his choices, gesturing to the bottle on the right. Richie bowed formally, placed the bottles on the table, and proceeded to open the Cabernet.

Everything about Richie's family and this house screamed splendor beyond Amy's comfort zone. She should have been better adjusted, especially after spending the evening with Richie at the Hampton house during the summer and having dinner here a few weeks ago for Thanksgiving. But for some reason, she wasn't. In comparison to her own laidback family who savored a grilled dinner in the garden followed by a race to the beach, Richie's family were formal. From family traditions to the picture-perfect decor of the house, their families couldn't be more different in their approach towards holidays and family gatherings, and yet, personality wise, there were many similarities. Silently, she prayed the day would come that their families would meet and get along.

Sitting on the blue paisley chair across from the couch, Andrew loosened his tie. His fingers grazed the phone screen once again, the slightest tremor evident.

"Dad, phone away. We're officially on vacation." Abby surveyed the platter and settled on a square piece of cheddar cheese. Diane held the glasses for Richie to pour the wine.

"You're right, and consider it done." In a grand gesture, Andrew marched to the mantle and placed his phone on the shelf next to the family photo taken in Paris when the kids were much younger.

The only difference between Andrew and his son was coloring. He had chestnut brown hair peppered with gray, and green eyes that shone brightly when he talked. Both men shared the same mannerisms—both animated, motioning with their hands when expressing a point.

"Here we go." Richie handed everyone their wine glasses and came to stand next to Amy, the scent of his woodsy aftershave wafting in the air between them. She felt his fingers lace through hers, his large hand warm and possessive. As if on cue, Andrew began a toast, his voice even as if he were weighing each word carefully.

"It's been a great year for us, and I'm so very proud of the both of you. I'm the luckiest man alive to be blessed with an incredible family." Andrew paused briefly, exchanging a knowing look with Diane who immediately came to stand by his side, wrapping an arm around his waist. "Amy, we're so happy to have you with us and we're all praying for the white Christmas of your dreams." Andrew winked at Richie, a wan smile on his face.

The heat crept up her neck and stained her cheeks. With tears in her eyes, she squeezed Richie's hand, feeling so touched by Andrew's sweet words and his warm welcome. The family's acceptance of her made it easier to be away from home during the holidays. Richie leaned down and planted a wet kiss on her burning cheek.

Amy had been swimming upstream for weeks, fighting for her rightful place at work and, in a way, fighting for her relationship. And it had all led to this beautiful moment where she could take a deep breath and enjoy being present instead of trying to stay a few steps ahead of her life.

Beads of sweat formed at the nape of her neck from the heat radiating from the fireplace. She was never one to enjoy being the center of attention and that's exactly where she'd ended up. The once cozy family room now felt like a sauna, and she squirmed a little, eager for the family's attention to be diverted elsewhere.

"Thank you, Andrew. Let's hope the highly anticipated white Christmas doesn't freeze this LA girl." Her comment was met with laughter.

Growing up, Amy never wanted for anything and certainly never needed anything. She was raised in an affluent neighborhood, mere minutes from the beach. Her parents had done well for themselves through successful careers, smart financial investments, and their inheritance of the house from her maternal grandmother. Her fondest memories weren't of European vacations or beach resorts, they were of grilling parties and spontaneous picnics at the beach, unconditional love, and acceptance. The McKinsey clan prided themselves on being low key, fun, and unceremonious. The holidays were no exception. Friends and extended family flooded the house, their laughter echoing at all hours of the day and evening. Her heart squeezed a little thinking of home.

She clinked her glass with everyone, noting Richie beaming with pride next to her. God, she loved that man. The red wine felt velvety on her tongue, and she indulged in another sip, savoring the robust flavors teasing her senses. It was the perfect start to a magical Christmas.

Chapter Seventeen

T HE SWEET SMELL of cinnamon and French toast wafted through the air, and Amy's stomach growled enthusiastically in response, disrupting the sultry dream that had stretched deliciously throughout the night. She threw the plush duvet to the side and padded to the bathroom for a hot shower. Within thirty minutes, dressed and excited for Christmas day, she made her way towards the kitchen. The sound of raised voices in a heated discussion stopped her in her tracks. She couldn't imagine what would cause this uncharacteristic rancor from Richie or his dad.

"There's something you're not telling me, Dad."

"Son, it's time, that's all."

"No, I don't believe you. Something happened, or you wouldn't be in such a rush for this transition."

Andrew sighed loudly, followed by a long pause.

"All right. Your mother and I didn't want to tell you just yet because we didn't want to ruin Christmas, but you're right, there is something. I've been diagnosed with early onset Alzheimer's, and I'm afraid time isn't on my side. I prefer to transition the business to you while I'm able and while I can still guide you. Who knows what six months from now will look like? Maybe not much different, maybe very different."

"What?" Richie said.

"Dad, are you sure of the diagnosis?" Abby asked. "We should get a second opinion."

"It's early stages, and I've already had multiple opinions. There are medications that can keep the progression at bay." Andrew's voice broke, and Amy's heart broke with it.

The sound of soft sobs, sniffling, and chairs being dragged followed.

"There are a couple more tests coming up. Until then, we have to stay positive about this." Diane, the ever-present voice of reason in the family, tried to keep the peace.

"Mom, how can you be so calm about this?" Richie asked.

"Because worrying is a waste of time and it doesn't change the out-come of anything. Let's enjoy each other and cherish our time together. We can talk more after our follow-up with the neurologist."

"Your mother is right. Let us enjoy breakfast on this fine Christmas day. There's nothing to panic about."

"Dad, how—when?" Richie pressed. A stone settled in Amy's stomach eavesdropping on their private conversation.

"Son, I haven't felt like myself for months. At first it was little things, like forgetting where I put the keys or where I parked. I thought it was stress. A couple of weeks ago, I was supposed to meet your mom for dinner at Pastis, a place we've been to together at least once a month since we've been married, and I couldn't remember the name of the restaurant or how to get there. I felt lost and alone. It was a terrible evening. Thank God your mom called my phone and managed to track me down. She insisted I see the doctor. A series of tests and a long visit with the neurologist later and here we are …" Andrew's voice was subdued, tired, nothing like the high energy man Amy had met months ago. "Now listen, I know this is upsetting to you and it's upsetting to me and to your mom, but we have to be strong to get through this. Knowing there's a world of unknown ahead of us, I want us to enjoy Christmas together. The rest we will figure out together, later."

"Dad –" Richie's voice broke.

"It's all right son. Everything will be just fine. I will transition the company to you and Abby after the New Year, and since you have more experience, you will manage the company with Abby by your side. And I'm here for as long as you need me. Now, no more talk of business and no more talk of Alzheimer's," Andrew responded.

Someone sniffled followed by soft crying and a hiccup. Probably Abby.

"My sweet Abby. Don't worry honey, everything will be okay," Andrew reassured tenderly.

"There's nothing we can't overcome, and we need to stay positive," Diane said, sounding strong and full of conviction, unlike the typical soft tenor of her voice.

Once again, Amy found herself in awe of the woman holding up the family. The room went very still as Amy continued to hover outside the kitchen, feeling wretched about the turn of events and unsure whether to walk in or run back up to her room and give the family the privacy they needed. Suddenly, it all made sense. Richie and Abby had felt the change in their dad but couldn't pinpoint the cause. She sighed, her chest constricting painfully. Time was of the essence, and she found herself praying for a prolonged, healthy life for Andrew. Memories of her grandmother's battle with the same disease flooded a part of her brain that had locked the recollections away. When Amy was in elementary school, they moved into her grandmother's house because her grandmother, a feisty and very spirited woman, had wanted to travel the world and didn't want to be bogged down with a house and the responsibilities that came with one. Within a few weeks, the deed on the house was changed to Amy's mother and all her grandmother's belongings were moved to storage.

"You're inheriting the house anyway, so why wait? Just take it now," Amy's grandmother had told Amy's mom.

"Mom, are you sure? Where will you live when you're back from your travels?"

"With you guys, and don't worry, I wouldn't be staying long. I have big plans to see every inch of this beautiful world."

Sadly, fate had other plans. Within six months of the arrangement, her grandmother moved in with them, her memory failing her too often and too frequently to travel anywhere on her own. Alzheimer's had claimed her, and she was gone within three turbulent years. Unexpected tears stung Amy's eyes, and she fought to keep them in check.

She tiptoed back to the stairway intending to go upstairs, feeling like an intruder on sacred territory. Quietly, she planted her foot on the second step.

"Amy?"

"Richie – ah – good morning."

"How long have you –"

"Long enough. Richie, I'm so sorry."

He looked pale, his eyes hazy and unfocused. She closed the distance between them and wrapped him in her embrace, wanting to provide any form of comfort she could. The chatter in the kitchen stilled. Even Abby's cries seemed to subside for now. There were no words to offer comfort, only soft caresses to let him know she was here for him. She showered him with tender kisses, hoping her affections could verbalize everything she couldn't. He leaned into her, pulling her tighter against him. They stood silently for a few minutes, the clatter of dishes and silverware the only sound around them. A shroud of sadness seemed to have settled over the kitchen and everyone in it. Slowly, Richie pulled away, wiping at the tears with the sleeve of his navy, button down shirt. Unsure of what to do or say, Amy caressed his face, wishing she could sweep away the sorrow twisting his features.

"I should have known. I've felt something was off with him for a while, but I've been so wrapped up in my own world that I didn't push for answers. The signs were right there," he croaked, his voice breaking.

"Don't do that – you didn't know, and there's no way you could have."

"But he's been so forgetful lately. The repetitive questions, the micromanaging. His behavior has been out of character, and I should have pushed harder for answers. I should have asked him what was going on."

"Richie – don't." She put a finger to his lips to silence his outburst, their eyes locking for the briefest of moments before Richie closed his, tears streaming down his face. He wiped at his face frantically, his palms wet from his tears.

"Let's go in." Just as he said the words, Andrew, Diane, and Abby appeared in the archway dividing the kitchen from the foyer.

"Ah. Good morning," Amy said. It was uncomfortable to say the least.

"Good morning, Amy. Merry Christmas." Diane walked over and

hugged her tightly, kissing her cheek. Andrew and then Abby followed suit.

"Merry Christmas. Andrew … I'm so sorry about the diagnosis. And I'm sorry for intruding on your private family time."

"Don't be silly. We're happy to have you here, and thank you."

"I feel so horrible about all of this."

"Everything will be all right," Andrew said confidently, but the trapped tear clinging to the corner of his eye said otherwise.

A few minutes later, they all walked back into the state-of-the-art kitchen, naturally lit on this sunny morning. The snow clung to the tree branches outside, a red cardinal vibrant against the white canvas around it. He sang happily as if unaware of the mood on the other side of the kitchen wall.

The room smelled of maple syrup and felt as equally heavy, despite everyone's best efforts to be cheery. Andrew sat in his chair, picking at the fruit on his plate while Diane headed to the counter to ladle some sort of sauce into a serving bowl. Abby absently sipped coffee, her eyes glazed over and brimming with tears.

Nervous tension coiled and twisted in Amy's stomach. Her hands went to her belly to massage the painful spot, and she chastised herself for letting stressful situations affect her so easily. The magical pixie dust had evaporated. The family was dealing with a painful new reality, and while Andrew may very well live several years with minimal alteration to his daily routine, the wheels of change were already in motion. She understood the urgency of transferring the company out of Andrew's name and securing its future along with Richie and Abby's.

"How did you sleep, Amy?" Diane asked, shifting the subject.

"Great, thank you, Diane. The bed is so comfortable, and it was nice to wake up to natural sunlight."

They bantered for a bit longer about inconsequential topics, Diane and Andrew putting on a brave facade for everyone's benefit. Amy polished off two cups of tea without realizing it. Even during the toughest moments, Andrew and Diane conducted themselves with poise, and she found herself admiring their strength. Taking a deep breath, she vowed to be equally strong for Richie's sake. If Diane and Andrew could put their best foot forward and hope for the best, so could she. It was Christmas after all and a time for miracles. And she believed in miracles. Her stomach rumbled enthusiastically, temporarily shifting her attention to the mouthwatering food artistically arranged on Christmas platters. If she didn't know better, Amy would have thought the whole neighborhood was coming for breakfast. From savory to sweet, every inch of the marble countertop was covered—French toast to eggs Benedict and everything in between. In spite of herself, she licked her lips. Diane truly hadn't held anything back, cooking everyone's favorite dishes.

Richie sat next to her at the dining room table, his hand resting casually on her thigh, but he remained silent. His face was withdrawn as he stared absently into the distance.

When she was done with her tea, he led her to the counter to choose her breakfast. With her brightest smile secured firmly on her face, she beamed up at Richie, rubbing his forearm. She gripped the porcelain white plate with red holly along the edges, selecting a sample from each platter, and they returned to the table to join the others.

"Amy, you're going to love the eggs Benedict. Diane adds a secret ingredient to the hollandaise sauce that makes it out of this world." Andrew walked to the counter for a second helping.

Stuffing a huge forkful of eggs Benedict into her mouth, Amy forced herself to relax in her chair, savoring every bite. An immediate explosion of flavors hit her tongue, and she moaned softly with pleasure.

"This is so delicious, Diane, thank you."

Richie leaned in and kissed her cheek before he stood up to get a second helping, having wolfed down a good portion of the French toast already. He seemed onboard with putting on a brave front as well. "Didn't I tell you? My mom's the best cook, and during holidays, no one is allowed to think about calories or workouts or passing up a dish." The mood in the kitchen lifted.

On the surface, everything seemed so normal, just as Diane and Andrew wanted.

Taking a sip from her coffee, Abby seemed to rejoin the living, forcing a smile here and there. She craned her neck to look at the platters of food, contemplating a second helping herself. "Holiday meals are calorie free," Abby said, supporting Richie's excuse to pig out.

Sitting across from Amy, Diane chewed quietly, smiling at her children with fondness.

"After breakfast, we'll open presents, and then let's go sledding," said Andrew. "We'll burn off breakfast and work up an appetite for dinner. Your mother outdid herself again this year." He sat back in his chair, coffee cup in hand, the furrowed lines between his eyebrows smoothing out.

Amy silently regarded Richie's family, wishing that her own parents were with them—under different circumstances, of course. Amy's mom had been especially excited to visit an elephant sanctuary and interact with the animals during their bathing and feeding times. The trip sounded amazing, and it beat cooking all-day and cleaning up for hours afterwards.

As if reading Amy's thoughts, Diane reached over to pat her hand. "It must be hard to be without your family during the holidays."

"It is. But I'm also happy being here. It means a lot to me to celebrate Christmas with you."

"We wouldn't want it any other way."

An hour later, the Hendricks brood and Amy stomped through the hilly grounds of the villa, boots sinking deep into the snow. They each carried a sled, except Abby who preferred a round-shaped disc in bright pink.

Amy paused to admire the snow-covered vista around them. The villa was in the distance now, and the further they walked, the more it disappeared behind the hills. The air was biting, stinging Amy's exposed skin, but somehow, she didn't mind. The sun was shining bright, casting a luminous glow over the landscape around them. Gigantic trees were scattered around the grounds creating a miniature forest. An image of her dream materialized in her mind, and Amy remembered the scene vividly as she was running through the snow-covered forest looking for Santa. This exact spot was in her dream before she saw Santa's workshop.

"Hey, slow poke, keep up. We need to get to the clearing so we're not crashing into the trees," Richie explained, slowing down for her to catch up to him.

"I always forget about the long walk to get there," Abby complained, bringing up the rear.

"It's worth it once we're there." Taking Amy's hand in his, Richie pulled her along, leaning down for a quick kiss. "We're almost there, baby."

"Richie …" Amy hesitated. "Remember the dream I had about meeting Santa?"

He nodded, and Amy went on to tell him about the uncanny resemblance between the forest leading up to Santa's village and this place.

Diane turned to face them. "And what did you want to ask Santa?" she said, looking amused.

"Well … I wanted him to grant me a wish … I wanted inner peace. Work has been hell, and I've missed spending time with Richie … anyway, I didn't get a chance to actually speak with Santa but that was my intention," Amy replied, feeling sheepish.

"Ahhh … sometimes our dreams are to remind us of what matters to us. You know… the big picture stuff," Diane explained.

"Your dream was about us?" Richie whispered, pulling Amy to his side.

Embarrassed, Amy nodded, eager to change the subject, although Diane's words of wisdom about the big picture weren't wasted on her.

After what seemed like a marathon hike, they arrived at their destination—an open space with rolling hills covered in thick white powder. Panting heavily, Amy heaved the sled to her other hand, shaking out her sore fingers, which were slightly numb now.

Within minutes, her discomfort was forgotten as she rocketed down the hill on her belly, holding on to the sled for dear life. Happiness consumed her.

"Abby, I'm almost certain people in space can see that pink sled of yours," Diane teased.

The easy banter among the group reminded Amy of her own family, and she felt more convinced than ever that her beach loving parents would get along splendidly with this sledding crew. She couldn't help but chuckle at the thought of their families together, doing something fun and outdoorsy, and if she had anything to do with the planning, it would be at the beach.

Amy was surprised by Diane's agility and athleticism. She was keeping up with Richie without complaint. That was much more than Amy could say for herself. She was feeling more winded with each passing minute, not to mention her aching thighs from trudging up the hill with sled in tow.

At the bottom of the hill, she plopped down on top of her sled, giving her shaky legs a break. She watched everyone zip past her, a deep joy glowing within her. Nothing but sunshine nestled inside her heart, and Amy found herself counting her blessings, filled with gratitude at the abundance of joy and love in her life. Then she said a silent prayer for Andrew, her heart breaking for the tough road awaiting him.

"A penny for your thoughts," Richie said, squatting next to her and gently placing a hand on her shoulder.

Startled, Amy blushed, shaking her head slowly. Richie nestled behind her on the sled and pulled her against him so her back was resting against his broad chest.

He kissed her neck, pulling her pink turtleneck down to have better access. "I love you so much. I can't wait to have you all to myself later. Maybe we can come back here for a little bonding with nature."

A small moan escaped her throat, and she bit her lower lip to keep her emotions under control, tipping her head back.

"That sounds amazing, except I don't think I can do this hike again. Perhaps a closer destination?"

"You're driving me nuts. Let's head back to the house." With one quick motion, he stood, lifting her up with him.

"We can't just leave." Amy gaped at him in surprise.

A pair of smoldering eyes held her gaze, daring her to oppose his plans. "Like hell we can't. Come on." Taking her by the hand, Richie tucked her sled under his free arm and walked over to retrieve his, with

Amy still in tow. Dropping both sleds to the ground, he unraveled a coiled rope from under both sleds, lashed them together, and proceeded to drag them behind them.

"We're heading back," he called to the others. "See you back at the house."

"Richie, would you mind turning on the oven to 350 degrees?" Diane called. "I'll be there in about twenty minutes or so to start cooking."

She waved them off before turning to say something to Andrew that had him roaring with laughter. This was the most relaxed Amy had seen Andrew since breakfast.

Richie quickened his steps, and Amy practically ran to keep up with him, giggling happily. Looking down at her, his eyes twinkled with mischief.

"We don't have much time. You don't know my mom. She's very regimented when it comes to her holiday cooking."

They raced through the forest, panting and laughing. Once at the house, they discarded the sleds in the side yard and bolted through the front door, slamming it shut behind them. Richie took the stairs two at a time with Amy running close behind him, her short legs no match for his long ones. Remembering the stove, he thundered back down. A couple of minutes later, he was back, dragging Amy up the stairs.

Inside his room, he locked the door before pulling Amy against him. Excitement bubbled inside her with anticipation. He kissed her feverishly, and she reciprocated, holding nothing back.

A knock at the door had them both jumping with disbelief.

"Honey, I'm sorry to bother you. I need your help," Diane called from the other side of the door.

He cursed under his breath, running his fingers through his disheveled hair, shaking his head with frustration. "I'll be right there, Mom," he said tightly, rolling his eyes.

Amy stared at Richie, mouth hanging open. She could have sworn Diane had mentioned staying behind a little longer. Wasn't that the reason she asked them to turn on the oven for her?

"I'm sorry, baby. This isn't what I had in mind when we snuck back here. This isn't like her." Richie held Amy close, kissing the corners of her mouth.

They walked into the kitchen hand-in-hand to find Andrew sitting at the kitchen table, his skin as pale as the snow covering every inch of the landscape outside. Abby was rubbing her father's trembling hands while Diane stood at the counter pouring tea into a mug.

Releasing Amy's hand, Richie rushed to his dad's side, dragging a chair to sit next to him and Abby. "What happened?"

"Dad got disoriented and couldn't remember where he was."

"I'm sorry. I don't know what happened. I'm feeling better now. Let's go back out," Andrew said, his voice lacking conviction.

"I'm happy enough hanging inside. Besides, we all know Mom and her strict cooking schedule," Abby chimed cheerily, determined to lift her dad's spirits.

"I'm ruining Christmas for everyone." Andrew's eyes glazed over with tears. He wiped at the drops, self-conscious with everyone fussing over him.

Amy drifted to the kitchen counter, busying herself with tea, feeling heartbroken for the family at the rapid change of events. Richie's tenderness towards his dad was very sweet, and her love for him only intensified. She smiled softly at him, unsure of how to help. Only a few minutes ago, Richie's face had been flushed with excitement and passion, and now he looked pale with his mouth downturned. That was the wretched thing about Alzheimer's, it was unpredictable and cruel and selfish.

"Don't be silly, Dad. We're together, and that's all that matters." Richie leaned over, wrapping a protective arm around his dad's shoulders. "Let's have some tea and then maybe hang out by the fireplace."

On cue, Diane set the ceramic mug on the kitchen table in front of Andrew, kissing the top of his head before sliding into an empty seat, Abby hovering at her dad's side.

"This is actually perfect. I was getting a bit chilled, and my favorite way to enjoy the snow is from a toasty room with hot chocolate," Amy volunteered, wanting to offer some words of comfort. Then a stroke of genius buzzed in her mind. She would make dessert and have everyone help, including Andrew.

"Diane, would it be okay with you if I got started on dessert? It's a Christmas tradition at my house, and I thought I'd share it with you all. I actually brought the ingredients with me." Amy smiled, pleased with herself.

"That would be lovely. Thank you, Amy." Diane glanced up, beaming, before she returned her attention to Andrew.

"Great. In my family, we all chip in to make it, and I was hoping we could do the same here. Andrew, would you like to do the honors of manning the mixing bowl?"

Andrew's eyes flickered towards her at the sound of his name. He held her gaze for a few seconds before a slow smile crept across his face. "I would be delighted, Amy."

Richie came to stand beside her. "Amy, you didn't tell me. I love it already. What are you going to make?"

Amy licked her lips, feeling nervous all of a sudden. "S'mores cake, a guaranteed crowd pleaser. My mom makes it every year."

"Sounds delicious." Diane stood, following Andrew to where Amy stood by the stove. "I want to help too."

Amy quickly assigned everyone a task. Andrew at the large mixing bowl, Diane at the stove melting the oversized marshmallows, Richie and Abby chopping chocolate squares and layering the pan with graham crackers. The somber mood lifted. Sadness was temporarily replaced with laughter and the heavenly smell of melting marshmallows.

"I know the perfect complement to our work," said Richie as he rummaged through the fridge for a few seconds. "Ta da," he said, holding a bottle of champagne up in the air like it was prize.

With dessert cooling on the counter, champagne consumed, and many belly laughs, mostly at Richie's helplessness in the kitchen, Amy felt relieved at having a small hand in helping Andrew feel better.

Chapter Eighteen

THE MORNING SUN filtered through the open drapes, a soft white glow settling over the room, inviting and warm, fitting of the perfect family portrait the Hendricks clan portrayed. The home was thoughtfully architected right down to the baseboards, cream colored and at least an inch higher than most baseboards she had ever seen, undoubtedly a custom job, like every square inch of this mansion. Even the welcome mat outside had the family coat of arms embossed on the thick wheat-colored fiber. She shuddered a little, hoping Diane didn't expect her to have the same devotion to domestic details.

By the time Amy walked into the kitchen, breakfast was cooked and on the kitchen table.

"Good morning," Amy said. "Diane, this looks so delicious. Can I help with anything?" Amy smiled from ear to ear as she surveyed the platters of mouthwatering breakfast dishes. Did Diane cook like this all the time? Amy hoped Diane didn't go through all this trouble for her sake.

"Good morning, dear. I hope you slept well."

"I haven't slept this soundly in ages. I feel better than I've felt in a long time," Amy confessed, walking to the kitchen counter in search of a mug and tea.

"Mugs are in the top cabinet," Diane said, pointing. "And tea bags are here. We have an assortment, so hopefully you'll like one of these." Diane placed an expensive looking rectangular wooden tray on the counter. The carvings along the sides curved and twisted purposefully, and Amy couldn't help but run her fingers along the indented shapes. Inside the tray was an endless variety of small packets of loose tea tagged with ornate labels identifying the flavor—some familiar—others intriguing but not temping enough to try.

"I'm not sure what's more fascinating, the variety of tea bags or this tray." Amy said, chuckling.

"I love tea and, some days, I prefer it to coffee especially in the afternoon when I'm relaxing with a book. The tray is from a friend in New Zealand. It's hand-carved and the Māori symbol on the side is called koru. The circular design represents creativity and perpetual movement," Diane explained, running her fingers gently over the markings.

Amy eyed the tray closer, intrigued by Diane's interest in Māori culture and artwork. "What drew you to Māori—" her words were interrupted by Richie trailing into the kitchen, muffling a loud yawn with his hand.

"Good morning, everyone," he said, still looking sleepy. He walked toward Amy and planted a soft kiss on her cheek and then beelined for the coffee maker.

"How long have you been up?" he asked.

"Not that long," Amy replied, diverting her attention back to the tray. "Diane, what drew you to Māori art?" she asked again.

"After college graduation, Andrew and I traveled to New Zealand and we spent over a month there, backpacking through the North Island and then the South Island. We both loved New Zealand, but for me, it was more than an incredible trip. It was a spiritual awakening of sorts. I felt this unexplainable pull towards the Māori culture, art, and food. I've been a devoted admirer since," Diane said, her voice whimsical.

"You and Dad have been back a few times, right, Mom?" Richie chimed in, large cup of coffee in hand.

"Yes, at least a half dozen times. I was hoping to go back later this year," Diane said, her voice dropping a little.

"You still can," Amy and Richie said at the same time.

"Yes, maybe. We'll see what the future brings." A wan smile touched her delicate features.

Amy watched Diane silently, Andrew's diagnosis surely top of mind when considering any future plans, especially long-term ones. Amy felt gutted and helpless, unsure of how to comfort the woman who has been kind and loving toward her.

Within minutes, Abby and Andrew straggled in, dressed and much more awake than Richie had looked a few minutes ago. After pleasantries were exchanged and coffee mugs were filled, they all sat at the kitchen table, the earlier sad tenor in the air replaced by lighthearted banter.

"Amy, how are your parents doing? Richie tells us they're in Bali," Andrew said, sounding happy and relaxed this morning.

"They seem to be doing great. They left a couple of days ago, they texted when they arrived, and said they'll call me at some point this evening."

"That's so cool. Why Bali?" Abby asked in between mouthfuls.

"My mom has always wanted to go, so my brother Peter and I chipped in and bought them the tickets for their anniversary. We found a great deal through a travel agent that Peter knew and booked it. In hindsight, we should have planned it better so my parents weren't away for the holidays, but I know they'll love the trip." Amy sipped the tea, notes of Bergamot wafting around her.

"Richie, maybe you and I should do the same for Mom and Dad and buy them tickets to New Zealand," Abby offered.

Amy and Richie exchanged a knowing look and, smiling, they turned to watch Diane. She was also smiling softly.

"What?" Abby asked.

"We were just talking about New Zealand before you and Dad walked into the kitchen. Amy got the lowdown on Mom's love for the place," Richie explained.

"Ah, got it." Abby beamed. "Then it's a sign that you should go," she said looking at her mom and then her dad, sitting on opposite ends of the table.

"I think it's a great idea," Andrew said, winking at his wife.

After breakfast was done and the kitchen was cleaned, they all meandered to the family room for a game of Monopoly, a long-standing family tradition for the Hendricks clan. Andrew and Diane took turns asking Amy more about her family, their interest genuine, and she appreciated it greatly. And even though it wasn't her intention to divulge the stressful details of her job since Sarah joined the team, she ended up spilling all the beans and got plenty of sound advice and sympathy in return.

"As tempting as it may be, don't bait her and don't celebrate her shortcomings. Rise above the petty stuff but be smart about it. Keep a running log of your contentious interactions, and especially incidents of verbal abuse or harassment. Write it all down," Andrew said. "I hope it doesn't come to that, but in case things get worse, you might want to share your document with HR."

"That's the same advice Richie gave me a while back," Amy said, nodding in agreement.

"I'd love to know why she left LA in the first place," Diane said, rolling the dice and moving her piece on the board, coincidently causing Andrew to declare bankruptcy.

"Well, I'm out and I'm starving," Andrew said, standing to stretch his arms over his head. "Anyone care for a drink or a sandwich?"

"I'll come with you, Dad," Abby said.

"Hey, what about the game?" Diane quipped.

"Mom, you've whooped us three times in a row. I think we need a break," Abby said over her shoulder, halfway to the kitchen. "Who wants a sandwich?"

Diane laughed, her eyes twinkling with joy. The strange shift in energy Amy had sensed earlier in the kitchen and the day before had vanished and she couldn't be happier.

"I'll come help. I'm kinda hungry too. Turkey sandwiches okay?" Diane asked, making quick work of packing up the Monopoly board before joining Andrew and Abby in the kitchen.

Amy and Richie nodded enthusiastically.

"Are you having fun?" Richie asked, joining Amy on the couch, their legs outstretched in front of them on the coffee table.

"I'm so happy and relaxed beyond words. Thank you, Richie, for all of this," she said, slipping her hand in his.

"You're welcome, and thank you for saying yes to being part of our holiday traditions." He leaned his head tenderly against hers.

"Your dad has kept to his promise. I haven't seen him on his phone since yesterday. He seems to be more relaxed."

"He does, right?" Richie said, closing his eyes.

Their conversation was interrupted by Abby approaching, their plates gingerly balanced on one arm and, in her other hand, stacked cans of seltzer water for each of them. Turkey sandwiches on fresh baguettes, salad, and sliced fruit. "The Hendricks don't do anything halfway," Amy thought.

"Thanks, Abby. We could have helped," Amy said, grabbing the plates and then the seltzers to set them down on the coffee table.

"This looks amazing. Thanks, Abby," Richie said, opening their seltzers.

Diane and Andrew followed with their food and Abby's, making themselves comfortable around the coffee table where the Monopoly board had been a few minutes ago.

Surprisingly, they all ate with relish, the food coma from the hearty breakfast forgotten.

"It's not a holiday without indulgence," Andrew joked.

"And on that note, I'm going upstairs for a little nap," announced Diane, standing. She reached down to grab her plate, but Richie waved her off.

"We'll do that, Mom. Enjoy your nap," Richie offered.

"Would you mind taking my plate too?" Andrew asked, rising and putting his arm around his wife's waist.

"We've got this," Amy said.

"What are you guys up to this afternoon?" Abby asked.

"I haven't given it much thought. Maybe we'll watch a movie or go for a walk." Richie eyed Amy for a reaction.

"I'm good with either," Amy said, "What do you want to do, Abby?"

"I think I'm going to head into town, run some errands."

"Errands?" Richie eyed her dubiously. "Come on, where are you really going?"

"Errands and that's all I've got," she smirked, clearly not ready to share anything else.

Once she was gone, Richie asked Amy if she and Abby had talked about anything in particular the day before, perhaps...a guy.

"She didn't mention anything," Amy said.

"I think she's seeing someone, and I think it's fairly new," Richie said, a smug look on his face like he'd just figured out a great mystery.

They decided on a movie, some action-packed thriller that Richie wanted to see. Cuddled in his arms under an afghan, Amy dozed off and on throughout the movie. At the sounds of talking and pots and pans being taken out in the kitchen, she opened her eyes to find herself alone on the couch, happily burrowed under the blanket. Richie must have laid her down and tucked a cushion under her head. She remained still for a few minutes longer, savoring the blissful feeling of a delicious afternoon nap.

Somewhere from the kitchen, Richie and Diane's voices echoed around her. Reluctantly getting up, she folded the blanket and returned it to the large wicker basket next to the fireplace, fluffed the cushion, and ran her fingers through her hair before walking into the kitchen.

"Hello, sleepy head. How was your nap?" Richie teased. He sat at the kitchen counter with a cup of coffee in hand facing Diane who was on the opposite side, chopping vegetables. The woman never stopped.

"Hi, Amy," Diane said, pausing from whatever food prep she was doing.

"Amazing. Why didn't you wake me?" She was secretly glad that he hadn't.

Richie pulled out a high barstool for her. "You needed the rest. Can I get you anything?"

"Just some water, thank you. Diane, can I help you with anything?"

"Thanks, but I'm almost done. We're having roasted chicken and vegetables for dinner and chocolate mouse for dessert," Diane announced, smiling.

Amy returned the grin, vowing to double up on her workouts post holidays. The thought of eating another morsel had her jeans protesting, the typically comfortably pants were now snug, the waistband pinching her rounded belly mercilessly. She exhaled, hoping no one noticed.

After dinner, they enjoyed a spontaneous game of cards, shared a couple of bottles of wine, and finished the night standing around the kitchen counter for a snack before bed. The evening was mellow and cozy and perfect in every way.

Amy's fondness for Richie's family swelled by the minute, and she found herself daydreaming of the day her parents would meet them and Richie. From conversations about community efforts to encourage recycling to the charity events that Diane organized, the evening had exceeded her expectations. By the time Andrew, Diane, and Abby turned in for the night, Amy was floating on clouds.

Richie squatted in front of the fireplace, adding a few logs and poking at them cautiously until the flames engulfed the wood. Yellow and orange tongues danced in the fireplace, the wood crackling. Richie's dark blond hair shimmered in the soft light. Even with his back to her, she knew the compounded stress from the last few weeks had melted away. The worst seemed to be over for Richie and for her, though only time would tell. But for now, she intended to enjoy every minute of her time here. A part of her wanted to leap from the couch and wrap herself around Richie but she refrained until he was done.

Richie left the family room and returned with three more logs cradled in his arms. He knelt down and stacked them methodically against the exposed red brick wall alongside the fireplace. Even with such a simple task, he was thorough and thoughtful. The extra logs on stand-by hinted at a long, romantic evening. She loved watching him do anything. Like the time he'd taken her sailing and expertly maneuvered the sailboat, occasionally hurrying to turn the sail in time to catch the wind. Little had she known that fateful day would mark the beginning of their relationship. She had been afraid to be hopeful for something too good to be true.

Folding her legs under her, she retrieved the plush afghan from the basket where she had placed it earlier, its heavy weight comforting over her lap. The flames twisted seductively, casting a golden glow over his profile. So handsome. As if sensing her gaze, he turned to look at her, his hazel eyes smoldering, an easy smile tugging at his mouth. It was nice to see him so relaxed and happy. He sauntered towards her, settling on the couch next to her, the couch cushions sinking beneath his heavy frame. Slowly, she inched toward him, pulling the afghan with her, covering them both. A deep chuckle vibrated in his chest, and she squirmed closer. She didn't realize how much she'd craved their uninterrupted closeness until her cheek rested against his side and her hand pressed over his heart. The scent of his sandalwood aftershave and burning logs seduced her, and she burrowed against him, her need for him overpowering. Not just a physical attraction, although she didn't have any complaints in that department. It was so much more than that. Very early on in their relationship, they'd both recognized the deep connection they felt to one another. They used to spend hours talking—in bed, in the park, on the phone—but lately, they barely texted. She missed the intimacy that had come so easily to them.

"Thank you," she murmured.

"For what?"

"A perfect white Christmas."

"It's not Christmas yet, and you don't have to keep thanking me. I'm so happy you're here, and there's no question about how my family feels about you."

"I'm so happy, Richie, I'm almost a little afraid to be this happy."

"Don't be silly. Let's enjoy the evening. I have big plans for you."

"Oh?"

"We're alone, and I don't think anyone will be coming down." Richie turned to face her, eyebrows raised with amusement.

"No way. What if you're wrong?"

"No one's coming, I promise."

"Still no way." She chuckled, his persistence adorable.

For the remainder of the evening, Richie showered her with sweet words, their hushed voices and soft laughter the perfect harmony to the stillness of the room. The evening felt enchanted, and everything they needed to remember how special they were to each other.

As they lay on the couch, exhausted and sleepy, the wood crackled in the fireplace, its charred smell taking Amy down memory lane to camping trips in the rich forests of Big Bear. She sighed at the happy recollections, dreaming of the day Richie could experience it with her. Her hand absently caressed Richie's arm, and at her touch, he snuggled closer. Cradled in his arms, wrapped around the blanket, was romantic and exactly what she needed to reconnect to him. She squirmed, perching on her forearms so they were eye to eye, loving their alone time together and wishing he could sleep next to her. But she knew better than to upset his parents by being so brazen.

"We should turn in, my love. Tomorrow is Christmas. Our first one together." He kissed the tip of her nose.

"I know, baby. I can't wait."

"I love you."

"I love you too."

They shuffled upstairs, exchanging chaste kisses before going to bed in their respective rooms.

The perfect Christmas holiday in picturesque Greenwich was turning out to be even better than she imagined.

Once she was alone, she dialed her mom. Suzanne answered after the first ring.

"Hi, honey. I was just about to call you," her mother said.

"Mom, it's so good to hear your voice. How's Dad? How's your trip?" Amy asked, sinking onto the bed.

"He's doing great. You and Peter have outdone yourselves with this trip for us. The hotel is beautiful. Marbled floors and verandas that overlook the gardens. It's so serene here, just like the brochure promised," Suzanne rattled on, excitement lacing her voice.

The two chatted for the better part of an hour thanks to the app Amy had downloaded allowing them to talk for free. She told her mom about the Hendricks, their generosity and hospitality toward her, the winter wonderland outside, and about Andrew's diagnosis.

"I'm so sorry to hear the awful news," Suzanne said, sounding sad.

"I know, it's going to be a tough road ahead for them," Amy said. "I don't want to keep you. It must be almost lunchtime there. I love you. Check in when you can so I know you guys are okay."

After they exchanged I love yous and promised to stay in touch, Amy changed into her pajamas and slid under the covers, the soft sheets and cozy comforter lulling her into dreamless sleep.

Chapter Nineteen

T HE DRIVE BACK to Manhattan was uneventful, the hum of the engine the only sound cutting through the silence in the car. It was soothing in comparison to the emotional roller coaster from the previous couple of days. The cruel grip of Alzheimer's was imprinted, and with each passing day, the struggle Andrew had been hiding from his kids was now more obvious even though physically he looked unchanged. The confident man she'd met seven months ago was now reserved, at times unsure of his movements, hesitating before speaking in fear of losing his train of thought. When she'd first met him and Diane at the Boathouse restaurant in Central Park, Andrew was the life of the party with his easy charm and eyes that glittered with excitement when delivering the punch line to a story. Looking back, early signs of Alzheimer's were already prevalent… occasionally misplacing his words or repeating the same story a couple of times, but somehow, the change didn't phase him then. The staff at the Boathouse hung on his every word, roaring with laughter at his jokes. Of course, he and Diane had been regulars for years, but it wasn't his loyal patronage that yielded such a cheery response from the staff. It was him. It was all Andrew. Charming, charismatic, and funny Andrew.

Her chest constricted tightly, the air seeping from her lungs without being replenished. The mood in the car felt thick and heavy, like a humid August day in Manhattan, but worse because it was saturated with sadness.

The gift exchange was subdued in spite of Andrew and Diane's efforts to maintain a cheery disposition. Richie had given Amy a beautiful silver bangle encrusted in emeralds that she loved, and she had given him a new leather laptop bag embossed with his initials. Everyone seemed to have received what he or she wanted for Christmas, but even the most festive evening had paled in the face of the changes around them.

"What can I do for you?" asked Amy.

"Thank you, baby. You've done so much already."

"I made dessert. That hardly qualifies as so much."

"You made my dad laugh and you lifted the tension on Christmas Day. That's more than any of us have been able to manage."

"I love you, Richie. And I'm so sorry your family is going through this."

"Thank you."

"Do you want to stay for dinner tonight? We can order in."

"I wish I could. I need to get to my place, pack a few things, and get back to my parents' house. We're meeting with the lawyer first thing tomorrow morning."

"I know. Everything will be fine. Well, it won't…but with time, it will be a new normal."

"How long did your grandmother battle it?"

"Just a few years. But she was much older than your dad, and it was many years ago. There's been a lot of progress with treatment since then."

"But there's no cure, Amy. And the thought of my dad not knowing who we are is devastating."

The tough part was knowing exactly what Richie was referring to because she had lived it herself – except it was easier to accept because her grandmother was old and old people were expected to get sick and pass. With Richie's dad, that was hardly the case.

Richie pulled up in front of her brownstone, the street light already on; its reflection creating a shimmery layer over the semi-melted snow. It took her a couple of steps to gain her footing, the leather soles of the trendy boots the wrong pairing with the sleek surface beneath her feet.

"You all right there, LA girl?" Richie teased.

"Yup," she said over her shoulder, grabbing the stair railing for dear life.

They climbed the few stairs leading to the front door with Amy latching on to the railing for balance and Richie chuckling at her side. It was the first time he'd laughed all day.

Once inside the apartment, she hurried to the thermostat on the wall by her bed and cranked the heat up. Then she kicked off the damp boots, the plush carpet comforting beneath her feet.

"Good night, baby. Sleep well."

"You too and drive safe. Text me when you're back in Greenwich so I know you got there okay."

"I will."

Amy stood on tiptoe to kiss him goodnight, sad to see him go.

Richie's hurried footsteps echoed in the hall outside as he ran towards the staircase. The car was illegally parked curbside with the hazard lights on in hopes of deterring a police officer from slapping him with a parking ticket. With the kind of day Richie was having, she hoped the traffic violation gods spared him tonight.

After unpacking, taking a hot bath, and having a quick dinner of a peanut butter and jelly sandwich, she decided to check her work email. Typically, she wouldn't while she was on vacation, but she figured it had been a slow week with everyone being away for Christmas, so it couldn't be that bad. Her heart sank as soon as her email opened. Sarah's name filled her inbox.

Her eyes roamed over the small screen of her phone, her mouth gaping with shock at the flood of emails. She had only been gone a few days with a day and half being an office holiday. Every subject line stared back at her with the word urgent in all capital letters followed by the topic of the email. From budget questions to production timelines, at least a dozen unopened messages awaited her response. Dread seeped into her bones, and she fought the anxiety prickling her skin. With the sender being none other than Sarah Mitchell, she had reason enough to break out in hives. But she didn't. She refused to fall victim to Sarah's games. She breathed deeply, ignoring the boulder wedged in her stomach, jilting her momentarily.

While Amy was basking in the natural beauty of Greenwich, Sarah had been a busy bee at work. She couldn't imagine what could have come up over the course of three days that warranted such urgency. She forced a deep breath, refusing to react, because that's what Sarah was counting on, and that's what Amy had done in the past. But this was a new, evolved Amy, and she wasn't going to fall into the same trap.

Annoyed, she stomped to the kitchen, poured a generous helping of pinot noir, and returned to the oversized chair, pulling the soft chenille blanket across her lap with her free hand. She forced a deep breath before grabbing the phone and opening each email to read it carefully. A loud groan sliced through the silence in the apartment. Not surprisingly, nothing had changed. The emails all had the same condescending tenor peppered with fake niceness. "Hi Amy, I hope you're enjoying the holiday – I don't mean to bother you, but you seem to have forgotten to provide an update for our launch campaign. The advertising team has been anxiously calling me for answers, but since you didn't connect with me before you left, I couldn't help them." Another email said, "Amy, it's so nice to be on the same team again. I couldn't help but notice the line items on the budget didn't all match the line items on the production timeline. Shouldn't our deliverables be in sync with what we're spending? Please clarify ASAP." And on and on the emails went. To her satisfaction, none of the urgent questions were actually urgent. In fact, they were on the agenda for the upcoming staff meeting, not due for another week. Sighing, Amy tossed her phone on the coffee table in front of her and took a generous gulp of wine.

She shook her head with disbelief at Sarah's reluctance to peacefully coexist in the same workplace. Outside, fluffy snowflakes floated through the air, clinging to the windowsill and treetops. There was nothing more beautiful than snow falling, except maybe a Southern California sunset. In spite of her stomach churning with misery at Sarah's ploy to ruffle her feathers, she smiled, remembering the last few days with Richie and his family. After the gift exchange, she was able to spend more alone time with Richie talking and snuggling by the fireplace while Andrew and Diane retreated to their bedroom for a little nap. Thinking of Richie lessened her anxiety about work and reminded her to keep things in perspective. She fingered the delicate sterling silver bracelet from Richie, her index finger tracing over the infinity sign molded into the charm. Grinning, she reached for her phone to check for a message from him, then returned the phone to the coffee table. She sighed thinking of the long icy drive ahead of him and said a silent prayer for his safety.

The more she analyzed Sarah's ridiculous behavior, the more clearly she saw Sarah for what she was, insecure and petty. In that moment, it dawned on her that Sarah felt threatened because there was something to be threatened by – Amy's experience and competence. Something Sarah seemed to be lacking in spades. And that realization brought a slow satisfied smile across her face. She was a force to be reckoned with, and that was a wonderful thing. Briefly, she allowed herself to revel in her accomplishments and success. Sarah's behavior was still annoying, like a pesky mosquito that refused to buzz away, but in the big picture, a mosquito was hardly a reason to lose her cool. Besides, she had bigger things to worry about—like Andrew and how he had been coping since this morning. Richie – heartbroken over his dad's condition. Abby—who cried off and on the last couple of days, and Diane, the brave matriarch of the family who was most likely freaking out on the inside.

Sighing softly, Amy grabbed the phone and set her alarm before padding to bed, making a mental note to check on Diane and Abby the following day. With the comforter pulled under her chin, she said a prayer for the family before closing her eyes and succumbing to sleep.

THE NEXT MORNING, she woke up extra early to attend yoga before work. Every ounce of serenity was necessary, she reminded herself as she headed down the street, hunched forward against the punishing wind whipping at her.

The office was fairly quiet. The days between Christmas and New Year's were typically unproductive, with many employees stretching vacation days until after the New Year. Christmas decorations still hung from doorways, and someone had plugged in the Christmas tree lights so they twinkled festively on this frigid December morning.

A couple of voices carried across the hallway as she meandered to her office, the rubber soles of her shoes soundless on the hard wood floor. Just as she was rounding the corner to the kitchen, she heard Sarah's hushed words, and Amy's steps faltered.

"I really like her, so it's hard for me to say this, but I don't think she's qualified to make decisions that impact the entire Valentine's Day campaign."

"Oh, really. That's surprising to hear. Amy has been an invaluable member of the team. I think her ideas are well received, and she's certainly very well liked around here," said Josh, the Creative Director.

"Oh, totally. She's lovely. I'm not bad-mouthing her at all. I really like her as a person and she's well liked by everyone. I was only commenting on her experience level and recommending that a more senior member of the team have final approval."

"Someone more senior does have final approval, and Jane is a huge fan of Amy's, as am I," Josh retorted.

"Look, I didn't mean to offend you. I was only thinking of our marketing campaign."

Sensing the conversation was ending, Amy scurried to her office before she was discovered eavesdropping. It was only after she was settled at her desk that she was able to breathe more easily. Her body pulsed with tension at Sarah's audacity, fully aware that Jane was on vacation until after the New Year, as was Joan, leaving Sarah to her own venomous devices. Josh's defense of her was a small victory, but she couldn't help wondering whom else Sarah had approached with her concerns. Refusing to surrender to defeat, Amy sat up straight and began sorting her inbox, her heart racing the entire time. Perhaps it was time to address things with Sarah once and for all. Let the chips fall where they may.

Fed up with Sarah's nonsense, she marched down to Sarah's office, determined to address the devious behavior. The hallway was empty, the glass panels on each side of the wooden doors were dark, confirming Amy's suspicion that no one but Sarah was looking for urgent answers about the Valentine's Day campaign. That was all part of a ruse, and she intended to find out why.

Outside Sarah's office, she stopped short at the sound of Sarah talking to someone on the phone. "I just don't understand why everyone likes her. She's meh at best." Followed by silence and then, "I just want her gone, and sooner or later, she'll screw up. No one is perfect." Amy's blood ran cold, and she shuddered at Sarah's heartless words.

Her phone vibrated in her hand, Richie's handsome face popping up on the screen. She swallowed the lump in her throat and walked quickly away before answering the phone, reminding herself to be his cheerleader, not the person he needed to cheer. He had enough on his plate.

"Hi, how are you?" she chirped.

"Not great. It's been a hellish morning. We transferred the company over. I've dreamed of this moment since grad school, and now that I have it, I would do anything to have things go back to the way they were."

"I'm sorry, baby. This is just awful. How's your dad holding up?"

"He's business as usual for the most part, cracking jokes, but he's a little deflated. As soon as he signed the company over, his demeanor changed. The company has been a proud accomplishment for him and now he's handing it over before he was ready. I feel so sad for him."

"I know it's hard, and you're doing all the right things. Just continue to be there for him. This is all new to him too, and it's hard for him to adjust to needing someone when he's been independent his entire life. How long will you stay in Greenwich?"

"I'm not sure yet. I think for a little while. I'm going to work from here for a few days alongside my dad. I think we need to keep him busy and maintain a normal routine. Abby went back to the city last night and she'll work out of the office there."

"Oh – yes, of course. Your dad needs you."

"Thanks for understanding, Amy. I know this gets in the way of us, and I will figure out a way to make it all work. Just give me some time."

"Don't worry about me or us. We'll be fine. I love you."

"Thanks, baby. I'm trying. How are things at work?"

"Brutal because Sarah is on a rampage of sorts. Cruella Deville, the puppy tormentor, is at it again," she admitted and regretted the decision immediately. It was so easy to talk to Richie, she couldn't hide things from him if she tried—and she did try.

"Now what?"

Sighing, she said, "Sarah has been bad mouthing me to anyone who will listen."

"Don't let her get to you, and you should find a way to talk to her in person. And keep track of all communication with her in writing. And if talking to her doesn't work, go to Joan and Jane."

"Yes, Mr. Hendricks."

A few minutes later, she was perched outside Sarah's office, adrenaline pumping through her veins, twisting her insides with nervous tension. Her hands trembled slightly, reminding her of previous altercations with this relentless woman who was so set on making her work life miserable. Groaning, she willed herself to remain rooted, knowing if she didn't confront Sarah, the alternative was much worse, and she couldn't live with that. She had walked away once. It hadn't served her then and it wouldn't serve her now.

She took a deep breath and knocked softly on the door, prayed for the best, and waltzed in, but remained close to the door. Sarah's mouth opened as if to say something but quickly shut, a sneer plastered on her face.

"Sarah, I was hoping you and I could talk."

"Ah, sure. What's this about?" Sarah spoke loudly, too loudly given the short distance between them.

"Well, for starters, I wanted to address your urgent emails and answer any questions you may have for me."

"I think I was clear with what I needed answers on."

"I'm a little confused, because during our last staff meeting, we addressed all the questions you emailed me about. Do you want me to resend you the meeting minutes?"

"No, Amy. I don't need the meeting minutes again. It's your job to update the team on the project, and we shouldn't have to wait for meetings and minutes to have the latest information."

The two women stared at each other. Sarah was rigid in her chair, menacing, her blue eyes icy cold, lacking any glimmer of emotion. In that moment, Amy knew without doubt Sarah would never be her advocate. But it was worse than that. Sarah wanted her gone. The motive was unclear and frankly, it didn't matter.

Sarah's freshly manicured nails tapped impatiently on the desk, the same condescending look fixed on her otherwise flawless features. Amy nodded slowly as if finally understanding the terms of the game, stepped deeper into the office, and slid into the chair across from Sarah.

"Sarah, our staff meeting was right before the holidays—three days ago. Nothing has changed since then."

"This is exactly the type of behavior that differentiates a leader from everyone else. Waiting for meetings to provide an update is an excuse for not doing your due diligence and following up."

Despite her best efforts, there was a tremor in her voice confirming her rage. "With all due respect, Sarah, your comment is unfounded. A detailed update was provided to the team before the holiday break, and since then, literally nothing has happened. Christmas Day is a national holiday. Offices are closed. No one is working."

"I'm just trying to help you."

"How exactly are you helping me?"

"By trying to teach you how to be a leader."

Sitting up straighter, Amy laughed out loud. "And is that why you talk about me behind my back to anyone and everyone lending an ear? Is that also part of the helping me efforts?"

"What are you talking about?"

"Sarah, I heard you. I know what you're up to, and honestly, it's a shame. What are you gaining by doing that?"

"Gaining? Don't flatter yourself by thinking I would waste my time on you."

"I heard you and I am flattered. Your behavior is disgusting and deplorable. Instead of coming here for a fresh start, you came here with the same baggage you lugged around at Glitz."

"You're the one being ridiculous. I've been nothing but complimentary of you, even when it was undeserved."

"Come on, Sarah. We both know you've never been complimentary of me."

"I have nothing against you. I think you misunderstood what you heard and now you're making a mountain out of a molehill."

"Right. Okay. We're clearly not going to see eye to eye on this. I'll let you get back to work."

Amy stood gracefully, a wan smile masking her feelings for the conniving fraud glaring at her. Sarah looked uneasy with their interaction, and that gave Amy a measure of satisfaction. The old Amy would never have confronted Sarah. The old Amy would have slunk away to her desk, wounded and defeated with the afternoon spent in the bathroom crying in private. The old Amy threw in the towel and found another job. But not the new and evolved Amy. This Amy didn't turn the other cheek. She was more confident in her abilities and she certainly had no intentions of finding another job. This Amy was ready to fight for the job she worked so hard to achieve. Taking a page out of Richie's book of advice, she drafted a letter to Jane and outlined the entire interaction, ending the letter by asking for her guidance. It was a new day!

Chapter Twenty

T HE DAYS LEADING up to New Year's Eve dragged with more of the same childish antics from Sarah without change or resolution. With each day, Sarah got a little braver, showing her true unprofessional colors by either rolling her eyes when Amy happened to walk by, ignoring her completely, or giving her the once-over with complete disdain. At one point, Sarah's behavior was so bizarre that Amy laughed out loud. If Sarah was trying to bait her for a reaction, she wasn't succeeding.

Sarah was entitled and spoiled, and her family's elite social standing opened many doors for her. Sadly, Sarah didn't appreciate any of it, and not once had she applied herself in the role handed to her because she never had to work for anything – until now. Jane was a demanding boss who led by example and had very high expectations of her team. At this rate, Amy didn't need to worry about surviving Sarah because Sarah might not survive Jane. And that was just fine. The next few months were gearing up to be interesting on every front and especially because the magazine was launching their biggest marketing campaign in years. From the creative team to the lowliest assistant, it was all-hands on deck with Amy leading the project. Everything was at stake. Sarah's antics were an unwelcome distraction.

With Richie occupied with his family and Megan still on vacation, Amy felt alone and vulnerable. Facing Sarah's daily passive aggressive behavior without a support system to rally her was tough and, at times, took its toll on her spirits. There had to be some karmic reward for choosing the high road when the low road presented immediate gratification, she mused.

The glass panels rattled violently against the howling wind wreaking havoc on the helpless tree limbs. Since arriving in Manhattan, Amy had developed a habit of checking the daily news and weather in Los Angeles, and today, it was eighty degrees and sunny—much more appealing than the ice age outside. She shimmied under the thick blanket on the oversized chair, shivering along with the trees, missing the warm LA sun. She reached for the mug of hot chocolate on the side table, the sweet scent of cocoa and melted marshmallow comforting and a soothing remedy to the bruising week at work. The heat from the ceramic mug warmed her palms, momentarily easing the painful day from her memories. This moment was the perfect beginning to a quiet and peaceful evening. New Year's Eve was the following day, and she looked forward to spending the evening with Richie and his family. Richie's presence at home was reassuring to both his parents as they adjusted to their new normal. And she understood that, mostly.

The phone vibrated loudly with a text message, and her heart practically leaped from her chest with hopes of hearing from Richie. She carefully set the mug down and retrieved the phone from the coffee table to see a text from Megan.

"Hi Amy. Miss you. Aspen is amazing. Call me when you have a sec. I need to talk to you."

Dubious, she touched the call button on the screen and waited for Megan to pick up.

"Wow, that was fast." Megan laughed.

"Hi. Of course I was going to call as soon as I saw that cryptic message. What's up?"

"Aspen is amazing. We should plan a girls' trip here or you and Richie should come here."

"I'm not much of a skier but I do want to see it. But that can't be the reason you wanted me to call."

"It's not, but first I want a quick recap of Christmas with your perfect boyfriend."

Amy giggled. "Well … you know … he is perfect. He's so easy to be around and he's so attentive and loving and hot …"

"Am I sensing a but?"

Within minutes Megan was caught up with Andrew's diagnosis,

which was met with a gasp of shock.

"I'm taking the train to Greenwich tomorrow morning to spend New Year's with Richie and his family. We're having dinner at a nearby restaurant they love."

"That will be good. Listen, I hate adding more to your full plate, but I need to tell you something. Sarah has been telling a few people that you're very difficult to work with and that you're combative."

Amy gasped, her hand fisting in her lap. "Combative?"

"Amy, have you been fighting with her?"

"No, and how could you ask me that?"

"I'm sorry. I'm not doubting you. I guess knowing that you're not her biggest fan and knowing that she can be a tough personality, I thought things came to head this week."

"I can't believe you wouldn't automatically be on my side. You know me. I've never been combative with anyone in my life, and for the record, she's been undermining me every chance she gets. Just yesterday she scheduled a meeting with me about timelines. Timelines?" Amy shrieked into the phone, the week-long tension with Sarah pushing her over the edge.

"Calm down. I didn't mean to upset you. I just wanted you to know so you're careful with your interactions with her."

Amy squeezed her eyes shut long enough to keep the tears from trickling down her cheeks and betraying her. "Thank you. I appreciate the warning, and I'm sorry for flying off the handle. She's a nightmare. I don't understand why once again I'm the target of her nastiness. And what makes it worse, I'm now her equal, and she's still treating me like I'm scum of the earth."

Megan sighed softly on the other end. "Don't give it any more thought. Jane will be back in the office in a few days, and hopefully this will all be resolved."

"Yeah. True," Amy choked out, defeat seeping in.

"Have a great time with Richie. Wish him a Happy New Year from me and tell him I'm sorry about his dad."

"I will. And you do the same with your family. Love you."

"Love you too. Keep your chin up."

The pipes whistled loudly as the heat kicked into gear, startling her. It was part of the old building's allure, except tonight, the whistling was more torturous than charming. She stretched her legs in front of her, a million tiny little pins prickled her right calf, the one that was folded neatly beneath her, and she winced from the discomfort, willing her toes to wiggle around and speed up the flow of blood through her limbs. The phone was still in her hand. The conversation with Megan was unsettling, bringing back many emotions, mostly bad ones. Sarah was a nightmare to work with.

Catfights in the office were career suicide, and now thanks to Sarah's pettiness, she was in the midst of one. The toxic feelings were slowly poisoning her otherwise sunny disposition. This wasn't fair, and it wasn't deserved. Not that anyone deserved Sarah's venomous treatment. But why her? If what she'd read about the law of attraction was true, then she was drawing this behavior to her, subconsciously. Was it because she was too nice or was it because she needed to behave in a different way where Sarah was concerned? She groaned at the thought of facing Sarah after the New Year, just three days away. She slunk deeper in the chair, wishing she could hide in her apartment forever. It didn't help that Megan wasn't outwardly blaming Sarah. Worse, Megan seemed unsure of what to believe, and that hurt, deeply. Amy had been fighting feelings of defeat for weeks and now, she felt a little beaten. With her legs extended in front of her, she rested her head back, welcoming the soft cushion cradling her neck. She sighed. Sarah was like an oil spill in the ocean. No matter how minimal the damage seemed on the surface, the oil contaminated everything in sight.

The next evening, back in Richie's loving embrace, the two drove to Greenwich Village from his parents' house for an early New Year's Eve dinner. This was the first time Andrew had ventured out since Christmas, and the family was eager for a glimmer of normalcy—for his sake and theirs. The roads were a slippery mess with the overnight rain turning the snow into slushy puddles at every intersection, but Amy didn't mind one bit. There was no other place she would rather be than in this moment with Richie's loving family. Besides, the conversation with her mom the evening before had boosted her spirits and reminded her to brush off the nonsense with Sarah.

The village was quiet this evening, with hardly anyone in sight. Richie was able to ease the car into a parking spot right outside the cozy Italian eatery where they were meeting his parents and Abby for dinner. The evening was the perfect distraction even though, selfishly, she wished for a quiet night alone with Richie and not with the entire family. Richie had been at his parents' side almost the entire time, working from his dad's office in Greenwich and commuting to the city for meetings. She hadn't seen him since he drove her home the day after Christmas, with barely any communication between them. For the most part, she understood the gravity of Andrew's situation and loved Richie's loyalty and dedication to his parents. But there was a small part of her that resented his parents for needing him so much.

"Abby mentioned that she was bringing a friend to dinner tonight," Richie said as he sat in the car waiting for Amy to finish freshening up her lipstick.

"That's great," she said, feeling happy for Abby. "I'm ready." She slipped her arms into her coat while waiting for Richie to come around to open her car door. It was important to him that she accepts his chivalrous gestures, and she gladly obliged, enjoying being treated like a lady.

Richie extended his hand to help her out. Feeling spontaneous, Amy leapt into his arms, causing him to stumble backwards from surprise at her boisterous out of character performance. He chuckled, recovering quickly, and turned the tables on her by covering her mouth in a knee-buckling kiss.

"Mr. Hendricks ... that was one hell of a kiss." Amy remained in his embrace, standing on tippy toes so their lips were inches apart. God, how she'd missed him.

"There will be more of that later ... come on, let's get inside." He gave her bottom a playful smack, pulling her along with him through the heavy glass panel doors trimmed with oak wood, a striped white and beige awning over the door accentuating the already charming exterior.

Briefly, everything felt like old times.

The interior décor was breathtaking with polished oak floors from wall to wall, high ceilings and intricate woodwork on the square columns separating the bar area from the formal seating area. The aroma of sautéed garlic wafted through the air, and Amy's stomach responded by growling loudly.

Spotting his parents and Abby at the back of the restaurant, Richie waved and began walking toward them with Amy's hand firmly clasped in his.

"Hi Mom, Dad, Abby." Richie hugged and kissed everyone, and Amy followed suit before they took their seats. A waiter appeared quickly to fill water glasses and take their drink orders.

"How was everyone's day?" Diane asked, sounding chipper.

In Amy's brief conversations with Richie, he'd mentioned that his mom was leaning on him quite a bit for every doctor appointment and decision involving his dad, even though his dad was still capable of making all his decisions on his own. Naturally, Richie was concerned about his mom's fragile state. Tonight, a glimmer of the bubbly, confident matriarch of the family chatted easily. The relaxed tenor in Diane's voice warmed Amy's heart.

"Great," said Richie. "We just hung at the house all day."

"I had an awesome day," said Abby. "I had a facial and massage and then did a little shopping."

Amy wondered whether Abby had changed her mind about inviting a friend to dinner.

"We indulged in a couple's massage and some shopping," Andrew said, articulating each word as if worried the very language he'd known his entire life would somehow abandon him. But his spirits were high as he scanned the restaurant for their waiter, who came rushing to the table and jotted down their order of appetizers and wine.

"Sounds like everyone had a great day," Richie said, eyeing Abby curiously.

The waiter returned with two bottles of cabernet, and Andrew happily carried out the ritual of swirling, smelling, and tasting before giving it his glowing approval.

Abby stood abruptly, her cheeks flushed, as she waved to someone. A tall, handsome man with red wavy hair approached their table, all smiles with twinkling blue eyes fixated on Abby.

"James, you made it. Mom, Dad, this is James Whitfield. James, this is my dad, Andrew, and my mom, Diane, and this is my older brother, Richie, and his girlfriend, Amy." The waiter hurried over with an extra chair for James, squeezing it between Abby and Amy's chairs.

"It's very nice to meet you, James," said Diane. "We're always delighted to meet Abby's friends," she added, stressing the word "friends."

"Thank you for having me. I'm delighted to meet Abby's family."

James was good-looking, polite, and confident. Amy liked him already.

"James and I met at a charity event last year," said Abby, "and then we kept bumping into each other at work functions and always ended up talking most of the evening. So we decided to meet for coffee one day." She spoke evenly, only her smile giving away how much she liked him.

"And what is it that you do, James?" Andrew leaned in.

"I'm a lawyer," he said. "I handle acquisitions and mergers."

With that, Andrew smiled affectionately while Diane bombarded the poor guy with questions about his family, his job, and everything in between. Amy was surprised Richie's parents didn't ask James for his W2 and a list of references. To James's credit, he didn't seem bothered in the slightest.

"I'm very surprised our paths haven't crossed until now. Abby has done a great job hiding you," Richie said, teasing.

Course after succulent course was brought to the table with wine pairings that knocked Amy's boots off. From the roasted asparagus and poached egg drizzled with bacon-black truffle dressing to the pan-roasted salmon, Amy barely came up for air between bites, grateful she'd worn a dress with a forgiving waist.

Over cappuccino and the restaurant's signature dessert, Richie and James made plans for a double date in the city for the following week when everyone was back to their normal routines. Abby and Amy exchanged smiles, both delighted at the opportunity to hang out. Amy was especially grateful to have Richie back in the city. Andrew paid the bill and led the way outside the restaurant, seeming relaxed and happy, the way Amy remembered him at the Boathouse months ago. Diane seemed rather mellow herself and shocked everyone by hugging James goodbye. Maybe the tide was turning for smoother sailing, or perhaps the several glasses of wine were worth their weight in gold.

"We'll be home in a little while," Richie said. "We're joining Abby and James for a drink. Happy New Year." He hugged his parents, thanking his dad for dinner and his mom for a perfect New Year's. Amy did the same.

"So how long have the two of you been seeing each other?" Richie pressed, once they were inside a pub down the street and comfortably seated in a back booth with cocktails for everyone.

"Three months," Abby and James said simultaneously, gazing into each other's eyes, the way couples do during the early stages of falling in love. Amy smiled, squeezing Richie's hand, and he returned the squeeze.

"But why keep it a secret?" Amy asked, her eyes darting between the lovebirds, noting the way James caressed Abby's hand resting on the table.

"I wanted to be sure we liked each other first," said Abby. "There's no point going through Mom and Dad's brutal interrogation for someone I barely knew and wasn't sure I wanted to stick around."

Abby was a poised and well-spoken woman, and Amy admired her more with each passing day. Some of her most noticeable attributes were the same ones that Amy had seen in Sarah—affluent background, elegance, and the ability to navigate any conversation with ease and confidence. The difference between Abby and Sarah though, was that Abby didn't rely on her looks and bank account to secure her future. She was a hard worker who had carved her own career path by putting in the time and effort. And even though Amy had never worked with her, she doubted that the sweet and compassionate woman sitting across from her was capable of attacking anyone for pleasure. Hopefully those dark days were over for Sarah as well.

"I don't blame you for keeping James to yourself at the beginning. And thanks for bringing him to dinner tonight." Amy leaned into Richie, enjoying their closeness. She wiggled her shoulders, loosening the tight muscles. Richie must have sensed what she was trying to do, as he placed his large hand on her shoulder and kneaded the sore spots.

At the stroke of midnight, a few patrons sitting at the bar howled and clinked beer glasses. Richie pulled her against him for a tender kiss. And then they hugged Abby and James, well wishes exchanged all around.

A couple more drinks later, exhaustion was settling in, pulling her body into the chair. No one had ever accused her of being a night owl. Her watch said 1:30 a.m.

"Maybe we should have gone to couple's massage this morning," Richie whispered in her ear.

"Nah … I like our tradition much better, especially the post-breakfast snuggling."

"I'm relieved to hear that. You ready to head home?"

"I'm ready when you are," Amy said, pressing her lips to his for a quick kiss.

"All right, you two," Richie said to Abby and James, "we're headed home. Abby, are you okay to drive home or do you want to come with us? He stood and helped Amy into her coat before he slipped into his.

"Hmmm … I guess it's getting late," said Abby. "As much as I would love to stay out, I should get home too. I'm headed back to the city tomorrow afternoon. My car is around the corner."

She stood, retrieving her own coat, and James held it as she slid her arms through the sleeves. The foursome walked outside into the freezing air that whipped at them mercilessly, shivering uncontrollably from the sudden drop in temperature.

Amy's skin prickled at the glacial assault on her face, remembering that she'd forgotten her scarf in Richie's car. They were all parked on the same block outside the Italian bistro and began running like mad toward their cars, the anticipation of heat a wonderful motivator.

Waving goodbye, Amy slipped into the passenger seat and waited for Richie to come around the car to the driver's side.

"And this is when I wish we lived in LA," she said as soon as Richie was settled into his seat, her teeth chattering violently.

"I know, baby. I wish the same thing, and I'm from Connecticut."

The car engine roared, slowly defrosting in the frigid night air. The heater blew hot air over Amy's chilled, stiff body, but she didn't feel any relief just yet, finally understanding the full meaning of chilled to the bone.

Too cold and tired to speak, she closed her eyes and leaned into the heated seat, savoring the comfortable quietness between her and the handsome man next to her. She loved that they could sit in silence, both lost in their own thoughts, neither anxious about filling the air with meaningless conversation just for the sake of talking.

When she eventually felt the car slow down, Amy fluttered her eyes open, the headlights on the side mirror catching her attention. She saw a third set of headlights and wondered if James was spending the night. Within seconds, the headlights backed away, and turned and drove off into the night. James must have driven behind Abby to make sure she got home safely. As far as Amy was concerned, James was a keeper and when the right moment presented itself, she decided to tell Abby just that.

Inside the house, Richie and Amy said goodnight to Abby, wanting a little alone time to say their own private words.

"Stay with me tonight," he insisted between kisses.

"We can't. I don't want to upset your parents."

"They don't care as much – they have bigger things to worry about. And with me being here so much, they know we haven't seen each other in over a week. Come on, I miss you."

"Hmmm ... I miss you too, more than you know. But staying with you will upset your mom. My overnight bag was placed on the bed in the spare bedroom, not your bedroom. That little gesture wasn't by accident. So the answer is still 'no way,'" she murmured, standing on tippy toes to kiss his mouth. She wished him goodnight and moseyed into the guest bedroom, shutting the door behind her before her resolve weakened. Besides, she needed sleep. The lack of sunlight was wreaking havoc on her sleep and her mood. Her body felt lethargic and groggy. Maybe she was coming down with something, and if that was the case, she needed a good night's sleep.

In the ensuite bathroom, Amy washed her face and brushed her teeth, examining her windswept skin closely. Her cheeks were still blotchy from the blast of icy air. So this was winter in the northeast. Shrugging her shoulders in acceptance, she walked back into the bedroom, peeled off her dress, tights, and boots, and put on warm pink flannel pajamas and matching socks. She climbed into bed, pulling the duvet up all the way around her shoulders, burrowing deeper into the plush sheets.

At some point soon, Amy would need to address Richie returning to the city and picking up where they left off. But she knew she needed to tackle the sensitive subject delicately. On the one hand, his presence at home was priceless in terms of the comfort it gave his parents, but on the other, his dad had seemed fine at dinner. Maybe she could offer to come up every weekend.

She tossed and turned in bed, her mind refusing to quiet down despite her body's need for sleep. Amy's thoughts spiraled in a million directions as she struggled to regain peace of mind. The thought of Richie relocating to Connecticut permanently was devastating and would certainly put a wrench in their relationship.

Fully worked up and anxious beyond logic over something that hadn't manifested yet, Amy got out of bed and opened the curtains, the night sky inky and speckled with stars. Think about the big picture, Amy. Have faith that everything will work itself out.

Chapter Twenty-One

T HE OFFICE KITCHEN looked stark, the bright florescent lights overshadowed by the sunbeams streaming through the oversized windows. Frost clung to the exterior glass panels, a keen reminder of the frigid temperatures outside. Amy stood at the coffee maker to use the hot water dispenser for her tea. She hummed to herself, joy bubbling inside her, the last few days with Richie renewing her spirits and reconnecting them.

"I've been looking all over for you," Megan said, wrapping her arms around Amy.

"Welcome back, snow bunny. God, I've missed you."

"Me too. How was New Year's?"

"Amazing, and guess what?"

Megan reached around her for a mug from the cupboard above the coffee maker and queued up for a fill. "What?"

"Richie is coming back to the city today." Amy sipped slowly, eyes twinkling with excitement.

"Well, that's exciting and worth celebrating." Megan fixed her coffee with a generous amount of half and half and sipped carefully, sighing with pleasure.

The two walked to Amy's office. "Do you have a few minutes to catch up?" Amy asked.

"Yeah. Jane is in a meeting upstairs and everyone is taking their time settling back in." Megan sat in the chair across from Amy's desk and Amy joined her on the chair next to it.

"I'm sorry about the other day."

"No, I'm sorry. I shouldn't have doubted you. I've only been back at my desk for an hour and I have a pretty good idea of Sarah's antics."

"What do you mean?"

"I got here early to catch up on email, thinking no one would be here. But Sarah was already in. She was on a call to someone, talking about you. She was telling them that your skill level is well beneath where it should be for middle management and that your decisions are hasty without a well thought out strategy. When she saw me walk by on my way to the kitchen, she looked flustered and lowered her voice. She shut her door after that so I couldn't hear anything else."

"Oh wow. So you heard her mention me by name?

"Yup, several times, and she even referenced Glitz as your old stomping grounds where similar mistakes were made."

"She's really out to get me."

"Don't let her get to you, Amy. Other people are on to her. How's Richie's dad doing?"

"We had a nice New Year's Eve dinner, and he seemed in great spirits. I'm heartbroken for what's to come for him but for now, everything is pretty much the same. For the record, I hate myself for feeling resentful of how Andrew's disease has taken a huge toll on Richie and me. I mean we barely talk or text. He's always busy with his parents."

"I know it's rough, especially when everything else is stressful, but don't be like that. Be patient. You love him, and it's his world that's blowing up. This can't be easy on him either." Megan leaned in, elbows on knees and her hands tightly clasped with Amy's.

"I know, Megs. I said I hate myself for feeling that way and I do. I just miss him, you know."

"I understand, babe. Listen, let's have lunch and finish catching up."

The two friends hugged quickly before Megan scurried to her new desk in the photo department on the other side of the floor. As miserable as Amy was with Sarah's relentless attempts at creating pitfalls the size of craters, she was genuinely happy her friend had landed her dream job.

I'm in the city, baby, and I can't wait to see you.
Come to my place tonight? xx Richie

Rainbows might as well have beamed from the phone at the end of

Richie's text, and she fumbled to respond, giddy and a little embarrassed that a simple text from Richie could have such an impact on her mood. Richie was back in the city and all was good in her world.

That was until a whiff of orange blossoms exquisitely blended with just the right hint of woodsy trail hung in the air—Sarah's signature perfume. Damn it! Amy had just picked up her phone to text Megan as Sarah barged in, a fake exaggerated smirk plastered on her glossy lips.

"Amy, I'm sorry to interrupt seeing that you're so busy ... with personal texts ... but I need you to forward me the latest creative files for the print ads so I'm in the loop. Or are you purposely trying to keep me out?" Sarah leaned against the doorway, her face passive, giving away nothing.

"I don't have the latest files. The creative team has until end of the week to finalize designs. It's on the timeline," Amy said, still smiling from reading Richie's message. Intentionally, she turned to face the computer. Sarah's request wasn't out of line in the least. After all, she was a senior director in the department, and she had every right to review anything she wanted. This wasn't about the request or the work. This was much more personal. This was in part retaliation against Sarah, the half dozen times she'd been caught talking about her unabashedly. It was about the ongoing passive aggressive nature of their interactions that drained her.

"Someone woke up on the wrong side of the bed this morning?" Sarah taunted, still perched in the doorway, looking flawless as usual with perfectly coifed hair and an outfit that would set the average person back a month's salary, at least.

"Nope, couldn't be happier, actually. Was there anything else you wanted to ask, or are we done here?"

Sarah raised her hands up in submission and walked away, shaking her head, her long silky blond tresses bouncing between her shoulder blades. Amy rolled her eyes and returned her attention to work. It was just a few hours until she was home, with Richie.

MORNING CAME TOO soon, and Amy wished for a few hours more of sleep. The honking of cars blended with the rhythmic thumping wheels making their way through the congested Manhattan streets. Even at this early hour, the city was vibrating with activity and in constant motion. It was the very essence of organized chaos that made the city so special and unique.

"Good morning, beautiful." Richie turned on his side to face Amy. Strands of disheveled, dark blond hair covered his forehead, giving that him that effortlessly sexy appeal she loved so much.

"Good morning," she murmured, raising an arm to shield her eyes from the bright sun flooding the room. "Did you sleep well?"

"Mmmm." He nodded, hazel eyes locked with hers. "I slept better than I have in weeks. I'm glad you came over. I wish we could stop time or do anything but deal with reality."

"Why don't we then? Play hooky from work. You need a little time to yourself to recharge. We could grab a late lunch ..."

"Baby, I wish. I'll make this up to you very soon. I promise," Richie said, sounding tired in spite of his admission of a restful sleep. Reluctantly, he pushed the covers back and dragged himself out of bed.

"I'm sorry, I didn't mean to pile on. I thought a day off would energize you. You've been working around the clock, and when you're not working, you're at your dad's side. You need a break. It's well-deserved and—"

"I know and I will ... but not today. The timing is a little rough. I've been joining all my dad's meetings so when the time comes, the transition is smooth, and his clients are comfortable." Richie rubbed his hands over his face and disappeared into the bathroom, the conversation over.

A few minutes later, the shower came on followed by the bathroom vent, the low hum silencing the words on her lips. This was hardly the morning she expected. Of course, he apologized profusely before they went their separate ways for work, but the sting hurt just the same.

A little over an hour later, she sat at her desk, the frown lines bunching her brows together and pursing her lips. The morning was a disaster, and nothing like she imagined their first morning together would be like.

His family and business consumed his every waking moment, leaving him without peace of mind or free time to think about anything else. It was so unfair.

"Good morning, sunshine." Megan's singsong voice was a welcome interruption to Amy's rollercoaster of emotions.

Looking up from her desk, Amy smiled weakly at her friend. "Hey, Megs, how are you?"

Megan settled in the chair across from Amy's desk, coffee mug in hand. "What happened?"

Amy recapped the morning in a hushed voice. Nothing made more entertaining conversation than juicy gossip, and she had no intention of being the subject matter at the water cooler.

"It sounds like stress is taking its toll on him," Megan offered. "I know the last couple of weeks have been hard on you too, but try and see things from his perspective. He probably feels trapped but can't say it."

"I know, I was trying to be there for him, but I feel helpless."

In hindsight, she should have kept her mouth shut and just listened. Megan was right, Richie was between a rock and a hard place but couldn't verbalize it or do anything about it. Life was so unfair sometimes. She sent him an apology text and offered to bring dinner to his place and then set her phone back on the desk and turned her attention to the piles of spreadsheets she had to go through.

About a month after Richie returned to the city, life was somewhat normal. Though Richie was mostly distracted, and their time together was regularly interrupted by either calls from the office or his parents. He spent every weekend in Greenwich. Sometimes she was invited along and other times, she wasn't. Truthfully, she looked forward to being in her own apartment more often than not, and that intensified her longing for Richie. Even when they were physically together, it felt like oceans separated them.

Early February brought one of the roughest snowstorms the city had experienced in a couple of years with the accumulation rising faster than plows could manage. The city came to a complete standstill, bringing with it a soothing quietness. From lampposts to cars, a glimmering white carpet covered everything in sight. Newscasters urged city residents to stay indoors and off the roads. It was officially a snow day – no better day to spend with Richie without the constant interruptions from work. Giddy with excitement, she pranced to the side table by her bed and dialed him.

"Good morning, baby."

"Hey Amy. I can't really talk right now," he croaked.

Taken aback by the cool reception, she cleared her throat to compose herself. "Oh, I … I was just thinking with the city being shut down and nowhere to go … we could spend the day together. I miss you, Richie."

"Amy … I can't … I'm driving … I'm almost in Connecticut. My dad had a stroke a couple of hours ago. I'm on my way to the hospital." His voice sounded flat, lifeless.

"Richie, I'm so sorry. I had no idea. What can I do?"

"Nothing. Enjoy the snow day. It's your first one. Do something fun with Megan. Have a hot chocolate for me." His voice broke, and Amy's heart broke with it. "I have to run. I'm almost home. We'll talk soon, okay?"

"Richie, I love you. Please tell me what I can do for you."

"Maybe you can come up tomorrow or the day after."

"Yes, done. I'll do that."

After they said their goodbyes, Amy sunk into the oversized chair, hot tears streaming from her eyes, her heart breaking for Richie. She felt bad. Helpless. And selfish for wishing this was happening to someone else's boyfriend's family and not hers.

Chapter Twenty-Two

GOOSEBUMPS PRICKLED HER skin underneath the heavy wool sweater and knee length black coat, her steps muffled by the dozens of people coming and going through the reception area of the intensive care unit. Interesting artwork decorated every empty wall space, the only color in an otherwise very sterile environment. In a far corner of the square-shaped room sat a family huddled around one another, their hushed voices barely audible over the TV droning in the background. An older man looked up long enough to smile sweetly at her before returning his attention to the group around him. A woman's cry sounded in the distance. Shivers ran down Amy's spine. She hated hospitals. Ever since her grandmother had been admitted to one, she hated everything about them. The hospital was where she bid her beloved grandmother farewell for the last time. But today wasn't about her. This day was about Richie and his family and being here to offer support. Ignoring the painful memories that flooded her, she dragged her booted feet to the desk and waited for the red-headed receptionist to finish a phone call. The woman was young, bubbly, and beautiful. The caller seemed to be asking about a patient that had been transferred to hospice.

"Hi. How can I help you?"

"I'm here to visit Andrew Hendricks."

"Are you family?"

"No, I'm – a friend of the family. I can just wait with them … in the lobby area. I don't need to be in the room." Amy hesitated.

"Go the sixth floor, and reception will help you upstairs."

She thanked the woman and hurried to the bank of elevators down the hall, her heart thumping wildly in her chest the entire time.

The sixth floor was just as sterile as the main floor with even less warmth, completely stark of the landscape paintings that adorned the downstairs walls. Bright red chairs were the only splash of color in the otherwise gray waiting room. The minimal artwork on the walls was subdued and abstract, offering no comfort for families in anguish awaiting updates about loved ones. The TV was tuned to a news channel, yet another form of discomfort as the anchor reported about one tragedy after another. What happened to the days of soothing music or funny sitcoms to take the edge off? The news hardly provided either. In the background, the weatherman affirmed the recent snowstorm, reciting statistics from years past and a lengthy summary about streets still to be plowed. Great!

Her coat felt suffocating, or maybe it was the anticipation of feeling helpless at seeing Richie in so much pain and not being able to take it away. At reception, she was directed to the last room down the hall to the right. Nodding her thanks, she exhaled shakily, her chest caving in with nerves, her stomach twisting uncomfortably. Muffled crying and sniffling caught her attention before she spotted Abby, balled up in a chair, knees hugged against her chest with her head bowed. Amy hurried to her before the image fully processed in her mind.

"Abby, how are you holding up? Any changes?"

The two women embraced, and Abby wiped her eyes with the back of her hand, the rims red and swollen. It took a moment for the hiccups to subside enough for her to speak.

"Hi, Amy. I'm so glad you're here," she said. "There's been no change since yesterday, but the stroke took a bad toll on him. He's half-paralyzed. He can barely talk. He can't move. He can't do anything but lie there. Richie is with him now." Abby buried her face in her hands and sobbed. "Why is this happening to my family?" she cried.

"I'm so sorry, Abby. How's Richie holding up? How's your mom?"

"I don't know. Richie's overwhelmed, I think, but he's putting on a strong front. And my mom looks like a shell of herself. She barely speaks."

Amy wrapped an arm around Abby's shoulder and sat with her in silence.

"Hey, what time did you get here?" Richie stood in front of her. He kissed her cheek in greeting, his lips a thin white line, his face gaunt and gray.

She stood to greet him, wrapping her arms around his neck and holding him, her cheek warm against his cool one.

"How are you holding up?"

"I don't know. This feels so surreal."

"What can I do for you and your family?"

He shook his head in response, his Adam's apple bobbing up and down with each hard swallow. Instinctively, her hands reached for his, holding them tight. "Thank you," he choked out, an unreadable mask sliding across his handsome features. "I have to go back in."

They stayed at the hospital until almost eleven o'clock, well past visiting hours, but the nurse had made a special exception given that Andrew and Diane were generous donors to the hospital. Richie drove them home in silence, his motions almost robotic. Abby fell asleep in the back seat next to Amy, and Diane sat next to Richie, equally dazed, her eyes glassy with detachment. She thanked Amy for coming but remained silent otherwise. When they got home, everyone dispersed to their private corners, Richie disappearing into his dad's office to check work messages, barely acknowledging Amy who stood in the doorway of the office. From the open curtain, the full moon glistened, illuminating the blanket of snow clinging to tree branches and bushes. Under different circumstances, she would have marveled at the unexpected beauty. But not tonight. Richie sat behind the large oak desk listening to one message after another, but he might as well have been a million miles away. She wondered whether he realized she was standing there. When she offered to make him a sandwich, knowing he hadn't eaten anything all day, he looked startled, his eyes large with alarm. Whether it was a conscious decision or not, Richie had shut out the world, including her, and it hurt, deeply.

THE NEXT MORNING, Amy woke up early, dressed, and made her way to the kitchen. She couldn't take away the family's pain or worry but she could make breakfast. Already familiar with Diane's pantry, she moved around fluidly and with ease. First order of business was a strong pot of coffee, which everyone needed.

The aroma of black coffee brewing awakened her senses. She inhaled deeply, optimistic for a better day ahead. She moved quickly, mixing the egg batter for French toast, working rhythmically as she drenched the bread slices and set them in the pan. By the time she heard footsteps coming down the stairs, she had the table set, French toast and scrambled eggs ready for everyone.

"Wow. Amy, you didn't have to do this." Diane walked over, hugging her tightly. "Thank you."

Amy poured coffee in a large mug and handed it to Diane, who clasped the cup like a child holding on to their favorite teddy bear for comfort. Diane headed for the table, motioning with her head for Amy to follow.

Amy made a cup of tea, fixing it the way she liked, and sat down next to Diane. Silence descended for a few minutes, the two sipping their beverages, taking comfort from one another. The strong, composed matriarch of the family now looked like a fragile child, scared and unsure of everything. Dark circles stained the delicate area around her dim eyes, her skin sallow and her face gaunt.

"How are you holding up, Diane?"

"I don't know. Honestly. I don't know what I would have done without Richie. I'd be completely lost. I feel like I'm in a fog, but it's not clearing, and I'm scared it never will."

"You're dealing with a lot, and it was all so sudden. It takes time to adjust to a new normal."

"A new normal?"

"Yes, adjusting to Andrew needing around the clock care."

"Oh. I guess I hadn't thought about it in that way. I'm ashamed of my weakness, Amy. I've never been a woman crippled with fear but that's exactly how I feel now."

"It will get better. Don't be so hard on yourself."

Amy sensed Richie's presence in the doorway before he walked into the kitchen.

"Good morning." He shuffled to the coffee maker, poured himself a cup, and came to sit across from Amy. "Thank you for all this. You didn't have to go to all this trouble." He avoided her eyes by focusing on his coffee and then on the breakfast that he shoveled in at record speed.

Amy swallowed hard as she watched him keep her at an arm's length. "It's no trouble. Did you sleep at all?"

"Not really," he said between bites. "The French toast is delicious." Richie gave her a tight smile, one that lacked any warmth or intimacy. Her heart broke a little.

"Honey, slow down…" Diane urged before taking her plate and coffee mug to the sink, kissing Amy's cheek as she passed by. Then she excused herself for a shower before heading back to the hospital. With their first moments alone in days, Amy skirted the kitchen table and wrapped her arms around Richie, nuzzling his neck.

"I'm worried about you," she whispered, planting a tender kiss on his cheek. His body slacked a little, but only a little.

"I'm all right. I'm worried about my mom. She's not handling any of this well."

"I'm sorry, Richie. I know a lot has fallen on your shoulders."

"I'm all right," he said again, his voice flat.

"Please let me be here for you. I love you and I want to help."

"Amy, I'm so grateful for everything you've done and are trying to do. I'm sorry if I'm not reciprocating in the way you need. I'm just … in a weird headspace right now. I'm all over the place and I can't believe our lives turned upside down overnight. I'm in a constant state of panic and guilt and worry. I don't want to leave my dad's side for fear of something else happening to him, even though I know that's a crazy way to think. I'm drained and tired. I'm sorry I'm not a great boyfriend right now."

"You don't have to thank me, and you are a great boyfriend all the time. There's a lot going on, give yourself a break." She kissed the side of his neck, hoping her touch would melt the rigidness in his back. It didn't.

"I'm happy to help in any way."

The shuffling of footsteps sliding across the hardwood floor had them both looking up towards the door with anticipation to see Abby.

"Good morning," Abby mumbled, rubbing her eyes. She was still in pajamas. "Wow, this is really nice." Abby surveyed the mouthwatering breakfast. "I know this can't be Richie's doing," she teased.

"Can I fix you a plate?" Amy offered, her arms still wrapped around Richie's neck.

"I got it. Thank you, Amy. This is the nicest treat. How are you two holding up?" Abby said, her voice raspy from sleep. She scooped a generous helping of everything, slid into the chair across from Richie, and began eating with relish.

"Fine. I'm just waiting on Mom and then we're headed back to the hospital." Richie pulled out of Amy's embrace and strolled towards the coffee maker for another cup.

"I just talked to Mom. She won't be ready for another couple of hours. She mentioned something about buying dad comfortable clothes for the hospital." Abby made herself comfortable in the chair at the dining room table, one leg folded neatly beneath her and proceeded to eat in silence.

Richie nodded but didn't say anything, turning to face the kitchen window overlooking the snow-covered garden, brown patches peeking through in areas where the snow had melted. The dreary gray sky did little to cheer anyone up.

"How about a short walk to get some fresh air. You can show this Cali girl the wonders of winter wonderland," Amy suggested after Abby left the kitchen.

"Oh … Amy, I can't. I have a lot to do this morning."

"Richie, you need a little break. I'm not telling you to take the day off, just a short walk." She sounded harsher than she intended.

"Amy, do you have any idea of how much I'm dealing with?" he snapped, taking her off guard for the second time.

"I've never doubted the amount of pressure you're under. I'm just trying to help by offering a break, a small one. Your mom is taking one to go shopping for your dad, Abby is taking one, and you deserve one too. Why can't you?"

"Because I'm the only one holding up all ends of our lives from the business to my mom's well being and Dad's care and even Abby's health. They're all leaning on me and counting on me to take care of things. That's why they're able to take a break."

"Richie, I'm so sorry. I didn't…"

"Amy, I can't do this right now. This is all becoming too much."

"I know, that's why I'm asking you to take a break and take care of yourself."

"No, I mean … this … us … you deserve a more available boyfriend. We barely spend time together, and I don't know when that will change. And I'm in constant state of guilt about everything and everyone."

"Your family is going through a tough time. It will pass, and things will get back to normal. You're being too hard on yourself. You've done an amazing job holding everyone up and you're an amazing boyfriend. We'll get through this." She reached over and caressed his cheek.

He leaned his face into her palm, and on some level, she thought she'd gotten through to him a little. "Amy, I love you, but I can't give you what you need right now."

"I'll decide what I need right now."

"You're not hearing me. I can't do this. I'm falling apart watching my dad in this state, my mom … I just can't … a romantic relationship isn't what I need right now because eventually, this will become too hard to deal with and one of us will become resentful of the situation. I don't know how long this phase will last. I don't know what tomorrow will look like for my dad or my family. The only thing I do know is that I need to dedicate every available minute outside of caring for my family to the business so it doesn't fall apart too."

"I can't believe I'm hearing this."

"I'm sorry. I'm so sorry. This isn't what I wanted but it's what I need to do."

"So this is it? We're done without me even having a say?"

"I'm sorry, Amy."

THE COMMUTER TRAIN came to a grinding halt at Grand Central Station, another ordinary day as riders shuffled their way into the commotion of the city outside. The hour-long ride felt endless and unbearable as she sobbed on and off, avoiding the looks of pity from nearby passengers. Being with Richie had meant more than just an incredible romantic relationship; he was also her friend and she had come to rely on his advice, his jokes, and their banter. He was a ray of sunshine in a sea of turmoil at work with Sarah, tenderly taking the sting out of Sarah's verbal attacks.

The cold wind slapped at her raw skin as she queued up for a taxi. Once in the cab, she was grateful for the toothy driver who weaved in and out of traffic like a mad man on a mission. By the time she walked into her small apartment, every muscle in her body hurt. It was the kind of soreness she typically felt after a vigorous workout, except she hadn't worked out. The radiator clanked loudly, surprisingly comforting as she robotically unpacked, texted her mom, Miranda, and Megan, and then jumped into the shower before waiting for any of them to respond. The thought of dealing with Sarah on top of mending a broken heart felt like a cruel punishment from the gods who had granted her heart's desire not that long ago.

By the time she walked out of the cloud of steam, there were multiple voicemails from her mom, Miranda, and Megan and several text messages.

She gave herself a pep talk about finding inner strength before dialing her mom, who would be worried enough without Amy falling apart on the phone.

"Hi, Mom."

"Hi, honey, I'm so sorry. I've been waiting by the phone since I got your text message. Are you all right? What happened?" The sound of her mom's voice unraveled her, the sobs oblivious to the earlier pep talk.

"He said it was too much and he couldn't be the boyfriend I needed."

"I'm sorry, honey. Timing is everything, and right now, he can't handle anything more than what's been dealt to him. Give him some space. He might come around once his dad is settled at home and life goes back to normal." She was grateful for her parents' support. She couldn't imagine dealing with any of this without her mom's sound advice.

"That's easier said than done, Mom. He was so – distant and decisive. What if things don't ever go back to normal for him?"

"Listen, Amy, life has dealt him a crappy deck of cards. Overnight, he's become a caregiver, a business owner, a boss, and he's also looking after his mom and Abby. Its more than most people can handle. He'll either come around or this relationship wasn't meant for the long haul and you'll need to move on."

"How can you be so cut and dry?"

"Because there's no sense fighting what's already happened. You need to shift your focus to work and find something to keep you busy after hours."

"I don't understand how this happened. Everything was going great between us. He just shut me out."

"He didn't shut you out. He couldn't handle one more person needing him or wanting anything from him. And being someone's boyfriend comes with certain demands that are too much right now."

"I know … I know. It just hurts, and it still sucks. I love him. I thought he was the one for me."

"He might still be the one down the road but not right now. Besides, you have enough on your plate. You have a big project at work."

"And then there's Sarah," Amy complained.

"Don't worry about her. Don't let her push you around, but you shouldn't give her so much energy either. Stay focused."

"Okay. I love you, Mom."

"I love you too and remember to keep busy."

Right, keep busy.

Chapter Twenty-Three

T HE OFFICE BUZZED with everyone's adrenaline pumping, the energy creating an electrifying hum as the marketing team assembled in the large conference room awaiting Jane. Earlier that morning, Jane had sent a group meeting invite for a mandatory staff meeting, something about an important announcement. Amy sat adjacent to a perfectly coifed and outfitted Sarah, unfazed by the purring sound of chatter that filled the large room. The gloomy gray sky outside poured through the floor-to-ceiling windows, mirroring Amy's mood. The subzero temperatures and gathering clouds hinted at an imminent downpour of icy rain. She felt Sarah's gaze on her without looking, and on a dare with herself, she turned her chair slightly so her eyes locked with Sarah's. Amy returned the glare with a placid smile that didn't quite reach her eyes. Two could play this game.

"Good morning all," Jane said. "I don't want to keep you in suspense longer than necessary, so here's the deal. Our advertising and marketing Valentine's Day campaign deadline has shifted. And by that, I mean it's been pushed up by a week. What does this mean? All hands need to be on deck. There's no time for nonsense. Teamwork is the only thing that will get us to the finish line successfully."

"Why the change?" Amy asked.

"Great question. Our board members are meeting with financial investors a couple of weeks earlier than planned, and they want to share metrics on our Valentine's campaign during the meeting. Investors and advertisers keep us in business, and showing them our value in the market is what keeps them on as investors. So Amy, let's look at a revised timeline by end of day today. Sarah, start calling our production vendors and let them know of the change."

Amy swallowed hard, the lump in her throat painfully sliding down, wreaking havoc on her insides. Partnering with the devil would have been more pleasant than working with Sarah, but she would be damned if she gave Sarah the satisfaction of knowing it.

Facing Sarah, she smiled brightly, "I look forward to it."

After the meeting, Amy hurried to the kitchen for a cup of tea, looking forward to the distraction of an accelerated deadline. This was exactly what she needed to stay busy and keep her from dialing Richie. The thought of him brought fresh tears to her eyes. A million emotions nagged at her. Everything from missing him to feeling really bad for him to being angry with him for not being strong enough to resenting Diane for being so weak. She blinked the tears away, her fingers fumbling with the mug, and she hated herself for the awful thoughts running wild through her mind.

"Oh, the pressure finally got to you?" Sarah sneered from behind her. How long had she been standing there?

"What's your problem?"

"Me? I don't have a problem. It's you who should be worried that everyone will finally know you're not the fabulous buttoned-up person you pretend to be."

"Sarah, you clearly have issues, and more specifically your issue is with me. So let's hear it."

"Fine, I think you're a fraud."

"Fraud? The only fraud here is you. Or did you forget how you landed your first job? If it weren't for your daddy's money, you would never have gotten the job at Glitz, let alone be a manager anywhere. Unlike you, I actually worked my way up. What the hell qualifies you to do anything? The only thing you're good at is gossip and demeaning hardworking colleagues because they're actually doing something you're not capable of doing. We had a great department at Glitz until you came along, and now you're pulling the same crap here. Doesn't it get old?" Heat rose to Amy's cheeks, and a tear escaped, despite the deep breaths she took to keep her emotions from spilling over. Until that moment, she never dreamed of confronting Sarah, especially at work. A small crowd had gathered outside the kitchen, some visibly uncomfortable as they exchanged worried glances while others snickered with delight at fresh gossip.

Beet red with humiliation or fury or a combination of the two, Sarah's bright blue eyes glistened with tears. "Excuse me." Sarah defiantly stuck her chin up and stomped out of the kitchen, but not before glaring at Amy with disdain.

Amy glared back, arms crossed over her chest. She felt wretched for her part, but she was also fed up.

It wasn't a huge surprise when Jane knocked on her door later in the afternoon, and then shut the office door for privacy.

"What happened this morning?" Jane said, sitting in the chair across from Amy's desk.

"Sarah and I had an argument in the kitchen. It got out of hand."

"I gathered as much, but what happened to bring you both to that point?"

Amy paused, weighing her options, and decided to come clean with every ugly detail starting with Sarah assigning her random tasks meant to demean her. Jane listened attentively, nodding without interruption.

"Thank you for being so honest with me and I owe you an apology for not following up with you about your email from late December. At the time, I spoke with Sarah, and she assured me it was an innocent misunderstanding. I took her word for it without following up with you. And I will take that responsibility. When I met with Sarah earlier today, she was candid about her part in this morning. She also didn't deny her actions. I'm not blind, and I have eyes and ears all over this building. I'm fully aware of everything including Sarah's lack of experience. There's a lot going on behind the scenes that you're not privy to, nor should you be privy to, but it doesn't mean we have blinders on. I have willingly agreed to take Sarah under my wing and help with her professional development, just as I did for you. The difference between the two of you is that you came to us with experience and determination and a fighting spirit to want more for yourself. I can't say the same for Sarah, which is why I agreed to mentor her."

"I'm sorry I doubted you and I also should have followed up with you about my email. I didn't want to come across as petty and insecure. Truly, it's neither of these things. I thought I could handle it on my own without bothering anyone, but she's been relentless in her verbal attacks and has been undermining me almost daily. I felt she was getting away with murder – again—and my resentment of her got in the way."

"I understand, but this morning's explosion didn't solve anything."

"I know and I'm sorry for my part in it. I should have walked away."

"One of the things I detest the most is women going after each other, especially at work. There's no reason for it. It's time we raised the bar for ourselves by helping each other succeed instead of burying one another."

"I do feel the same way, and today was clearly a horrible judgment call on my part. She's been a nightmare to work with and she has no problem making me look incompetent in front of the team. I felt it was the only way to defend myself."

"I do understand, but I'll be honest. I'm a little disappointed. While she's wrong to have provoked you and undermined your work for the last couple of months, outing her for her lack of experience and past failures in front of the team doesn't help anyone's case."

"Now what?"

"Now we figure out a way for both of you to work together and succeed. You don't have to be her friend, but you do need to work with her. I'm happy to mediate between you two or you can both meet with Joan in HR without me. Either way, you need to figure this out."

Amy nodded miserably, determined to avoid another run-in with Sarah. Letting Jane down was the worst part of this whole mess, and she vowed to never find herself in a similar predicament at any cost. Jane left, and Amy was alone with her thoughts.

Sarah had gotten the best of her during a weak moment, just as she was vulnerable and heartbroken. It wasn't fair. Barely functioning from another sleepless night with thoughts of Richie swirling in her mind, the last thing she was prepared for was venomous Sarah, the girl who had it all in spades and who seemed to avoid any form of self-destruction. Bitterness and resentment were becoming a trend that Amy needed to break. She chewed on her bottom lip to keep from crying. How did everything go so wrong so fast?

Getting caught up in Sarah's tornado was foolish. While Sarah would always bounce back from bad judgment calls, Amy wasn't so sure the same could be said for her. That was reason enough to figure out a way to play nice in the sandbox.

A soft knock at the door had her sitting straighter, smoothing her hair with her fingers, and plastering on a calm smile to disguise the anguish eating at her.

"Amy, hey. Do you have a minute?" Megan stood in the doorway, looking as anxious as Amy felt.

"Of course, come in."

"I'm so sorry about things with Richie. Are you okay?"

Amy nodded.

"Everything will work out the way it's meant to. You met him when you least expected it, the stuff with his dad happened when you least expected it, and things might work out when you least expect them. That's the universal magic that keeps us on track with what's meant for us."

"I would never have pegged you for a philosopher, Megan, but I'll take it, so keep channeling the Dalai Lama. I need to hear this." Amy forced a smile for Megan's benefit, wiping at her eyes and cheeks with her fingers.

"Now what are we going to do about Sarah? Kill her with kindness? Kill her period?" Megan joked.

"I don't know, but she seems to be channeling forces from the dark side. She was ready for a fight this morning, that's for sure."

"Miserable cow. Listen. Kill her with kindness for now. What's that saying about keeping your enemies close?"

"All true, my friend."

"Good girl. Keep your chin up and we'll talk tonight. I'm working late to accommodate the accelerated deadline." Amy walked around the desk and hugged Megan tightly, grateful for their friendship. In spite of the crappy few days, life didn't suck completely.

Chapter Twenty-Four

THE PRODUCTION FOR the Valentine's Day campaign was in the home stretch, and the team was weary and drained and in desperate need of a night to blow off steam. When rumblings of happy hour made their way around the office, everyone eagerly accepted and decided to meet at a local bar just a couple of blocks from the office. Being busy had its pros, mainly keeping thoughts of Richie to a minimum, at least during the day. The nighttime remained torturous with a rolling reel of memories from their time together. The dream always ended with Richie saying goodbye, and Amy always woke up with a stream of tears soaking her pillow. She texted him a couple of times over the month asking about the family, and although he always responded promptly, his answers were polite and curt, closing the door on further communication. He might as well have been replying to a business partner. And that hurt, a lot.

Happy hour was fun and exactly what everyone needed. Amy made her way to the bar and ordered a glass of wine, surprised to find Sarah at her heels.

"Hi, Amy." Sarah forced a smile, visibly uncomfortable.

Amy smiled in return, ready to turn a over new leaf. "Hi, Sarah. I hope you have fun tonight."

"Of course I will. Why wouldn't I?" Sarah retorted.

"No reason. I didn't mean anything by it."

"Whatever, Amy. I hope you have a good time tonight."

"Sarah, you completely misunderstood …" Sarah didn't wait for her to explain and disappeared into the crowd, leaving her at the bar with wine in hand and mouth gaping open. Cleary, Sarah wasn't ready to leave the past behind. Oh well.

"What was that about?" Megan walked over.

"Nothing. She misunderstood something I said and walked away in a huff. Since when is she so sensitive?"

"Don't worry about her. Come on. Let's get a table, I'm starving."

By midnight, Amy was in bed contemplating calling Richie. With liquid courage throbbing in her veins, she dialed his number and to her dismay, got voicemail.

"Richie, it's me. I'm sorry to call so late. I hope you're well and the family too. I've been thinking about you and hope you're taking care of yourself. I miss you. You don't have to call. I understand you're dealing with a lot. I just wanted you to know that I was thinking about you and your family. Just because we're not together doesn't mean I no longer care. I still do. Anyway, have a great weekend. Say hi to everyone, or not. That's okay too. Okay bye."

Groaning she hung up before she rambled on any more.

Smooth Amy, real smooth.

VALENTINE'S DAY CREPT up on the city with Cupid leaving his mark on every post, store window, and street corner. It was nauseating. Given her recent membership in the singles club, Valentine's Day was a reminder of what she'd once had and lost. The day was also momentous because Diva's new ad campaign had launched earlier that day to rave reviews. From billboards in Times Square to signage all around the city, Diva ads were everywhere. And that made her smile. Jane had ordered bottles of champagne for the office, and together the entire team toasted to a successful launch.

"To my A-Team," Jane cheered proudly.

By the time she left the office, Amy felt like she was walking on clouds. It was the happiest she had felt since the break-up. Several members of the team, including Jane, had congratulated her. Even Sarah managed to squeak out a "nice job, Amy." It felt good to be recognized for her contribution, and it felt even better to prove it to her harshest critic, herself.

Her stomach growled, a stark reminder that she'd skipped dinner. She needed to eat something and didn't want to wait for delivery. Besides, she had dreamed of a white magical winter since moving to Manhattan and it felt wrong to shut it out by going to bed at eight o'clock. Somehow, succumbing to sleep this early in the evening on Valentine's Day and the day of the ad campaign launch felt downright pathetic. She reminded herself that she had been through a painful break-up with Adam and had come out stronger on the other side. This was no different. Well, it was, but no matter. She'd survive this too. Her soul depended on her surviving these unexpected pitfalls. And now she had something to celebrate, and by golly, she deserved it. Too bad Megan had made plans with the photo department.

The brisk walk outside could help physically exhaust her so that she would be guaranteed a full night of comatose sleep, oblivious to the pain that had ripped her heart in two. Without a plan in mind, Amy picked up her coat and purse and marched out of the apartment in search of food and Manhattan magic.

The cold air danced around her, and she paused in the middle of the sidewalk, relishing the feel of snow on her face and in her hair. Childlike, Amy tilted her head back, letting the snowflakes land on her nose and parted lips. In spite of herself, a small giggle escaped her throat. Leave it to the simplest act of nature to lift her broken spirit. With her eyes still closed, Amy contemplated a place to eat, glaringly aware that she was a party of one on Valentine's Day. The last thing she needed was looks of pity for the single girl dining alone on a holiday.

Zippering her coat all the way up to her neck, Amy shook the snowflakes from her hair before she began walking toward midtown, without a destination in mind. She'd eat at the first place that caught her attention, preferably somewhere that offered quick finger foods so she could eat while walking. Surveying the crowded street, it was hard to imagine that it was eight o'clock already. Didn't these people have somewhere to be? Ironically, they probably wondered the same thing about her.

A few blocks from her apartment, Amy spotted a neon green sign that said "Burrito King" and nearly leaped with joy. Bingo!

She hurried into the fast food eatery, ordering a burrito deluxe and a bottle of sparkling water. Treating herself to a burrito the size of her head seemed rather appropriate and necessary, even though she knew emotionally soothing with food was hardly healthy.

Amy paid, wished the man a happy Valentine's Day, stuffed the seltzer bottle in her purse, and walked back into the cluster of people crowding the sidewalk. She unwrapped the burrito, careful to keep the rolled-up insides of mouthwatering goodness from bursting out. Without a care in the world, she sunk her teeth into the delicacy and groaned out loud, a party of flavors dancing on her tongue. Either she was starving, or this was the best damn steak burrito she'd ever had. Coming from Los Angeles, she rarely found anything to beat the authentic Mexican fare she was accustomed to at home, but this was a close second.

With her hunger satisfied and her emotions momentarily under control, Amy trudged through the carpet of snow that continued to thicken with each passing minute as lights glittered and bounced off the white canvas covering Manhattan. The snow speckled her hair and clung to her thick down coat as she beelined forward; the only plan in her mind was to put one foot in front of the other. She wasn't ready to face her empty apartment just yet, craving pandemonium instead. The masses of people thinned out a little, glittery hearts adorned lampposts, more visible now with the crowds tapering.

The sound of blaring taxi horns rang from somewhere nearby. Out of curiosity, Amy craned her neck to get a better look around, her heart tripping at the sight of a Richie look-alike weaving in and out of gridlock at the intersection. He turned in her direction, as if sensing someone staring at him, and smiled. He was handsome, but he wasn't her Richie. Shrugging her shoulders, Amy continued walking. For once, the thought of Richie didn't make her cry, and that was a great step forward.

The crowd thickened again, and Amy found herself dodging elbows and long-stemmed roses. Calm down people! A row of restaurants dotted the busy sidewalk, some with lines outside. That explained the sudden increase in foot traffic. Feeling slightly frazzled, she stopped at an intersection to get her bearings and blinked a few times in disbelief at the brightly lit Macy's sign. She had walked nearly forty city blocks without realizing it.

A dull throbbing pain began to work itself through her stomach and up to the cavity of her chest, right into her heart. The last time she was here was with Richie, less than two months ago, when he instructed the taxi driver to drive up 5th Avenue so Amy could see the Christmas storefronts. Tears stung her eyes as she worked overtime to maintain her composure. Swallowing the lump in her throat, she shoved her hands into her coat pockets and stood still as shoppers moved around her, some bumping into her, others barely noticing her.

Amy didn't believe in coincidence. She never had. Ending up at Macy's was symbolic and perhaps significant, even if she didn't understand it yet. Not that long ago, she'd sat grinning in the taxi with Richie, excitement bubbling inside her at the thought of spending Christmas with his family, and now she was alone and heartbroken on Valentine's Day. She had come full circle and perhaps this was closure.

Amy's hair blew in her face as the wind swept the snow around her, briefly blinding her. Tucking the tangled hair behind her ears, she crossed the street and traipsed right through the revolving doors of Macy's, eager for any symbolic message of hope that awaited her.

A woman with a stroller was standing a couple of feet away, waving her arms frantically at Amy. "Miss, can you get out of the way please?"

Realizing that she was blocking the doorway, Amy apologized profusely, embarrassed for being caught in a daydream, and scooted out of the way.

Amy made her way past the cosmetic section, politely declining samples of perfume, lipstick and even a makeover. Seriously, a makeover?

Then Amy caught a glimpse of herself in one of the mirrors and gasped with horror. Blotchy skin and dark circles under droopy eyes stared back at her. Maybe she should have accepted the makeover. Good heavens. It was a surprise that shoppers weren't screaming with horror at the sight of her. With eyes averted away from the counter mirrors taunting her every few feet, Amy hurried out of the store.

As much as she hated the idea of going home and facing the reality of being alone for Valentine's Day, she knew she didn't have much of a choice. She walked at a leisurely pace—no point in hurrying. She pulled her phone from her purse to check the time. It was 10:00 p.m. No new messages. Had Richie moved on so quickly that he couldn't be bothered to return her calls? Shaking her head to clear thoughts of Richie from her mind, she stomped forward through the thick snow.

Bars and restaurants were still in full swing, the clinking of glassware and hum of chatter spilling out onto the sidewalk as Amy continued her stroll home. With the wind subsided and the snow settled for now, the walk was much more tolerable. She wandered past her and Richie's favorite bar, her feet turning to cement blocks, keeping her from moving another step. A couple, holding hands as they gazed adoringly into each other's eyes, shared a bottle of wine at the table closest to the window. The guy whispered something in his girlfriend's ear and she tipped her head back, laughter erupting from her throat. They noticed Amy watching them, and she took a step back from the window, embarrassed, until her eyes landed on the familiar looking blond sitting at the bar.

Intrigued, Amy watched for a few minutes as Sarah drank a dark gold liquid from a tumbler—whiskey, her favorite drink. Curiosity about the woman inflicting havoc on her professional life kept her rooted in her spot. The couple by the window looked annoyed at her presence now, but Amy ignored them. A few more minutes passed with Sarah drinking at the bar, dateless and alone on Valentine's Day.

Possessed by a force bigger than herself, Amy pulled on the heavy glass door and walked toward her nemesis; unsure what she would say once she actually came face to face with Sarah. Her heart thumped against her ribcage as she inched closer.

"Happy Valentine's Day, Sarah." Amy unzipped her coat and slung it over the back of the high bar stool, then slid next to Sarah. "Hi, Ryan. A cabernet please." She smiled brightly at the bartender. He'd served her and Richie many drinks on many date nights. Seeing a familiar friendly face boosted her confidence. This was Amy's territory with or without

Richie.

Sarah blanched at the sight of her, recoiling in her seat, eyes slightly bloodshot from tipping back one too many. Sarah was harsh and nasty when she could prepare well in advance, but caught off guard, she morphed into a spineless coward.

Pouring a generous amount of cabernet, Ryan pushed the glass toward Amy. "Hey, Amy. Happy Valentine's Day. Will Richie be joining you?"

"Not tonight, Ryan. And Happy Valentine's Day to you." Amy took a gulp of the wine, tempted to down it in one go, but she refrained. The rich full-bodied red surged through her, warming her up and giving her the liquid courage she needed for whatever was to come.

"What are you doing here?" Sarah glared at Amy, a hint of panic clouding her eyes.

"This is one of my favorite wine bars in the city, and it's become a regular spot for Richie and me. When I saw you from the window, I knew we were meant to have a Valentine's drink together," Amy said, her voice laced with sarcasm as she tossed her tangled hair over her shoulder. Damn it! She had momentarily forgotten how horrible she looked.

"Right. And where is this fabulous boyfriend of yours tonight? He wised up and moved on?" Sarah spat, taking a swig from her glass.

"Hardly. Last minute change of plans, that's all," Amy lied, hoping Sarah didn't notice her trembling hands.

"Whatever. I don't give a crap about you or your pathetic love life."

"Oh, Sarah, but you do. You care so much you couldn't stay away from me. In fact, you moved 3000 miles to work with me again. Why?" An inner calm had taken over Amy's body.

"Don't flatter yourself. I didn't move here for you. You're a loser, Amy, and you'll always be a loser. One successful marketing campaign doesn't change anything," Sarah sneered, turning in her stool to face her.

"I don't believe you." Amy sipped her wine, hiding the hurt at Sarah's venomous words.

"Yeah … well, I don't care what you believe."

"Listen, you should know something." Amy leaned back in her chair, crossing one leg over the other, exuding confidence. "You're not going to win this battle ... against me at the office, I mean. In case you haven't noticed, Jane isn't impressed with your crap and your horrible attitude. Do yourself a favor and focus on your own job, because I'm not going anywhere, and I'm prepared to fight you till the end." Amy gulped the last of her wine and nodded in Ryan's direction for another pour.

Sarah shifted uncomfortably in her seat, her eyes glassy, blinking rapidly as Amy's words penetrated her mind. Sarah downed the last of her whiskey and ordered another.

"Why are you here alone on Valentine Day?" Amy asked, enjoying having the upper hand for once.

"That's none of your business." She combed her fingers through her shiny blond hair, and Amy noticed the slight tremor in her hands.

"I thought you were going back to LA tonight?" Amy pressed. Every shred of hurt, anger, betrayal, and sadness as a result of Adam, Sarah, and Richie were now directed only at Sarah, threatening to unravel the petite woman hunched over her whiskey.

"Well, you thought wrong. Okay?" The tenor in her voice faltered, hinting at sadness or anxiety. That didn't make much sense. Sarah had the world in the palm of her very affluent hand.

"Why? Why didn't you go back to LA?" Amy asked, years of built-up anger exploding now, merciless in her quest to disarm Sarah. "Let me guess, you have a hot date later with some posh A-list celebrity and you're just killing time here?"

"Hardly. I don't have a date. Okay? Is that what you wanted to hear? That I'm alone and miserable?" Sarah's lips trembled before she turned away to compose herself, tears staining her perfectly made-up face.

Amy blinked in shock, not expecting the brutally honest confession that tumbled from her lips. Sarah was a social butterfly—a socialite who only declined fabulous parties because she was already double- or triple-booked. Never in a million years did Amy expect to hear those sad words from her.

"That's not what I wanted to hear," she said. "I know you hate me, Sarah. You've made that abundantly clear. But I don't hate you. I did for a long time, but I don't anymore. And I'm sorry you're feeling lonely."

Amy wasn't heartless, and even though Sarah had never shown her a shred of kindness or compassion, she couldn't be cruel and merciless toward Sarah during a vulnerable moment.

"Yup. Thanks for your pity, but I don't need it."

Sarah stared ahead, refusing to make eye contact, the whiskey glass clutched tightly in her manicured hand. Amy knew a little something about the misery of spending Valentine's Day alone. Hell, this year, she was the crowned queen of lonely and sad. Disarming Sarah had been wishful thinking, until the wish became a reality and now it didn't feel gratifying, it felt wretched.

"Do you want to talk about it? I'm a great listener." Amy leaned in, squeezing Sarah's arm.

Surprisingly, Sarah didn't flinch or shrug her hand away. "My parents are on the verge of disowning me, so if I don't make this job work, I'll be unemployed and homeless because my trust fund will be gone too. I was dating someone a couple of months ago until his wife found out, and then my parents. It's been a domino effect of disasters. Let's just say, things didn't end well on any front. It's why I left LA. My dad pulled strings to get me the interview at Diva and called in even more favors to secure the job on my behalf." Sarah's voice cracked, the truth finally revealed.

Amy refrained from gasping or reacting, but on the inside, she was screaming at the top of her lungs. So once again, Sarah's father had secured the position at Diva, yanking the opportunity from someone truly deserving of it, simply because he had the means. To add insult to injury, until now, Sarah hadn't displayed the slightest iota of humility. Her behavior had been the complete opposite of that.

Amy bit her tongue. She had already given Sarah a piece of her mind a few weeks back. Relishing in Sarah's misery was counterproductive. Sarah was too defensive and too arrogant, and most likely too drunk to listen to anything she had to say. Sarah was hurting and broken, and Amy didn't relish crushing her further. Instead, she decided on some tough love in hopes of getting through to Sarah's vulnerable side. Maybe if she was happier in her personal life, everyone around her would benefit too.

Amy placed her hand on Sarah's shoulder, gently twisting her to face her. Tears had filled her bright blue eyes.

"Sarah, I know you don't care for my opinion about anything and that's fine. But I'll say this anyway. Why in the hell were you dating a married man? You could have any single man you want."

"It didn't start out that way. He was a business associate and then he started showering me with attention and flowers and fancy lunches. It made me feel special. I liked being around him because I could do no wrong." Sarah shrugged her shoulders, wiping the tears with her thumb, careful not to smudge her makeup.

Taking a deep breath, Amy braced herself, hoping she wouldn't regret her decision to confide in Sarah. "I've been cheated on and it sucks. Why would you want any part of shredding another woman's heart?"

"I'm sorry, Amy. I didn't know. Is that why you're here without your boyfriend?" Sarah asked, grabbing her drink from the bar.

"No, Richie is great. That's not what broke us up." Amy choked back tears, reaching for a tissue from her purse.

"Wait, I thought you said you've been cheated on. So your boyfriend didn't cheat on you?"

"Richie didn't cheat on me, my ex boyfriend Adam did," Amy clarified, sitting up straighter.

"So what did Richie do?"

She hesitated at first, unsure whether to trust Sarah, but decided to throw caution to the wind. It not like she was telling her a secret.

Sarah rubbed her lips together. "I'm sorry."

"Thanks."

The two sat in silence for a few minutes, each lost in private thoughts.

"On my final day at Glitz, the staff clapped when I walked into the elevator for the last time. They didn't think I heard, but I did. And I know there was a party afterwards to celebrate being rid of me. They called it A Day of Jubilee. I saw the flyer on someone's desk."

Amy's eyes widened at Sarah's confession. She had prayed for a moment like this with Sarah for years. Being privy to her flaws and vulnerability helped Amy see past the hard exterior that she paraded around. This side of Sarah was refreshing.

"I'm sorry. That must have hurt."

Sarah nodded silently, downing the whiskey.

"Amy, I'm sorry for everything I've put you through. I shouldn't have gone after your job at Glitz and I won't come after your job at Diva. I felt so threatened by you; I just wanted you gone and out of my world. You were a reminder of all the things I wasn't—accomplished, likeable, and you had awesome girlfriends that adored you. I was jealous. I've never had a girlfriend."

"What? You have everything. What could you possibly be jealous about? And what do you mean you've never had a girlfriend?"

"Having money isn't having everything. I'm a trust fund kid surrounded by friends who enjoy my lifestyle, not necessarily my company."

"I'm sorry," Amy offered, leaning her elbow on the back of the stool, the wine working like magic to loosen her tongue and limbs. "Sarah, if you're serious about wanting to work at Diva, I'll help you learn the ropes."

"Thanks. I appreciate the offer, especially after what I've put you through. Wow, you really are nice." Sarah grinned, eyes sparkling.

Amy chuckled, enjoying their cordial conversation.

"I can't believe this is happening." Sarah rubbed her hands over her face.

"What? That we're having a civil conversation where you're not plotting my demise?" She exhaled, feeling lighter somehow.

"I know, right?" Sarah said, giggling nervously. "Listen, before the magic wears off, congratulations on the campaign. You did a hell of a job."

Sarah sounded sincere, and Amy nodded, taking the words in, appreciative of Sarah's uncharacteristic kindness.

"Come on, let's get out of here before we're too drunk to get home. I'm getting tired and you look like crap," Sarah said.

"Hey … not all of us can look picture perfect all the time, like you,"

Amy shot back, laughing. For once, the jab didn't hurt.

"Amy … I'm really sorry for everything I've put you through. I don't know what got into me …." Sarah openly cried, a trickle of black mascara rolling down her porcelain skin.

"It's okay, it's behind us now. I'm glad I saw you here tonight, and I'm really glad we talked."

Amy gently touched Sarah's arm, gazing at the woman she'd deemed a monster just a couple of hours ago. At least one hurdle had been resolved. In the grand scheme of things, Amy considered herself lucky—seeing Sarah could have gone either way.

Amy took out her credit card to hand to Ryan for her drinks and Sarah's too, in honor of the unfathomable truce they had forged between the two of them.

Sarah waved her hand at Amy. "I got this. It's the very least I can do after everything I've put you through," she said, sliding Amy's card back to her.

"Thank you, Sarah."

Chapter Twenty-Five

I<small>T WAS NEARLY</small> midnight when Amy and Sarah walked out of the bar, the street covered under a few feet of fresh powdery snow now. Their feet sank immediately, snow coming up to their shins as the two Los Angeles girls marveled at the beauty of an east coast winter.

Amy watched Sarah as she buttoned her white wool coat, pulled a stylish cashmere hat from her purse, and gingerly placed it over her head.

"Seriously, do you always have to look this perfect?" Amy griped, only half joking.

Sarah inched toward Amy, who instinctively took a small step back.

"Shut up. Get home safe and happy Valentine's Day." Sarah threw her arms around Amy's shoulders, holding on tight.

It took a few seconds for Amy to recover from the shock of being affectionately hugged by Sarah. Incredible how much had changed within a few short hours. Amy hugged Sarah back, sighing with relief at the overdue peace treaty between them, though still a little leery of the change of heart. She needed some time to get used to the idea of waking up and not dreading the day's interaction with Sarah.

Amy pulled slightly back to look at her. "Happy Valentine's Day, Sarah. You were a fabulous date, and thanks for talking to me tonight. It's changed everything … for me." Amy's voice cracked, the emotional intensity taking her by surprise.

"Oh … you're welcome. It's changed things for me too, you know. For a long time, I didn't want to think of you as a real person … it made it easier to live with my … horrible behavior. Talking to you tonight opened my eyes to the possibility of a friendship instead of a contentious hateful relationship. I don't want to be that person anymore." Sarah was crying again, wiping at tears with her coat sleeve.

"I'm open to the possibility of a friendship." And Amy meant it.

"Me too. You would be my first real friend."

"Well, that's worth celebrating, I think. Maybe we can grab dinner soon and talk about how we're going to survive another few months without the beach," Amy teased, and they both laughed. "Do you have a long walk home?"

"Nah, I'm only a few blocks south of here."

Amy was amused that they lived so close but couldn't be further apart in thinking and lifestyle, perhaps until now.

"I'm a couple of blocks up this way." Waving goodbye, Amy turned away from Sarah and strolled home, deep holes marking her footsteps in the snow. She lost a boyfriend and possibly gained a friend, or at the very least, made peace with an enemy. Small wins.

"Amy, Amy." She heard her name being shouted, the voice familiar, so familiar, she could have sworn it was Richie, but that was ridiculous because he was likely still living in Greenwich, over an hour from the city. The alcohol and the rollercoaster of a day were obviously playing tricks on her mind. So she kept walking, head held high, choosing to be in this moment and savor the peace with Sarah.

Arms waving over his head and panting heavily, Richie slipped and nearly lost his footing as he came closer, finally getting Amy's attention.

"Amy, wait." He was breathless and rosy-cheeked from the cold. He held up both hands to stop her, closing the gap between them. He hunched over, hands on his knees to catch his breath.

Instinctively, Amy grabbed his biceps, supporting him while his breathing leveled out. "Richie, are you okay? What are you doing here?" The questions flew out of her mouth, she was so shocked at seeing him. She bit her lip and waited for him to answer.

Pulling himself up tall, he snaked an arm around her waist and drew her against him. "I came looking for you, Amy. I've been walking around for the last hour. I went to your apartment and then to the ice rink in Central Park, Serendipity 3, back to your apartment … and then it dawned on me to check the bar when I saw you walking out. Who was that blond girl you were hugging?"

Amy turned her head, wondering if Sarah was still within earshot. She turned back around to face Richie. "Richie what are you doing here? Is everything okay with your family?" Amy said, purposely dodging the question so as not to divert the conversation from more pressing issues. "How's your dad?" She looked away, her eyes filling with tears.

"Everyone is fine. They miss you, and I do too. My dad is home and we hired a private nurse to care for him around the clock."

"That's great news, Richie. And your mom? And Abby?"

"They're both great. They miss you. Abby gave me an earful about my part in blowing the best relationship I've ever had."

"I see."

"My mom wasn't too happy with me either. You have quite the fan club among my family."

"I'm happy to hear it, and the feeling is mutual."

"Amy, I'm sorry for everything. I'm sorry I crumbled. I don't think I can explain the amount of pressure I was feeling, and instead of leaning on you for strength, I pushed you away. You're my whole world, Amy, and I need you in my life. I love you." Leaning down, he brushed his lips lightly against hers, sending an electric shock through her body.

"I love you too, Richie, and I'm glad that your dad's comfortable at home with reliable help. I should have been more sensitive to what you were going through. I only meant to comfort you." Amy sniffled, burying her face against his chest, his coat damp from the snow wetting her cheek.

Richie placed his fingers under her chin, tilting her face for a kiss that deepened instantly. Pulling back slightly, Richie's breath hitched, hazel eyes boring through her chocolate brown ones. He took her hands in his and brought them up for a tender kiss on the knuckles. The temperature was dropping rapidly, but Amy hardly minded. She had all the warmth she needed from her gorgeous boyfriend who'd come back looking for her.

Amy could have sworn she felt him tremble under her touch. She rubbed her hands over his shoulders to warm him up and then cupped his face, tenderly kissing his eyelids, his forehead, and then trailing kisses down his nose and landing on his lips for a passionate, knee-buckling smooch. A soft moan escaped her lips, or maybe it was his. Richie's large hands were tangled in her hair, tugging to pull her closer against him. Hot lava coursed through Amy's veins.

A whistle in the background snapped her attention to her surroundings, on the street, in the middle of the night. Reluctantly, she pulled away, her breath coming in short raspy gasps. They couldn't get to her apartment fast enough.

Tugging on his arm, Amy motioned with her head for Richie to follow. "Let's go home."

"Wait. There's something else …" Richie held a hand up.

Amy stopped, turning to face him, the blood draining from her face at the prospect of whatever he was about to tell her.

Taking both of her hands in his, Richie bent down on one knee in the snow and smiled nervously at Amy.

"Amy Charlotte McKinsey, would you make me the happiest man alive by marrying me?

She gasped, her heart beating so fast and loud, her ribcage nearly cracked open. Her hands trembled in Richie's steady ones and an inner calm spread through her, filling her with a love and joy she never dreamed possible. It made all the years of struggling and swimming upstream worth it for this moment in time when everything she wanted fell into place so perfectly.

The corners of her mouth tugged upwards as she glanced down at Richie, still watching her, his warm breath fogging up the frozen air between them.

"Yes," she cried, cradling his head against her chest as happy tears streamed down her cheeks. Immediately, his arms wrapped possessively around her middle, and he buried his face against her, still on bended knee in the snow, holding her tight. Her heart soared to new heights at the gorgeous man promising eternal love. At least that was her wish, and if things took a turn for the worse, she knew she could handle it because she was much stronger than she had ever given herself credit for until now.

"Yes, I would love to marry you, Richie," Amy repeated, getting down on both of her knees, molding her body to his, wrapping her arms around his neck and kissing him with everything she had.

"I love you, future Mrs. Hendricks," he whispered between kisses, tears pooling in the corners of his eyes.

In the distance, Amy heard clapping and cheering, and she giggled, a little embarrassed at being the center of attention. Richie chuckled, showering her with more kisses, unfazed. Breaking their embrace, he stuck his hand into his coat pocket and pulled out a velvet blue box, opening it to show Amy her engagement ring.

Her jaw dropped at the sight of the sparkling pink diamond surrounded by more round white diamonds in a brilliant silver setting. The ring was fit for a queen and it was breathtaking.

"Richie, this is too much." She gaped at the ring as Richie slid it on her frozen finger. "My gosh, it's so beautiful."

"Nothing is too much for you. I'm glad you like it."

Holding up her hand to admire the ring, Amy cried tears of joy. It was an evening of miracles. "I love it, Richie, and I love you."

Taking her by the hands, Richie stood and pulled Amy up to her feet, kissing her diamond-clad hand. Their gazes locked, his smoldering eyes looking more silver than hazel. She arched an eyebrow at him, on the same track of thinking.

"We should head back to your place before we freeze to death. What do you think?"

Amy nodded. "Yes."

Richie kissed her cheeks, smiling. "I already told you, you're my entire world. And we're not missing anything. We'll drive to Greenwich this weekend. My mom, dad, and Abby are excited to see you."

Relieved, Amy wrapped her arms around him. "That sounds perfect. I'm so happy, Richie. For the longest time, I didn't believe that true complete happiness was in the cards for me … until now."

"I'm sorry you felt that way, and I'm so sorry if I contributed to that feeling at all," he said, pressing his lips together in a thin line.

Taking him by the hand, Amy threaded her fingers through his, propelling them toward her apartment.

"It wasn't just you, Richie. It was a combination of a million things— from not dealing with past hurt and then holding on to it, to Sarah making my life miserable at work, to doubting myself. I felt like I couldn't get a break. Being in Manhattan on my own, succeeding at Diva, reminded me that I wasn't as worthless as Adam and Sarah made me feel. And you loving me and supporting me and showing up tonight restored my faith that things always work out the way they're meant to."

Richie slowed his pace to look at her, his hair spiking up at the top from the moisture and wind. She loved it when his hair looked wild, the way it did tonight.

"I'm sorry that you've had such a bad run. I've actually been thinking about your work situation. Maybe you should come work for the family company. It wouldn't be less work or stress, but you'll be treated great and you'll have a solid career path and it will get you away from Sarah."

The street around them was finally quieting down, fewer pedestrians and taxis passing them as they continued the short walk.

"Well ... there have been some developments on the work front," she said. Richie raised an eyebrow, watching her intently.

"Developments, eh?"

Amy nodded, recounting the last couple of weeks and entire scene tonight, from seeing Sarah sitting alone at the bar to her heartfelt apology and their goodbye outside the bar.

"She hugged me, and it felt genuine," Amy marveled as they walked into her building, shutting the front door behind them.

Scratching his head pensively, Richie chuckled with surprise. "Wow. I'm glad you resolved things with Sarah, but I still wouldn't trust her if I were you." He squeezed her hand as they climbed the stairs to the third floor.

Inside her apartment, Amy peeled the cold clothes from her frozen limbs and sauntered into the bathroom to turn on the hot shower, motioning to Richie to follow. Grinning, he obliged, undressing in record speed, piling his damp clothes on top of hers on the floor by the bed.

Later that night as Richie slept soundly, his chest rising and falling rhythmically, she pondered the unexpected turn of events, marveling at having her Christmas wish come true, although delayed in delivery. It was at that moment that she realized the true magic at the heart of all wishes – it wasn't Christmas miracles or shooting stars. The magic lay within having faith that everything happens in due time and only if it's meant to happen. She didn't have faith in her ability while working with Sarah the first time around and so she let Sarah run her down and run her out of Glitz. With Adam, she didn't love herself enough to walk away from a toxic relationship, choosing to believe his lies over her truth. And with Richie, deep down she didn't believe she deserved a happily ever after so at the first sign of a curveball, she lost faith in their ability to face whatever was thrown at them. It had been a year of life lessons and gifts from the Universe to remind her of the real magic, the one that lived within her.

Succeeding at work certainly helped shift her confidence in the right direction and more importantly, it solidified feeling valued. Standing up to Sarah was monumental in ending the vicious cycle of being a punching bag. And as uncomfortable as it was, Jane was also right in teaching her to handle conflicts in a more productive way. And then there was Richie – the beautiful Adonis who came looking for her just when she had started to move on. Without realizing it, she had helped tear them apart. She had depended on him for happiness, and that was too big of a burden for anyone to shoulder. With Richie out of the picture, she was forced to gain her footing again, on her own, and was reminded of her dear grandmother's words to her growing up. "The best unions are when two complete people come into a relationship, not when two halves make a whole." It had taken her over a decade to fully understand the wisdom behind the advice, but she finally got it. And the timing couldn't be better.

The End

Other books by Engy Neville

Time Travel Historical Fiction
A Leap In Time (The Travelers series)

Women's Contemporary Fiction
Fool's Luck – (A Manhattan Dream series Book 1)

A note from the author

With every accomplishment and measure of success comes countless hours of hard work behind the scenes. Writing *A Christmas Wish* was no exception. As a working mom, time isn't always on my side and I had to prioritize, sacrifice and juggle a million things to make this happen. The process taught me so much about myself and I'm so grateful for every expected and unexpected blessing along the way.

I'm especially grateful for the circle of dear friends and colleagues that have championed this book. First and foremost, to my tribe, my girlfriends, my sisters, your love and support anchors me. Your presence in my life has only made it richer and I'm a better person because of each of you.

To my beautiful friend and editor Marlene Roberts Engel, you believed in this story from the very beginning and it was your nurturing guidance that kept me on track.

To my wonderful editor, Patricia Eddy, thank you for your thoughtful direction in bringing out the book's magic. I'm eternally grateful for your talent and collaboration throughout this process.

To the team at Aurora Publicity, there are not enough words in the English dictionary to describe what you guys mean to me. Your creativity and partnership have been a godsend. I'm so humbled to have you in my corner.

To my parents and brothers, I love you more than words can express.

And finally to my husband and best friend, Brian, I love you more every day. Your unconditional love grounds me in what's important and I'm so grateful to have you by my side as we explore this life journey together.

To Liam and Reagan, you light up my life and fill my heart with endless love and joy. I'm so proud of you both and I'm so honored to be your Mommy. I love you so much.

About the Author

Engy started her career in the entertainment industry and years later, she worked in brand consulting. Some of the interesting personalities she met along the way have inspired the characters in her books.

She's a Southern California native and finds solace in being outdoors. Meditation and yoga help her maintain a Zen outlook in the midst of life's chaotic blessings.

Engy lives with her husband, two kids and dog on Long Island, New York.